THE HILL
OF THE RED FOX

'. . . a magnificent adventure story. It recalls
Stevenson and Buchan . . . The reader should be
swept away by the swift narrative, the splendid
vision and the magical atmosphere of Skye which
pervades the story.'   *Times Literary Supplement*

'This is an admirable story, well written and with
an authentic background which anyone who has
visited, or even seen films of the Highlands will
appreciate.'   *Teachers' World*

'With each successive book Allan Campbell McLean
grows in stature as an author.' *Children's Book News*

Also by Allan Campbell McLean
in Lions

THE YEAR OF THE STRANGER
MASTER OF MORGANA

THE HILL
OF THE RED FOX

Allan Campbell McLean

COLLINS · LIONS

First published 1955 by William Collins Sons & Co Ltd
14 St James's Place, London SW1
First published in Lions 1973
Second Impression 1975

© Allan Campbell McLean 1968

Printed in Great Britain
by William Collins Sons & Co Ltd, Glasgow

FOR CALUM BEAG OF RIGG

'This life has joys for you and I;
An' joys that riches ne'er could buy,
An' joys the very best.'

Chapter I

If I had not caught a bad cold and developed bronchitis, and if I had not upset the supper tray one night in June, I might never have taken the long road from my quiet street in Chelsea to the Isle of Mist in the Hebrides. It happened as simply as that. I suppose it had to happen that way. Like the strange message, thrust into my hand in the darkness, that sent me to the Hill of the Red Fox and made me lie shivering in the wet heather watching the shadowy forms of my pursuers.

But I can feel Duncan Mor's* big hand on my shoulder and hear him saying in that deep, commanding voice of his: 'A story should start at the beginning, Alasdair Beag.' And so it should.

It all started one night in June when the three of us, my mother, Aunt Evelyn, and I, were sitting in the little flat above Aunt Evelyn's bookshop. It was quiet in the flat. The only sounds were the muffled rumbling of traffic in Sloan Square, the busy click of my aunt's knitting needles, and the chink of crockery as my mother prepared the supper things in the tiny kitchenette that lay off the living-room.

I was sitting on a stool by the fire reading an adventure story, but my eyes scanned the words on the printed page without really taking in their meaning, for I could feel my aunt's eyes fixed upon me.

After a while, she said: 'What are you reading, Alasdair?'

'A book,' I said, not looking up, conscious of the disapproval in her tone.

'Alasdair, you really are a most aggravating child,' she exclaimed angrily.

* There is a glossary at the end of the book giving English equivalents of Gaelic words and phrases.

She knew I hated being called a child, and I raised the book so that she should not see the hot flush that spread over my cheeks.

'Of course you are reading a book,' she went on. 'But what book? Don't tell me it is more nonsense about Prince Charlie and his precious rebellion.'

'Yes, it's about the Jacobites and Prince Charlie and the men who sheltered him even when the English put a price on his head.' I paused for breath. 'And it is not nonsense' I added defiantly.

The busy needles stopped clicking, and I knew I was going to catch it, but I did not care.

'*The English* put a price on his head,' said Aunt Evelyn coldly. 'You are not English, then?'

'No,' I said, 'I am a Scotsman.'

'A Scotsman who has spent almost all his twelve years in London,' she mocked.

'I was born in Skye,' I said stubbornly, 'and so was my father, so I must be a Highlander.'

My mother came in with the supper tray and placed it on the low table in front of the fire. She took the book from me and said wearily: 'Alasdair, you really must stop arguing with Aunt Evelyn. It is terribly bad of you.'

'I was simply trying to get that boy's nose out of his book,' said my aunt. 'It is not good for him. Just look at the hours he spends reading when he should be outside in the sunshine. You know he is supposed to be convalescing after bronchitis. Really, Anne, you should do something about it. No wonder he is so pale and thin.'

'Whom can I play with?' I said. 'All the other boys are at school.'

'There was plenty of time before supper when they were not at school,' retorted Aunt Evelyn in a tone that brooked no contradiction.

I stuck my hands in my trouser-pockets and looked down at my shoes.

'Well, I like reading,' I said loudly.

Aunt Evelyn laid her knitting on her lap and looked at my mother.

'Anne, anyone can see that that boy has never had a father to keep him in order,' she declared. 'You are far too lax with him.'

I knew what would follow and I wanted to say I was sorry, to help my mother, but the words choked in my throat and I sat there dumbly, looking down at my feet, not wanting to catch my mother's eye.

'Alasdair was two when his father's ship went down,' said my mother quietly. 'You know I can't take his father's place.'

'My dear Anne, that does not alter the fact that the child is developing into a dreamer and a bookworm,' replied my aunt, 'and it is our duty to make a man of him.'

'Aunt Evelyn doesn't like me,' I burst out. 'She is always nagging at me. It's – it's not fair,' and so saying I jumped up from my stool and made to rush out of the room.

As I straightened up, my right elbow caught the corner of the tray, knocking it off the table and scattering the supper things all over the carpet.

There was a horrible silence that seemed to last for minutes on end, and I stood quite still looking down sheepishly at the smashed cups and the spreading milk and tea stains on the pale pink of the carpet.

When my mother spoke I knew she was really angry.

'Everything Aunt Evelyn says about you is true,' she snapped. 'You are rude and careless and clumsy and if your father could see you now I am sure he would be ashamed of you. Don't stand there gawking so. Run and get a cloth and a basin of water before this carpet is ruined.'

I did as I was bidden, feeling my mother's words worse than the cut of a cane. But worse still was the knowledge that I had deserved it, and that my aunt had triumphed. I expected her to say something scathing, but she picked up the broken crockery and helped my mother sponge the carpet, and never said a word.

It was later, when we were taking our supper, that she spoke.

'Anne, I think it would be a good thing,' she said thoughtfully, 'if you sent Alasdair to Skye for a long holiday.'

My mother put down her cup so hurriedly that the tea splashed into the saucer. She swallowed.

'Send him where?'

'To Skye,' said Aunt Evelyn calmly. 'By the time you get everything arranged the school holidays will be almost here, and there is no point in sending Alasdair back to school for a week or so, not after his illness. A long holiday in Skye would do the boy a world of good.'

I could see the bewilderment on my mother's face and something else too. If they had not been discussing me I would have said she was frightened. She glanced at me, and rubbed the palm of her hand along the edge of the table, as if to reassure herself with the feel of something solid.

'But where could he stay?' she stammered at last.

'At Achmore, of course,' replied Aunt Evelyn. She smiled one of her rare smiles. 'I never can pronounce those Gaelic names properly. I think Highlanders must be born with a special sort of tongue.'

'Achmore,' said my mother, as if she had never heard the name before. Indeed, I had not.

'Why,' went on my aunt, and she smiled a second time, 'Alasdair is a property owner at Achmore, is he not?'

'The croft and cottage at Achmore belong to Alasdair,' said my mother slowly, not looking at me at all, but keeping her eyes fixed on a spot above my head. 'When he comes of age he can take over the croft if he wishes.'

'But how is it mine?' I asked. 'In Skye.'

'It was your father's croft,' she answered, 'and his father's before him. You were born there during the war.'

'But I don't remember,' I started.

'Of course not, silly,' smiled my mother. 'You were only two when I came back to London.' She sighed and the smile left her face, leaving it pinched and drawn. 'I came back to

London after Black Alasdair's ship went down. And a few months later the war was over.'

Black Alasdair was my father's name. Alasdair Dubh in the Gaelic.

'But why didn't you tell me I had a croft in Skye?' I persisted.

My mother fingered the plain gold ring on her finger and it seemed to be a long time before she spoke.

'You are only a boy at school, Alasdair,' she said at length, 'and the croft at Achmore is one of the things that won't really be yours until you are a man. Besides, Skye is a long way off.'

Aunt Evelyn glanced sharply at her, and said briskly: 'Well, there you are. Alasdair really owns this cottage and croft at Achmore and this relation of his who has been staying in the place for nothing all these years should be only too pleased to have him for a few months.'

'But he isn't really a close relative,' protested my mother. 'He is only a second cousin of Black Alasdair's.'

'Nonsense,' said my aunt firmly. 'You know perfectly well, Anne, that it is quite different in the Highlands. Even a second cousin is looked upon as a member of the family, and I am quite sure that Mr . . . Mr . . .'

'Mr Beaton,' said my mother. 'Murdo Beaton.'

'Well, I'm sure that Mr Beaton and his wife will look after Alasdair as if he were one of their own family.'

'His wife is dead,' said my mother, in a curiously expressionless voice. 'He has a daughter, but she is only a child about the same age as Alasdair. His old mother keeps house for him.'

Aunt Evelyn clicked her teeth, a sure sign that her patience was being tried.

'That is neither here nor there,' she declared. 'Alasdair has had too many women around him, anyway. It will do him good to have a man to deal with for a change.'

'But Murdo Beaton might not like to take him in,' protested my mother.

'Has he ever paid you rent for the use of the cottage and croft?' inquired Aunt Evelyn.

'Well, no,' admitted my mother. 'After the *Empire Rose* went down I had a letter from Murdo Beaton saying that Black Alasdair had given him permission to use the cottage and croft when we were in London. At that time I didn't care what happened. I didn't want to go back to Skye, and Alasdair was only a baby.'

'And Mr Beaton has occupied the cottage ever since,' prompted my aunt.

My mother nodded.

'That settles it then,' declared Aunt Evelyn briskly. 'The man can hardly refuse to take Alasdair when you have been so generous with him.'

My mother cast me an anxious glance.

'But the journey,' she said helplessly. 'All the way to Skye from London.'

'You can take him as far as Glasgow,' said Aunt Evelyn, who liked nothing better than organizing people. 'Stay the night in Glasgow and put him on the morning train to Skye. Alasdair isn't helpless. As long as he has a tongue in his head he can find his way about quite easily.'

'But he is so young to be going there alone.'

'Anne, unless you are careful you will be tying this boy to your apron strings,' said my aunt severely. 'After all, his father was at sea when he wasn't much older than Alasdair, and as far as I can see it did him no harm. How do you suppose he rose to be a sea captain before he was thirty?'

'But Alasdair is so small for his age,' protested my mother. 'And he is only twelve.'

I saw my aunt's contemptuous gaze on me, and the words burst from me in a breathless rush.

'I'm nearly thirteen,' I cried, 'and if I have a croft in Skye I want to go and see it, and I know the way because I've looked it out on the map dozens and dozens of times.'

That clinched it. My mother's protests were swept aside, and when I went to bed that night she was already writing a letter to my father's cousin in Achmore.

I don't know why, but somehow or other I never really expected my mother to get a reply from Murdo Beaton in Skye. To me, Skye belonged to the land of make-believe; to stories of Prince Charlie and his hurried flight across the island disguised as a spinning maid; to clan feuds of long ago, and to old sad songs. It was another world from the one I lived in. My world was bound up with the smell of new books in Aunt Evelyn's shop; with escalators and tube trains; with endless streets and hurrying people, and dead flies in the window of Mr Goldsmith's antique shop on the corner, where I waited for the bus to take me to school. It did not seem possible that I could step out of my drab world into that other far-away world where Prince Charlie had rallied the clans and the Fiery Cross had flamed on the hills.

But one Tuesday morning the letter came. I knew it at once because it was postmarked Portree. My mother took it from me and sat down. She did not seem to hear me when I urged her to open it, although Aunt Evelyn was caught up in my excitement.

'Oh, do open it, Anne,' she exclaimed. 'Can't you see Alasdair's just dying to know what the man says?'

My mother opened the letter without a word and unfolded a single sheet of crumpled notepaper.

'What does he say?' I cried. 'Can I go?'

My mother cleared her throat.

'Dear Mistress Cameron,' she read. 'You know what a great friend I was of Alasdair Dubh, poor man. I shall be pleased to welcome his son to Skye. But it will be strange for the boy after life in the city, so do not be surprised if he gets homesick and I have to send him back to you.'

She paused.

'Well, go on,' said Aunt Evelyn.

My mother handed her the letter.

'That's all,' she said.

'Dear, dear,' clucked Aunt Evelyn, as she scanned the brief note. 'What a strange man. You would have thought he would have had more to say than that.'

'I don't suppose he writes many letters,' said my mother.

No more was said about it. The shortness of the letter was soon forgotten in the excitement of planning the journey. Aunt Evelyn took command and drew up a list of the things I would need, but my mother was strangely silent and withdrawn, and I could not help feeling that she should have been pleased with me now that I was setting out on my own for the first time. I felt sure my father would have been, if he could have seen me.

As soon as supper was over, I went to bed. I was already travelling, in my imagination, through the purple hills on my way to the west – travelling over hills and lochs with names like proud battle-cries. For a long time I lay awake, saying softly to myself, over and over again, 'By Tummel and Loch Rannoch and Lochaber I will go,' until the words gathered momentum, like the wheels of an express train, and I was plunged into an uneasy sleep.

I dreamed I was striding through the heather, when I saw an old woman with a creel of peats on her back. I took the creel from her and she straightened up and I saw that it wasn't an old woman at all, but Prince Charlie, and I cried out in astonishment.

My mother's voice whispered: 'Hush, Alasdair, you've been dreaming.'

I tried to tell her that I had seen Prince Charlie, but before I could speak I felt her cool fingers stroking my forehead, and I fell into a deep, dreamless sleep.

Chapter 2

AUNT EVELYN saw us off at Euston Station on a sunny Monday morning. In the dim cavern of the station all was bustle and movement. Porters rushed here and there with trucks piled high with baggage; long queues formed outside the ticket offices, and latecomers hurried for their trains. At regular intervals a voice blared over the loudspeakers announcing train departures.

'Attention, please,' boomed the voice. 'The eight-thirty to Glasgow will be leaving Platform Twelve in five minutes' time, calling at Rugby, Stafford, Crewe, Carlisle. . . .'

'Oh, hurry,' I urged, one eye on the large black minute-hand of the station clock, slowly creeping round to the half-hour mark, 'or we will miss the train.'

Aunt Evelyn was calmly selecting magazines at the bookstall, and all she said was: 'Don't fuss so, Alasdair. I have never yet missed a train, and I do so hate spending hours over farewells.'

She collected several magazines and paid the girl, then added in a kindlier tone, doubtless conscious of my squirming impatience: 'Don't worry, I promise you we shan't miss the train.'

Aunt Evelyn was as good as her word. She found us two corner seats, settled our luggage on the rack to her own satisfaction, and kissed my mother good-bye before the guard's whistle shrilled.

She shook hands with me through the open window and when I withdrew my hand I discovered a pound note in my palm. I blurted out my thanks, but the train was already moving slowly out of the station, and I doubt if Aunt Evelyn heard me. But she smiled and waved, and I felt, without knowing why, that she was pleased with me, and the realization of this was so unexpected that I wanted to cry out to her that I was sorry for all the things that I had said and done in the past. But such thoughts always come too late, and, as if to make up for all that I had left unsaid, I waved and waved until she was a tiny speck in the distance. I was still waving when the platform could no longer be seen, and my mother called to me to come away from the window.

I hardly remember anything about the journey to Glasgow, although most of the time I gazed out of the window watching the green fields go spinning by. My mother never spoke, except to answer my questions, but from time to time I felt her eyes on me. Whenever I looked up she smiled and went on with her reading, but I knew that something was troubling her. I could not understand why she could not accept my holiday in Skye in the same happy spirit as Aunt Evelyn had shown. But such dismal thoughts were soon forgotten in the growing excitement of the journey ahead. In a few hours we would be in Glasgow, and the very next morning I would be starting out on my own, like any lone adventurer from a tale of long ago.

We stayed overnight in Glasgow at an hotel near Queen Street Station, for the train to Mallaig left at four minutes to six in the morning. After dinner I had a bath and got into bed. I lay with my eyes closed, listening to the noise of the traffic in the street outside, hardly able to believe that I was at last in Glasgow and that tomorrow I would be in Skye.

My mother came into the room so quietly that I did not hear her until she whispered: 'Alasdair, are you asleep?'

'No,' I said, opening my eyes. 'I was just thinking.'

She sat down on the side of the bed and I noticed how tired she looked.

'What were you thinking about?' she asked presently.

I rubbed one foot against the other, feeling pleasantly drowsy in the cool comfort of the bed.

'Just thinking,' I answered and then, knowing the angry retort that would have sprung to Aunt Evelyn's lips if she could have heard me, I added: 'I was thinking how good it is going to be staying in Skye.'

'Is it?'

The words were spoken gently, sorrowfully almost, certainly not with any bitterness or malice, but I was suddenly angry. I struggled into a sitting position and said hotly: 'You don't think I am old enough to go to Skye on my own, do you? You think I am just a baby.'

My mother put a hand on my arm and shook her head.

After a while, she said: 'I don't want you to be disappointed, Alasdair, that's all.'

'Why should I be disappointed?' I demanded, not wanting to argue with her, but still feeling angry.

'Well, it is all so different to your life in London,' replied my mother. 'It is all so . . . so much rougher.'

'Aunt Evelyn says it will make a man of me,' I retorted.

'Aunt Evelyn hasn't the faintest idea of what it is like to live in a black house in Skye,' she said quietly.

'What's a black house?' I asked. It was the first time I had heard the phrase.

'It's an old thatched cottage,' said my mother, 'with poky little rooms and great thick walls with tiny windows that let in hardly any light at all.'

'Is my cottage a black house?' I asked eagerly.

'Yes, it is a black house,' she said quietly, 'with bare stone floors and no water and no electric light.'

'But what has that got to do with it?' I cried, caught up in a sudden surge of resentment. 'It's not fair, you spoiling it all for me like this. Why can't you be glad like Aunt Evelyn?'

'I am glad, Alasdair, awfully glad that you are not afraid to go to a strange place by yourself,' said my mother gently.

'But it's not strange to me,' I insisted. 'I know all about it. I have read dozens and dozens of books about Skye and the Highlands.'

'I know,' she said. 'That's the trouble.'

'Why?'

She smiled, a strange, crooked smile, and said earnestly: 'Can't you see, Alasdair, I don't want you to get hurt.'

'But I'll be careful,' I said. 'Promise. Cross my heart.'

It was an old game of ours, and my mother laughed as I marked a cross on my pyjama-jacket.

'Not that sort of hurt,' she said seriously. 'A hurt inside of you. You see, Alasdair, you have read too many books about things that happened a long, long time ago. You think that everything in the Highlands is wonderful, that it is all flashing tartans and pipers playing and noble clansmen. But all that sort of thing died out a long time ago, if it ever existed. It is as far away as Prince Charlie. Why, some of your Highlanders are mean and nasty, just like some people in London. Some of them would lie to you and be deceitful, if they thought it would help them. They are just the same as other people, no better and no worse. I do want you to realize that, Alasdair, or you are going to get hurt.'

'But you are English,' I said stubbornly.

'Well, that makes you half English,' she said, smiling.

'But I was born in Skye,' I said quickly. 'Besides, I am going to a friend of my father's.'

'Was Murdo Beaton a friend of your father's?' said my mother softly, half to herself.

'You know he was,' I retorted. 'He said so in his letter.'

'I don't know,' she said, frowning, 'I just don't know.' She bit her bottom lip, and I could see that she was undecided whether to continue or not, but then she went on: 'Black Alasdair never spoke to me of Murdo Beaton. He spoke of many of his friends in Skye but never of Murdo Beaton.'

'But my father let him have the croft until we wanted it again. You told me so yourself,' said I, trying to keep sufficiently awake to digest this bewildering piece of news.

'Murdo Beaton *said* your father let him have the croft,' my mother replied slowly. She sighed and shook her head wearily. 'I just don't know for sure, Alasdair, that is what upsets me. I never saw Murdo Beaton when we were in Skye. He was work-

ing somewhere on the mainland in those days. It was only after
. . . after your father was lost that I got the letter from him.
You were only two. But now – well, now I am not so sure.'

'Well, I wouldn't worry about Murdo Beaton,' I declared.
'He must have been a friend of my father's or he would never
have dreamed of writing you in the first place.'

'I suppose so,' she said doubtfully, and then, smiling: 'I
don't know what made me indulge in all this silly talk. What
I really came in for was to give you this present.'

My mother handed me a small rectangular parcel. The
wrapping was sealed with Sellotape and the package felt hard.
I turned it over in my hands and looked at her wonderingly.

'It's a present for you to take to Skye with you,' said my
mother.

'But what is it?' I asked. 'It feels awful hard.'

'Go ahead and open it,' she smiled.

'Oh, but what is it?' I cried, fumbling at the adhesive tape on
the wrapping paper.

'It is something you will be looking at an awful lot,' answered
my mother, but more than that she would not say.

I broke the tape with impatient fingers and ripped off the
wrapping paper, disclosing a small cardboard box. I plucked
off the lid and there was a wrist-watch with a leather strap.

'Gosh!' I exclaimed. 'It's just what I wanted,' and I tried
to strap it on my wrist, but I was so excited that I could not get
the metal prong through a hole in the stiff new leather of the
strap.

My mother fastened it for me, but there were not sufficient
holes in the strap to fasten the watch securely to my thin wrist.
She saw my disappointment and hurried to her room to fetch
a hatpin, and pierced a new hole in the strap so that the watch
fitted snugly against my wrist. I wound it up and set it to the
right time by my mother's watch, and held it to my ear and
listened to the steady tick.

'It has got luminous hands,' my mother said. 'You can tell the
time in the dark.'

I burrowed under the blankets, making a dark cave to test the luminous dial of the watch.

My mother laughed when I emerged with tousled hair, and said excitedly: 'You can too, it's as clear as can be.'

'Well,' she said, 'I am glad you like it,' and we sat together in a companionable silence as we often did in the flat at home when we were alone together.

After a while, we started to talk again, but this time it was of small things, like looking after the kitten while I was away, and arranging to write home as soon as I got to Achmore, and we laughed together when we remembered the fat woman who had got into our compartment at Crewe and eaten her way steadily through an enormous box of chocolates.

My mother went on to tell me about the first time she had gone away from home on a school trip to France, and I felt myself becoming steadily drowsier. I struggled hard to keep awake, but there were leaden weights on my eyelids dragging them shut, and my mother's voice merged with the sound of the traffic in the street outside, and that too faded, and was suddenly still.

From a great way off, I heard her say: 'Alasdair, are you asleep?'

I rubbed my eyes and stretched and yawned.

My mother bent down and kissed me lightly on the forehead.

'Off you go to sleep,' she said. 'We have to be up at five in the morning, and you have a long journey ahead of you.'

I wriggled down in the bed and she tucked in the blankets.

'And Alasdair.'

'Yes?' I said.

'Always remember, whatever happens, that you are Black Alasdair's son, and that everybody you meet in Skye will be thinking of him when they see you. Just try to be a man . . . like him.'

'Be a man,' I murmured drowsily.

I rolled over on my side and was asleep before the door closed behind her.

Chapter 3

IT was raining in the morning, a fine persistent drizzle, and Queen Street Station, without the noise and bustle of hundreds of holidaymakers, looked as drab as an empty football ground. My mother and I walked down the long platform in silence, and I climbed aboard the train and stowed my luggage on the rack. Now that the time had come to part, I did not know what to say, and my stomach felt curiously empty, although I had just eaten a good breakfast of bacon and egg and sausages.

I leaned out of the window, wishing that the guard would blow his whistle, and my mother stood on the platform, one hand resting on the carriage door.

'Don't poke your head out of the window when the train is moving,' she said, 'and when you get to Mallaig just follow all the people and the porters from the station to the pier. You get on the *Lochnevis* and stay on her until you reach Portree. If Murdo Beaton doesn't meet you, get on the red bus at the pier and ask the driver to put you off at Achmore.'

I nodded absently, because I had heard the instructions so many times before that I knew them off by heart, and an awkward silence came between us. It is strange how some silences affect you more than words, so that your skin tingles and you feel that if you don't speak you will have to creep away and hide, but you remain rooted to the spot, speechless and tongue-tied.

Before I realized what was happening the guard's green flag was waving up and down, and the train had started with a sudden jerk. I was caught unprepared and the sudden movement threw me off my balance. By the time I had regained the window the train was moving out of the station and I could only clasp my mother's hand for a brief moment.

I leaned out of the window, waving furiously, and felt a lump rise in my throat at the sight of her standing there alone, waving back. I had never thought of my mother as being small; indeed, she was a good head taller than Aunt Evelyn, and Aunt Evelyn was not a small woman. But seeing her standing there on the almost deserted platform, dirty with the unswept litter of the previous day, she looked curiously small and frail, and I waved and waved long after she had disappeared from view and the train was clanking over the network of points outside the station.

I stood by the window until I felt myself shivering in the chill morning air, then I turned and made my way blindly into a compartment and sat down and gazed fixedly out of the window. The window was misted with rain, but I could see row upon row of dingy houses, tall factory chimneys and the spidery network of cranes down by the river. It was all drab and grey, and I had a sudden longing for the familiar, cosy flat; supper on a stool by the fire with a book on my knees, and lazy Sunday afternoons in the park or on the river. For the first time in my life I was alone, and instead of rejoicing in my freedom I felt utterly defenceless and afraid.

I wished that the sun would come out and shut my eyes and counted ten and said to myself, when I open my eyes again the sun will be shining.

I had counted up to eight when a man's voice said: 'Where are ye bound for, laddie?'

I started and opened my eyes, and he laughed, seeing the evident astonishment on my face.

'You were in a wee bit dream,' he said, in the broad friendly dialect of the Scottish Lowlands. 'You didna notice me at all.'

'No, I didn't,' I stammered. 'I didn't see you.'

He was a very fat man with a red, kindly face, and when he laughed the watch-chain across his waistcoat joggled up and down.

'I didna think I was the kind to be overlooked sae easily,' he said dryly, 'but maybe you had mair things on your mind than admiring the likes o' me.'

'I am going to Skye,' I said proudly.

'Well, well,' he exclaimed, 'that's a gey long road for a wee fellow.'

'I'm nearly thirteen,' I said, flushing.

I half expected him to laugh, but he did not. Instead he looked at me with kindly eyes, and said slowly: 'This is your first time away from home, is it no'?'

'Yes,' I said, swallowing hard, and thinking that my voice sounded like a stranger's. 'But how did you know?'

'Och, well,' he said, stroking his chin thoughtfully with a great ham of a hand, 'Jamie Finlayson was no' born yesterday. You see, laddie, I'm a man who was travelling the world when I was no' much older than you are yoursel', and I'm thinking that the first time I took the lang road frae home I was looking much the way ye're lookin' yoursel' this forenoon.'

'Well, I'm glad to be going,' I declared, although I did not really feel very glad at that moment.

'Good for you, laddie,' he cried. 'And what's your name?'

'Alasdair Cameron,' I said.

'A good Hielan' name,' said he, 'and if I may say so, Alasdair, it's mysel' wishes I were away to Skye along wi' you. A good man is a good man onywhere, but a good Heilan' man is a king o' men.'

'Have you been to Skye?' I inquired timidly.

He slapped his thigh and let out a great bellow of laughter.

'Man alive!' he roared. 'Have I been to Skye! See that?' — and here he patted his great belly — 'it wasna always there. Listen, Alasdair, I've climbed Sgurr nan Gillean in the Black Cuillin; I've scrambled my way to the top of the Storr Rock and walked by Beinn Edra all the way to the Quiraing; I've lain in the heather up beyond Earlish watching the sun setting over Uig Bay, and many's the braw salmon I've lifted out o' Glenvarragill River an' no' with a fly either. Have I been to Skye, laddie? I've tramped the hills o' Skye from Ardvasar to

Duntulm and ye can take it from me there's no' a place like it on the face o' God's earth if ye're strong in the leg and no' afraid o' a good drooking.'

'I suppose you have got lots of friends in Skye?' I said.

'Och, I was aye blessed wi' good friends,' he replied. 'But, mind you, Alasdair, there's mony a gamekeeper in Skye would like to lay hands on Jamie Finlayson.' He laughed his great, roaring laugh, until the tears started in his eyes. 'Ye'd hardly credit it tae see me now, but there wasna a keeper in Skye could get his nose to my heels. But those days are lang past, lang past.'

My friend got out at Helensburgh, but before he left he shook hands solemnly and wished me luck.

He was easing his great bulk out of the door, when he turned and said quietly: 'I was aye a friend o' the tinkers, Alasdair, guid folk too, for a' that's said aboot them. If ever you need the help o' a tinker in Skye, tell them Jamie Finlayson sent you.'

And then he was gone with his great rumbling laugh echoing through the corridor, and I little thought that the name of Jamie Finlayson would come to my rescue in the dark days that lay ahead.

I was sorry when he left, but his company had cheered me, and I watched eagerly as we made our way north by the sea-lochs, past Garelochhead to Arrochar into the heart of the great hills of Argyll. The train cut through the glen, to Loch Lomond, and I craned my neck out of the window trying to get a glimpse of Ben Lomond, but the mountain was shrouded in mist. The rain dripped down steadily, and the sound of running water was everywhere as the rushing burns streamed down the flanks of the hillsides. Everything was grey and weeping, so much so that a thin spiral of brown smoke, rising from a newly kindled fire in a wayside cottage, made a splash of colour.

We reached Ardlui, the gateway to the Highlands, and I remembered how many times I had traced the route on my atlas at home. From Ardlui the train climbed steadily through silent hills, with never a house in sight, until we were speeding across the desolate wastes of Rannoch Moor. Two fishermen in oilskins, their rods slung over their shoulders, got out at Rannoch Station, then the train moved on again into a grey, featureless wilderness.

On and on over the unending moors, pitted with peat bogs and lonely lochans and north by Loch Treig into the Glen of Spean. The rain drifted down unceasingly, and, looking out at the wet moors, I was sure that the sun never shone on this lonely land. We travelled along by the side of the River Spean, until we were under the mist-wreathed shoulder of Scotland's highest mountain, Ben Nevis, and the train slowly came to a standstill in Fort William.

We were a long time in Fort William, and I leaned out of the window watching the restaurant car and two coaches being uncoupled and shunted away. The station was crowded with holidaymakers, and dotted with islands of luggage. Everyone seemed to be talking at once and the noise and bustle and shouts of laughter made me feel my own loneliness and isolation more keenly than when we had been travelling through the silent hills. Nobody on the station, it seemed to me, was alone. Everyone seemed to be happy and excited, as one should be when starting a holiday, and I was miserably conscious of my own wretchedness. If only I had someone to talk to, I thought, I would not be feeling like this, but I comforted myself with the thought that once I reached Skye and the welcome of my father's friends my loneliness would vanish.

The crowds had drifted away from the station, and a porter was clearing up the last island of baggage, when the train moved forward again. The porter looked up and saw my face at the window, and he smiled and waved to me. I waved back, wondering if he knew how much his friendly gesture meant to me.

The train was winding round the bend at Corpach when I first noticed the strange behaviour of the man in the corridor. He was standing with his back to my compartment, his hands behind him gripping the bar that crossed the window. At first

I glanced at him idly, then turned to look out of the window again. I don't know what made me look round a second time, but when I did, I noticed his hands. They were clenched so tightly on the window bar that the knuckles stood out whitely. There was a scar on the man's left hand; a long red weal stretching in a jagged, diagonal line, from the knuckle joint of his little finger to his wrist. I watched the man's hands for a long time. They were straining at the window bar as if trying to snap it in two, relaxing for an instant only to grip it again in a desperate clasp. I never took my eyes off those hands. They were gripping the window bar in the way that a drowning man would seize a life-line. But this man was not drowning. He was standing in the corridor of the Glasgow to Mallaig train with people within call on either side of him.

I could not see his face, or even the back of his head, only his shoulders and his clenching hands, but I knew there was something wrong. I knew that even before he turned round and slid the door open, and I saw his face.

Chapter 4

I LOOKED at the man framed in the doorway, and he stood stock-still looking back at me. He was a young man, dressed in a shabby fawn raincoat and a soft hat. His face was damp with sweat, and he passed the back of his hand across his forehead, and glanced quickly down the corridor before closing the door. He crossed the carriage in two quick strides and stood towering over me.

I followed his gaze and discovered that he was looking at my suitcase. There was a leather-bound label hanging from the handle of the case, bearing my name and address in Skye in large capital letters. Aunt Evelyn always insisted on attaching labels to our suitcases if we were going anywhere. The stranger glanced at the label for a moment, then tucked it under the case so that it was hidden from view, and sat down beside me.

For one wild moment I thought of running out of the compartment but he could have caught me easily before I reached the corridor, and even if I managed to call the guard, or another man, what could I say? That his hands had clutched the window bar in a desperate grasp? That he was sweating, although a cold wind, sweeping down from Ben Nevis, was blowing through the open window and chilling the air? That he had pushed the address label on my suitcase out of sight? There was nothing wrong in what he had done, however sinister it might seem. I would be laughed at, and told I had been imagining things. They would ask me how old I was, and tell me I should stay at home with my mother.

It is easy to scoff at one's own fears, but it is not so easy to dispel them. I could reason with myself, say to myself I was behaving like a silly girl, but I could not stop the quick fluttering of my heart. My senses were suddenly magnified. I could hear the rapid beating of my heart. It was loud in my ears, and I thought that the man next to me must hear it too.

I was looking out of the window at the wild, wet landscape, and all the time I knew that the stranger's eyes were fixed on me. I wanted to get up and run, but my legs felt paralysed. I could not even turn my head to look at the man by my side.

I sat quite still in a silent agony of apprehension, made worse by the growing certainty that at any moment I would be seized by those clutching hands in the same desperate grasp that had almost wrenched the window bar from its sockets.

The sound of the door sliding open jerked me round like a puppet on a string. A man stepped into the compartment, closed the door, and sat down in the opposite corner by the door. The newcomer was wearing a brown tweed suit and a tweed cap pulled well down over his eyes. His face was lean and weatherbeaten, not like the faces one sees every day in London. It was the face of a man who has spent most of his life out of doors in places where there are no city streets to block the driving wind and rain or break the fierce rays of the hot summer sun. But it was his eyes that I noticed most. They were a brilliant, light blue, and they never wavered from the face of the man sitting beside me.

Presently he took out a nail file and started to file his nails. I watched him carefully but his eyes never once looked down at his hands. They were fixed unblinkingly on the man in the raincoat. I was reminded of a snake I had watched one Saturday afternoon at the zoo in Regent's Park. It had the same sort of eyes. The same coldness and the same unwavering stare.

Nobody spoke, but I felt sure that it was not the first time these two had met. There was a tension in the air that did not spring from my own imagination; a feeling of two wills pitted one against the other in deadly combat. Although neither of them moved, they were like two boxers poised in the centre of the ring, each one watching warily for the other to strike the first blow.

The man with the light blue eyes went on filing his nails. He did it with quick, dexterous strokes of the file, never once looking down at his hands. He had broad, square hands and powerful fingers, but he handled the nail file as delicately as a woman. I had never before seen a man using a nail file in public, but there was nothing womanish about him. Those brown strong hands, I reflected, could have held a horse's bridle or the wheel of a car, or a gun, just as capably as they were holding the tiny metal file.

The man beside me never moved, but I could feel the tenseness of his body. I thought again of moving out into the corridor into the company of people who chatted and laughed and read magazines and fell asleep and did all the normal things people always do on train journeys. But I was rooted to my seat by the silence as much as anything. There was something sinister about it. I felt that if I moved I would break it, and something would happen. So I sat quite still in my corner, listening to the scrape of the nail file and the quick breathing of the man by my side.

The train was rushing westwards to the isles, by land-loch and sea-loch, through the land of Morar. This was Prince Charlie's country. It was into Loch-nan-Uamh that his ship came sailing, and the Prince landed, without an army, and attempted to win a crown. And it was in Morar, a year later, that the Prince fled through the heather, a fugitive with a price on his head.

I wondered if the man with the scar could be a fugitive; was it possible that he, too, was being pursued through this land of the heather and the mist? But all my wild thoughts vanished as the train slowed down and drew into Glenfinnan Station.

Far below, at the head of Loch Shiel, I could see Prince Charlie's Monument with the stone figure of the Prince gazing out over the loch. The rain dripped down unceasingly, grey hills loomed up all around out of the grey mist, and the sound of running water was everywhere. It must have been a day like this, I thought, when his ship sailed out of Loch-nan-Uamh, and he left behind a lost cause and the broken spirits of his clansmen. I looked for a long time at the stone figure on the monument, and thought of the day the Prince had raised his standard here with his clansmen rallying to his call. And all that was left now was the monument, alone in the mist and the rain at the head of the loch. The small figure of the stationmaster, in his shabby uniform, went past the window, and I looked at him sorrowfully for he had no place in my dreams of Glenfinnan.

The train started with a jerk, shattering my reverie and bringing me back from dreams of the past to the hidden menace of the present. The same ominous silence prevailed in the compartment, but I felt a movement at my side. I looked round. The man with the scar had taken a small black diary from his pocket and was writing something in it. A few moments later he put the diary away, and sat hunched forward, his hands thrust deep into his raincoat pockets. The other man never moved. He continued filing his nails, but his brilliant blue eyes were watchful and intent.

They were sitting like that when the train entered the tunnel.

The compartment was plunged in darkness and almost at once a man's strong fingers fastened around my wrist. For some reason or other, probably because I was too frightened, I did not cry out or struggle. The pressure on my wrist compelled me to bend my arm, and I felt a ball of paper being thrust into my palm, then my fingers were forced down over it and my hand thrust into my raincoat pocket with my fist still doubled round the tiny ball of paper. Streaks of light filtered through the darkness, and the train passed out of the tunnel before I realized that the pressure on my wrist had relaxed and I was free.

The man with the scar was still sitting hunched forward, his hands deep in the pockets of his raincoat, and the man with the nail file was watching him as intently as ever. Everything remained the same as it had been before we entered the tunnel, except for the piece of paper I could feel in my clenched fist and the wild racing of my heart.

The man with the scar got up swiftly and stepped into the

corridor. He was no sooner through the door when the other man rose to his feet and followed him. I moved to the other side of the compartment where I could look down the length of the corridor. The man with the scar was standing by the outer door of the train some way down the corridor, but the man in the tweed suit had stopped just outside the compartment. He had his back to me, but I knew that his brilliant blue eyes would be fixed on the face of his quarry.

The train drew into Lochailort Station, and the man with the scar stepped back from the door to allow an old woman to get off the train. He slammed the door shut himself and, as the train moved forward again, took out a cigarette and lit it. I saw the taut back of the man in the tweed suit relax, and the train gathered speed out of the station.

What happened next was so unexpected that I found myself standing in the corridor without realizing how I had got there.

The man with the scar spat out his newly lighted cigarette, threw the door open, and leapt off the train. The man in the tweed suit swung round and faced me, and I was conscious of those brilliant blue eyes taking in every detail of my face and figure. It was as if he were photographing me in his mind. Then he raced down the corridor to where the open door was swinging crazily backwards and forwards and for one dreadful moment I thought he was about to throw himself off the train. But he had hesitated too long, and with every passing second the train had gathered speed. Suddenly he threw up his arm and pulled the communication cord. I heard the shriek of protesting metal as the emergency brakes were applied, but before the train had stopped he had jumped out of the open door.

I saw him rolling down the embankment, head over heels, but he scrambled to his feet and made off in the direction of Lochailort. I caught a glimpse of him running hard with his head down before a clump of trees hid him from view.

The corridor was filling with people, all chattering excitedly, and I heard a woman's high-pitched voice say: 'It was a man in a brown suit. I saw him jump off the train.'

The guard appeared on the scene with a notebook in his hand. I heard the woman's voice again, and the guard moistened his pencil on his tongue and started writing. There was no mention of the man with the scar, and I slowly realized that I must have been the only witness to have seen him jump off the train.

The guard passed on down the corridor and when he drew level with me, I said:

'I saw him jump off, the man with the scar.'

He was an old man, and his jacket was too big for him, giving him a slightly comic appearance, but there was nothing amusing about his face when he turned to me. It was red and angry.

'Look here, young fellow-me-lad,' he barked, prodding me in the chest with a squat forefinger, 'there's no need for you to add any fancy trimmings of your own. It's wonderful what folk will remember when they think it might get themselves a wee line in the newspapers. There's a woman back yonder even got the colour of his eyes. Wonderful bright blue eyes she says.' He snorted. 'We're thirty-five minutes late, an' a passenger wanting off at Beasdale, so no more of it, d'you hear. No more of it.'

And so saying, he stamped off down the corridor, leaving me standing there helplessly, not knowing what to do. I went back into the compartment and sat down, and the train had started again before I realized that I was still clutching the ball of paper in my clenched fist. I smoothed it out carefully. It was a single sheet of thin paper torn from a pocket diary. Printed across it, in pencilled block letters, were the words: HUNT AT THE HILL OF THE RED FOX MI5.

I read the single sentence again and again, and the more I read it the more puzzled I became. This was the message furtively thrust into my hand in the darkness of the tunnel by the man with the scar, before he had risked his life in leaping from the moving train. Surely there must be some meaning in it. But a hunt could only mean a fox-hunt, and there were no fox-hunts in the Highlands, as far as I knew. The words spun round and round in my brain, and it was a long time before I thought I saw the obvious answer. To hunt could mean to search. Well, then, suppose I was intended to search for something at the Hill of the Red Fox? But how could the sender of the message know that I would be able to find the Hill of the Red Fox? And what on earth had M 15 got to do with it? Submarines, I knew, were often referred to by a single letter and two numerals, but what connexion could there be between a submarine and a hill?

I felt my heartbeats quicken as the thought flashed through my mind, perhaps there is treasure hidden at the Hill of the Red Fox. Perhaps the man with the scar had been travelling north to recover his hidden treasure, and his pursuer was a member of a rival gang. I thought of all the stories I had heard of ships being wrecked off the Hebrides during the war. Perhaps one of them had been carrying gold and her looted cargo had been hidden in the hills. But it still did not make sense. There was no point in giving me a message when I did not know where the treasure was hidden. Anyway, that sort of thing only happened in books.

I folded the paper in two and placed it in my wallet. Somehow or other, I had become involved in something beyond my understanding, and when I got to Skye I determined to seek Murdo Beaton's help. But although I had put the paper away, I still puzzled over the meaning of the message.

I never saw the golden sands of Arisaig, and I never realized that the train had stopped in Mallaig Station until a friendly porter tapped on the window and shouted that I had better hurry if I was bound for Skye. I snatched up my case and ran down the long platform, past the empty fish boxes, wrinkling my nose at the strong smell of fish.

Outside the station, on the way to the jetty, I stopped for a moment in sheer wonderment. There before me, across the grey green waters of the Sound of Sleat, stood the hills of Skye. For the first time in my life I smelled the tangle of the isles.

Chapter 5

THE Royal Mail Steamer, *Lochnevis*, chugged its way up the Sound of Sleat, past the rocky coastline of Knoydart and Loch Hourn. A friendly deckhand pointed out the white flag of the Royal Mail on her foremast, and on her mainmast, below the Red Ensign, the House Flag of David MacBrayne, Ltd, a red and white cross on a blue ground. Her single funnel was painted a gleaming red, topped by a broad band of black.

I stood on deck, watching the gulls wheel and circle round the ship, and a line from a poem I knew about the seabirds' lonely cry flashed through my mind. Old sailors thought they were the spirits of dead mariners, and there was certainly something strange about the way in which they wheeled around the ship, as if they were anxiously watching over its course.

A door opened on the foredeck, and I sniffed the savoury smell of soup, and realized for the first time how hungry I was. I went down below to the saloon, and sat at a table with a raised lip round the edges to prevent plates sliding off in rough weather, and ate a lunch of scotch broth and ham salad. At home I was always being chided for not eating enough, but the Highland air had given me such an appetite that I ate every scrap of the food set before me.

After lunch I went back on deck. It was still raining and great masses of thick grey clouds cloaked the peaks of the surrounding hills. I leaned over the rail, heedless of the rain, my eyes fixed on the rocky coastline of Skye.

The *Lochnevis* was steaming up the Kyle Narrows, and I saw the road winding down through lonely Glen Arroch to the little stone pier of Kylerhea. There was a house close to the pier, built on the water's edge, and a fishing boat lay at her moorings in front of the house. The road through Glen Arroch was the old drovers' road. In the old days the shaggy Highland cattle of Skye passed along this road in their hundreds. I saw the ruins of a long white building above the pier, and wondered if it could be the inn where the drovers once stayed before embarking on the hazardous crossing to Glenelg. They rowed across the swift waters of the Narrows, and drove the cattle all the way to Falkirk where the great cattle sales were held.

At Kyle of Lochalsh the hatch covers were lifted and we took aboard boxes and crates from the quayside. I marvelled at the way the deckhands piled box upon box into a loosely built pyramid, held together by a rope sling, which was attached to a hook at the end of the derrick cable. The whole swaying structure was lifted high into the air by the derrick, swung aboard, and poised over the gaping hole of the hatch. Then, at a shouted word of command in Gaelic, from the depths of the hold, the derrick man slowly let down his load.

From Kyle we made our way round Scalpay to the Island of Raasay, where a family of four struggled ashore with several large trunks, fishing rods, guns and three red setter dogs. Half an hour later the *Lochnevis* rounded a rocky headland and came into Portree Bay.

The curving crescent of the bay was ringed by houses and the hillside rose so steeply from the shore that I had the impression of houses perched one above the other, like men in the rigging of a ship. The *Lochnevis* drew in slowly to the pier, and I looked up to the bridge and saw the burly figure of the captain standing outside the wheelhouse. At that moment, he raised his hand to sound the ship's hooter, and, although I was expecting it, I jumped at the tremendous, deafening blast. I expected to see doors flung open, and people rush out to see the cause of the commotion, but everything went on as before. The people strolling down the pier road continued at the same easy pace, as if nothing had happened.

As we drew near the pier, a seaman in the stern tossed a coiled heaving line ashore. Two men on the pier seized it, and hauled in the heavy mooring rope and secured it to a bollard.

Another line was tossed from the bows, and the steamer drew in to the pier.

I scanned the faces of the people on the pier as I walked down the gangway, but nobody gave me a second look. I had a curious sinking feeling when I realized that Murdo Beaton had not come to meet me, but I tried to shrug it off, and made my way past the rickety turnstile to the road. The red bus was parked by the side of the road a little way from the pier. I asked the driver if he would put me off at Achmore, and he nodded and went on talking to a thick-set man in plus-fours with a collie at his heels. I sat down on the front seat and watched the crowds streaming past.

Two hikers, bowed down under the weight of enormous packs, boarded the bus, but the rest of the passengers seemed to be local people. I noticed that most of the men were dressed in blue serge suits and cloth caps, and I looked in vain for the bright flash of a kilt.

After a while, the driver climbed into his seat and the bus moved off up a steep hill. It turned left into a street with shops on either side and swung into a wide, open square, joining the line of buses already parked there. The driver got out and I watched him cross the square and enter a shop. When he returned he carried an armful of newspapers and magazines, all done up neatly in small bundles. He arranged them in some kind of order, tucking them behind a leather strap below his window.

The driver started the engine again and was about to let in the clutch when a man dashed across the square and boarded the bus. He was carrying two large cardboard boxes and when he set them down I heard the muffled cheeping of day-old chicks. The driver spoke to him in Gaelic, and the man laughed, and they chatted away together. One by one the other buses in the square departed, and I began to feel their conversation would never come to an end. But at length the man with the chicks took his seat, and the bus moved slowly out of the square.

We took the road out of Portree, and I could see the whole

expanse of the bay laid out far below. I saw the roofs of the buildings at the pier; the bright green of the petrol storage tanks, and the *Lochnevis* lying still at her moorings. At that distance, she looked like a toy steamer set against a toy pier.

I glanced at my watch. It was half past six. When I looked up again we were moving across open moorland with never a house in sight.

The road was narrow and winding, and from time to time the driver had to pull into a passing place, a shallow arc of levelled ground extending from the road, in order to let an approaching car go by. We travelled on and on over featureless moors, scarred here and there with the fresh black face of newly cut peat banks. The cut peats were stacked in small cone-shaped heaps along the top of the banks. Small, black-faced sheep grazed in the heather by the side of the road, sometimes scampering hastily across the road when the bus suddenly rounded a bend.

We passed a long narrow loch, leaden and grey under the drizzling rain, and the water lapped the banking of the road. There was a house by the side of the road, built out on piles over the loch, and a boat was moored under the gable window. There was another boat in the centre of the loch, and the man in the stern looked up as the bus went by. As he moved, I saw the long line of his rod arching out over the still water.

The road twisted and turned and we crossed small bridges under which foamed the rushing hill burns. There was water everywhere. Miniature waterfalls cascaded down the rocky hillside, and the flat stretches of peat bog were pitted with small pools. We passed a solitary grey stone house, and I laughed to see two geese go squawking up the path to the house in an indignant flurry of strong white wings. The bus driver slid open his window and tossed out a newspaper.

The road wound round the cliff face, and I caught a brief glimpse of the sea hundreds of feet below. A low turf bank was all that separated the road from the cliff face, but the driver seemed unconcerned. He kept glancing over his shoulder and carried on a conversation in Gaelic with the man sitting behind him.

We crossed a hump-backed bridge and rounded a sharp bend, and there before us, spread out across the road, stood a herd of shaggy Highland cattle. They made no attempt to move, but stood there firmly on their short stocky legs, gazing at us with large, incurious eyes. The driver braked sharply and changed down to bottom gear, but he had to sound his horn before they consented to move slowly out of the path of the bus. I saw the rain glistening on the long hair of their coats, and I was glad that the metal frame of the bus lay between me and their great sweeping horns.

The bus jolted down a steep hill, and the driver slid open his window and pitched out a bundle of newspapers. In the distance I saw two houses, solitary sentinels in a waste of moorland.

We crossed an iron bridge over a deep gorge, and beyond the gorge I saw a large grey house surrounded by a stone wall. A wide drive led from the road to the house, and at the side of the drive, a little way back from the road, stood a wooden post-box. Across the green door of the box, in white letters, were the words ACHMORE LODGE. I looked back at the lodge until we climbed the hill on the other side of the gorge, and it could no longer be seen.

When the bus stopped on a deserted stretch of road, with not a house in sight, I sat there stupidly, not moving.

'This is Achmore, a bhalaich,' called the driver.

I scrambled to my feet and paid him, and stepped down on to the road. I watched the red bus disappearing into the distance, and my heart sank when it rounded a bend in the road and vanished from view. There had been something warm and friendly about the driver's ready laugh and the Gaelic voices, and the smell of strong pipe tobacco, and the cheeping of the chicks, but now I stood alone and was conscious once more of my isolation.

I put down my case on the wet road and gazed around. A faint smirr of rain was drifting down and a grey mist crept in from the sea. The moor rose sharply to the west of the road, and I saw several stone houses high up on the hillside. The fall of the hill below the houses seemed to be cultivated ground, and I picked out the line of a fence between the bottom of the hill and the great expanse of bare moor stretching to the road. There seemed to be no path to the houses, and I gazed up at them in a mood of hopeless despair, not knowing what to do.

When I looked round again a man was standing on the road a few feet away from me.

Chapter 6

I suppose he must have popped up suddenly from behind a dip in the ground below the road, but I never knew for certain.

He was wearing a faded blue denim jacket over a fisherman's jersey, torn army trousers tucked into homespun stockings, and big tackety boots. Everything about him was long and lean, and I noticed how all the lines of his face drooped downwards, as if his mouth had long since forgotten how to lift in a smile. Even his dog had a lean and hungry look. It sniffed around my heels, but every time I moved it slunk away, its ears down and its tail between its legs. It was only when I shifted my feet again that I realized it had crept back to sniff my legs. Like its master, it had acquired the art of moving silently, unobserved.

My eyes wandered back to the man's face. He had a long thin face, and his arms were so long that his hands seemed to hang loosely below his knees, but this may have been due to the forward stoop of his shoulders. He had small, almost colourless eyes, deeply set below bushy, sandy eyebrows, and a jutting beak of a nose. He took off his cap, and settled it firmly on his head, and I caught a glimpse of wispy red hair. But the stubble on his chin was white, and he looked as if he had not shaved for a week.

He stood in the centre of the road, plucking at his long upper lip, his eyes fixed on a point above my left shoulder. I knew who he was before he spoke, and from the very start I disliked him.

I suppose only a minute could have passed from the time I first saw him until he spoke, although it seemed longer.

'Well, Alasdair,' he said, and his great paw of a hand swallowed mine in a brief clasp that had neither warmth nor friendship.

There was an awkward silence, and I had the feeling he was fumbling for the right words.

'I am Murdo Beaton,' he went on, 'your father's cousin.'

'Yes,' I said, not caring if he thought me rude, knowing only that I was tired and lonely and miserable.

He picked up my case without another word, and set off across the moor in long, slow strides. He did not seem to hurry but I was almost running as I tried to keep up with him.

I picked my way as best I could, trying to step from one tuft of heather to another, but now and then I stumbled into a wet patch of bog and sank in up to my ankles. Before we had gone twenty yards my feet were soaked.

We crossed a swiftly flowing burn by means of a single wooden plank lashed to an iron stanchion with tying wire. The ground grew rougher and there were heathery hillocks, bright green patches of sphagnum moss and tiny streams bubbling through the bog. We skirted a long straight peat cutting with an exposed face of black wet peat fully five feet deep. There was a tiny lake at the bottom of the cutting where the water had collected.

Murdo Beaton led the way up an earthen bank topped by two strands of barbed wire, and we jumped down across a drain and were on to firmer ground. The grassland sloped steeply upwards, cut by the long fingers of parallel open drains.

There were five houses spread out at intervals across the top of the hill, and he saw my eyes on them.

'This is Achmore,' he said. 'We are at the foot of the crofts now.'

'Which is my house?' I cried, suddenly excited.

He glanced at me directly for the first time, and I sensed the smouldering resentment in those small pale eyes, but all he said was: 'It cannot be seen from here.'

We climbed steadily, moving away from the other houses in a diagonal line. When we were level with them we topped a rise in the ground and there, in a sheltered hollow hidden from all the other houses in Achmore, I saw the cottage where I was born.

It seemed to grow out of the ground as naturally as the clump of rowan trees beside it. The cottage was built of unhewn mortarless grey stone, and the thatched roof was secured against the fury of the winter winds by a covering of wire netting. Large stones were tied to the netting at intervals of a few feet, so that it was firmly anchored. The walls of the cottage sloped slightly inwards and the corners were rounded. Two deep-set, foot-square windows peered towards the main road, like empty eye-sockets. A thin line of smoke curled up from the single chimney-pot, and I sniffed the fragrant, never-to-be-forgotten smell of burning peat.

Murdo Beaton ducked his long frame under the massive slab of stone forming the door lintel, and I followed him through the tiny lobby into the kitchen.

It was dim in the kitchen, and I stumbled over the uneven stone flags of the floor. He gestured me towards the long wooden bench under the window, and I sat down and glanced around the room.

The walls were lined with rough boards, which had probably been painted once long ago, but were now darkly stained with peat smoke. There was a plain deal table opposite the open-topped black range, and two home-made wooden chairs on either side of the fire, and a small cupboard facing me against the opposite wall, and that was all.

Two tin tea caddies stood on the mantelpiece in the centre of which hung the faded printed text GOD IS LOVE. Murdo Beaton leaned against the mantelpiece, picking his teeth with the end of a matchstick.

There was a rough wooden door in the far corner, leading into another room, and an old woman shuffled through it. She was wearing a shapeless black gown and had a woollen scarf tied round her head, and I had never before seen anyone who looked so old. Her face seemed to have shrunk, so that the skin hung around her cheeks in sagging wrinkles. She took no notice of me but sat down in a chair by the fire, and I noticed with a start of surprise that she was wearing men's boots.

Murdo Beaton spoke to her in Gaelic, and she got up, muttering to herself. She took a plate from inside the cupboard and filled it with soup from the iron pot over the fire.

He picked up the other wooden chair and set it in to the table.

'Take your food, boy,' he said. 'There is nothing great here, mind you. We are poor folk in this place with nothing fancy in the way o' food or anything else. But eat up. Dulse soup is good for you.'

I sat in to the table, protesting feebly that I was sure it was very good soup, and waited for him to join me. But he sat down on the bench and I realized that I was expected to eat alone.

The soup was greasy and sickly, and the taste of the dulse turned my stomach. But I willed myself to eat it, and swallowed each mouthful quickly, determined not to show my distaste.

When I had finished, I heard him speak to the old woman again, and she placed an enormous dish of boiled potatoes on the table and a plate of cold meat. I helped myself to potatoes. They had been cooked in their skins and I sat looking at them, not quite sure how to proceed.

I could feel Murdo Beaton's eyes on the back of my neck, and I felt the colour rising in my cheeks.

'Maybe you don't like potatoes in their jackets, boy?' he said.

'No, I like them like that,' I replied, and plunged my knife into one of them and proceeded to eat it, skin and all.

I think that was the most uncomfortable meal I have ever had. It was worse than my birthday treat, when Aunt Evelyn took my mother and me to lunch in a smart restaurant, and I upset my soup plate over Aunt Evelyn's new spring dress.

The old woman never spoke, but I could hear her shuffling around the room, muttering to herself. Once I dropped my knife and the sound of it clattering on the plate was so unnaturally loud in the silence of the room that I felt I had done something wrong, like laughing aloud during the silence on Remembrance Day. And all the time, although he never spoke, I knew that Murdo Beaton's eyes were on me.

I had almost finished when the door opened and a girl came quickly into the room. She was small and dark and I could see no resemblance to Murdo Beaton in her eager brown face, although I guessed she must be his daughter. She stopped suddenly when she caught sight of me, and seemed about to speak, when Murdo Beaton said something to her in Gaelic. She turned at once, with a final quick glance in my direction and went out of the room.

I finished my meal, and pushed the chair back from the table. Murdo Beaton was still sitting on the bench, but when I turned round his eyes were no longer on me. He offered no explanation for the girl's sudden disappearance, but sat plucking at his long upper lip, gazing into space. The old woman was huddled forward in her chair, muttering to herself, and I wondered if anybody ever spoke in this house.

I was determined to break the awful silence.

'Was that your daughter?' I asked.

His eyes wandered to a spot above my left shoulder.

'Yes, that was Mairi,' he said, and added: 'She has gone to fetch home the cows for milking.'

I wondered if he had sent her away deliberately, so that I could not talk to her, and I doubted if I could endure the long summer holiday in this cheerless home.

At length he rose to his feet and said: 'Well, boy, you had best get some rest. I expect you are tired now.'

He ushered me into a tiny room on the other side of the lobby, and stood in the doorway watching whilst I unpacked my case.

'You won't be thinking much of this after city life,' he ventured at last.

If I could have been granted one wish at that moment it would have been to be back in the comfort of our flat in Chelsea, but there was something about him that made me want to hide my feelings, so all I said was: 'Oh, I expect I'll soon get used to it.'

'Aye, maybe you will,' he muttered, in a voice that left me in no doubt that it was the last thing he wanted to happen.

Then the door closed behind him and he was gone.

I looked around the room. It was lined with the same rough boarding as the kitchen, broken in places and unpainted. Most of the space was taken up by an old-fashioned brass bedstead, and the stone flagstones between the bed and the door had no covering.

I undressed quickly and got into bed. There were no sheets and the coarse grey blankets pricked my face and neck.

I thought of my foolish boasting; how I had scoffed at my mother's forebodings, and urged her to let me come to Skye. If I were to return home now, I knew she would be sympathetic, but I could not face Aunt Evelyn's gibes. Come what may, I resolved grimly, there could be no going back for me until the holiday was over.

My thoughts drifted to the mysterious message in my wallet. HUNT AT THE HILL OF THE RED FOX. What could it possibly mean? My mind went round and round on what was now a familiar track. No matter how hard I tried, I was no nearer a solution. But whatever the meaning of the message, I decided, Murdo Beaton would not hear of it.

I wondered how my father could have let such a man take over the croft. It was obvious that he did not like me and resented my presence at Achmore. But it is my croft, I told myself fiercely, and he has really no right to be here. But there was no real conviction in such thoughts. It was simply my dislike of the man finding expression. For all I cared, he could have the croft and the cottage as well. It was the most miserably depressing place I had ever seen.

I had a moment's self-pity, thinking I had been born here, and my father, and his father before him, and no friendly smile or welcoming hand had awaited me. I wondered what could have happened to all my father's friends, and I remembered my mother saying that every house for miles around would welcome the kin of Alasdair Dubh. I remembered her stories about my father. How he loved Achmore above all places; he who had sailed the seven seas. Why was I so different; I who

45

longed so passionately to be like him in all things? Could it be that my upbringing in London had thinned my Highland blood, so that the city streets meant more to me than the wet moorland?

I thought again of my mother's words to me in Glasgow. She had said something about it not being all flashing tartans, and perhaps that was the reason for my wretchedness. Not that I had expected to see everyone wearing the kilt; indeed, it would be hard for me to say what I really expected to find in Skye. Whatever images my mind had conjured up had been swamped in the overwhelming greyness and gloom of the bleak reality.

I pulled the blankets up around my head and tried to go to sleep, but I heard the outer door scrape open and the sound of voices in the kitchen. I strained my ears and heard a girl's voice, speaking softly, and then the harsh tones of a man's voice raised in anger.

There was silence again, and I turned on my side, wondering drowsily what it could all mean.

When I finally dropped off to sleep, I was thinking of my mother's final admonition. Always remember, whatever happens, that you are Black Alasdair's son. . . . Try to be a man . . . like him.

Now I understood her words for the first time.

Chapter 7

A SHAFT of sunlight, warming the pillow by my head, awoke me in the morning. I rubbed my eyes and yawned and stretched lazily. Blinking drowsily, I wondered how the sunlight had penetrated the high wall of the building outside my bedroom window. It was only when I opened my eyes properly, and saw my clothes hanging over the rail at the foot of the bed, that I remembered I had left London far behind.

I fished under the pillow for my watch. It was eight o'clock. Despite the lumpy chaff mattress and my troubled forebodings of the night before, I had slept soundly.

I dressed quickly and opened the door. No sound came from the kitchen. I tiptoed across the lobby, opened the front door quietly, and I stepped outside.

I stepped into a new world and the wonder of it stopped me short before I was a yard outside the house. Gone was the mist and the rain and the dismal grey of yesterday. The sun shone brilliantly from a bright blue sky flecked with wisps of the purest white cloud. The green crofts dropped steeply to the warm brown of the moor, tinged with purpling heather, and the moor ended in the sea. A sea as calm as a park lake, and of such an artificial looking shade of cerulean blue that I was reminded of paintings I had seen of Italian grottoes. It was the Sound of Raasay.

In the middle of the Sound, like a long Viking galley riding at anchor, lay the Island of Rona. I saw the silvery wash of spray, as the current creamed over the rocks on the northernmost tip of the island, and then my eyes wandered again over its dark purple shore. Rona of the long heather. But to me it did not seem possible that heather could grow on that jagged spine of rock.

To the south of Rona, clinging to the tail of the smaller island, Raasay curved across the Sound, seeming to merge with the coastline of Skye. My eyes lifted to the massive outline of the mainland hills beyond the Sound. Blue peaks standing shoulder to shoulder, like the massed ranks of a giant army, all the way from Torridon in the north to Applecross in the south.

My gaze wandered back across the still waters of the Sound and fastened on the main road, a white thread against the brown of the moor. I followed it south and saw the roof of Achmore Lodge and the gorge beyond. The road climbed out of the gorge, and I traced it across the moor until it was lost in the far horizon.

To the west of the road a long line of hills swept round in a wide arc, encircling Achmore, and extending in an unbroken line as far as the eye could see. Strange outcroppings of black rock pierced the blue of the sky, and directly to the west of the lodge towered a conical-shaped peak, trailing a white wisp of cloud. Below the peak was a black hollow, shaped like a large saucer, and the hill itself seemed to incline over it. The air was so clear I could make out every scaur and hollow in the hills, every corrie and precipice. On one green peak I picked out the tiny white dots of grazing sheep.

Mairi Beaton must have been standing beside me for a long time before she spoke.

'What is the matter?' she said.

I started, and looked at her blankly. She was barefoot and her legs were tanned a deep brown.

'What is the matter?' she repeated shyly.

'Nothing,' I said.

There was a silence.

'I was just looking,' I added lamely.

'But your face,' she started.

'What about my face?' I demanded, suddenly feeling foolish. 'What's wrong with it?'

'Nothing,' she said, curling her toes into the grass. 'Only you looked as if you were still asleep and . . . and dreaming.'

48

She had a soft, lilting voice, and she spoke English slowly, as if she were thinking first in Gaelic.

'I was just looking,' I repeated. 'I couldn't see anything yesterday for the mist and the rain, and I was sort of surprised, that's all.'

'Do you like it?' she asked.

I nodded. 'I always thought Skye would be something like this, but I never thought I'd be able to see for miles and miles around.'

I could not put into words the feeling I had of freedom and limitless space, but how could she know what it felt like to be cooped up in a city street.

'What is it like in London?' she asked eagerly.

'Oh, just streets and people and fog in the winter-time,' I said.

'Did you ever go to Buckingham Palace?' she wanted to know.

I nodded.

'Is it very big and fine-looking?' she asked.

'Yes, it's big,' I said.

'Did you see the Queen?'

The questions were fired at me quickly, one after the other.

'No, just the palace,' I said, as casually as I could, conscious of her wide eyes on my face.

'It must be wonderful to see the palace,' she exclaimed.

'Oh, I don't know,' I said. 'It looked sort of lonely to me. I wouldn't like to live in it, anyway.'

'Would you rather stay in Skye?'

'Yes,' I said, forgetting her father's long, gloomy face in the brightness of the morning. 'Wouldn't you?'

'I don't know,' she answered slowly. 'I have never been away from Skye.'

'Would you like to go to London?'

She giggled.

'The cailleach says everyone in the cities is bad. She says they will all go to hell-fire.'

'What's a cailleach?' I asked, puzzled.

49

'A cailleach is an old woman.' she explained. 'We call my granny the cailleach.'

'Has she been to London?' I asked.

The girl shook her head, her dark plaits swinging from side to side.

'Well, then, how does she know?' I demanded.

'Oh, but himself says people in the cities are bad,' she declared. She saw that I did not understand her, and added quickly: 'My father, I mean.'

At the mention of his name, she glanced back nervously to the house, as if afraid she would see him standing in the doorway.

A silence came between us. I was thinking of Murdo Beaton and his thinly disguised hostility to me, and I wondered why his own daughter was afraid of him. Perhaps it was because I was there. Perhaps she was afraid to be seen talking to me. That would explain her startled glance back to the house.

'You father doesn't like me, does he?' I said suddenly.

She looked down at the ground, tracing a nervous pattern in the grass with one bare foot.

I repeated the question, and she glanced back again to the house, and murmured:

'I don't know.'

'Yes, you do,' I burst out. 'What did he say to you last night, when I was in the kitchen?'

'He told me to go for the cows,' she answered quietly, and then, looking me straight in the eye: 'But when I came back he told me not to speak to you.'

'But why?' I asked, bewildered.

'I don't think he wants you here,' she said, and then, the words tumbling out in a sudden rush: 'My cousin in Broadford was going to stay with me at Easter, but he wouldn't let her come.'

'But why?' I repeated helplessly.

'Maybe he hopes you will go away again, if you have nobody to speak to,' she said.

If the croft did not belong to me, I thought, he would not have allowed me to come in the first place. And now it seemed he was determined to make my stay as unpleasant as possible. I wondered why.

'Well, anyway, you can't care, because you are talking to me now,' I said, brightening.

Her thin brown hand touched my arm for a moment.

'You won't tell him, will you?' she pleaded earnestly.

''Course not,' I said, 'but what will you say if he sees you?'

'We are safe enough,' she said calmly. 'He usually sleeps in until about eleven o'clock.'

'Whatever for?' I asked.

'I don't know,' she said. 'People here don't get up very early.'

I noticed that smoke was rising from the chimneys of all the other houses in Achmore, and I sensed something evasive in her manner, but I was too glad of her company to pay much attention to a fleeting expression.

'Have you any calves?' I asked eagerly.

'Come on, I'll show you them,' she said, and I could see she was glad to get away from the house.

I followed her down the croft to the byre. The byre was very little different from the cottage except that there were no windows in the walls, and the thatch was not so well kept. The walls were of the same mortarless, undressed stone as the cottage, and I wondered how men could have lifted such huge blocks of stone into place.

It was dim inside the byre, the only light coming from a small pane of wooden framed glass fitted in the roof, and it was some time before I made out the four stalls with the tethering swivels set in the walls. Two black calves were tethered in one stall, and when they saw us they twisted and tugged at their ropes, and gazed at us with large, pleading eyes. I scratched their heads and they thrust their moist noses against my arm. Two rough tongues, like coarse sandpaper, rasped over my skin, and I withdrew my hand quickly.

'Don't they ever go out in the sun?' I asked.

'My father will tether them on the croft when he gets up,' she answered.

I saw the two long tethering ropes hooked over a rafter. They had a steel swivel in the middle, a noose at one end, and an iron stake at the other.

'We could take them out for him,' I suggested.

'You try,' she retorted. 'They would drag you off your feet. Even a man can only take out one at a time. They are strong wee calvies.'

She patted their backs proudly, and I walked to the other end of the byre.

There was a pile of hay in the corner stall and two hens were nesting in it. They had scooped out hollows in the compressed hay so that only their backs were visible, and their small beady eyes watched me warily. I wondered how they had got in until I noticed a small opening in the thatch above the hay, and at that moment a hen squeezed through it and fluttered down to join the other two on the nest.

The calves were becoming increasingly restive, leaping madly about their stall. Mairi said they were hungry, and we had better go out and look for the cows, for the calves could not get their feed until they were milked.

'But how do you know where to find them?' I asked.

'Och, they will be out the back, on the common grazing,' she said.

'But where?' I demanded, thinking of the limitless waste of moor stretching for miles around. 'What's to stop them wandering to the other side of Skye?'

'Wait you,' she smiled. 'The cows know when it is near milking time, and they won't be far away.'

She led the way out of the byre, and up the hill by the side of the cottage. The cottage was built into a cutting so that its rear wall was almost a part of the hill, and before we had gone far, glancing back over my shoulder I discovered I was looking down on its neatly thatched roof.

The grass here was smooth and green and it ended in a turf dike. There was a deep drain on the other side of the dike, to prevent cattle from climbing back on to the arable land of the township. Beyond the dike it was all rolling moorland as far as the line of circling hills.

I looked again at the strange conical peak over the saucer-shaped black hollow, but Mairi beckoned to me from the top of the dike.

I scrambled up beside her, and she looked down at my sandals and said: 'You would have been better in your bare feet. Your sandals will get wet.'

We jumped across the drain, and made our way over the rough ground. There were no cows in sight, and I asked her where she was going.

She pointed to a grassy knoll.

'To Cnoc an t-Sithein,' she said.

'What's that?' I asked.

'The Hill of the Fairies,' she answered. 'When the cailleach was a girl nobody would go near it in the dark.'

'What rot,' I said, but I had to admit to myself that I would not care to be alone on the moor in the darkness of the night. At that time, I did not know what desperate moves fear would drive me to.

We jumped across a small burn, and picked our way through a thick bank of heather. I wondered how she could walk on the prickly heather in her bare feet, but she did not seem to mind.

'How do you go to school?' I asked her.

'We have a scholars' bus,' she said. 'I meet it on the main road in the morning, but I'm allowed off school to help the cailleach. She's been ill.'

'When are your holidays?' I asked, hoping she would not have to go back to school before they started.

'In a wee while,' she replied. 'They start on Friday.'

'I expect you have lots of friends,' I ventured.

'Only at school,' she said slowly. 'My father doesn't like me to be talking with anyone here. He says they would be after wanting to know everything about the croft, and what himself was doing.'

I wondered again how my father could have been friendly

with such a strange man, and I recalled the doubt in my mother's mind about their friendship.

We climbed the green knoll, and the whole moorland lay before us. I could see a river winding its way east from the heart of the hills to the deep cleft of the gorge below Achmore Lodge, and I thought some day I will trace its course up into the hills.

Mairi tugged at my sleeve.

'There you are,' she cried. 'What did I tell you!'

Several cattle were grazing in a hollow, not thirty yards away from us. We raced across to them, and she went up to a great black beast and slapped it on the flank, and it moved off in the direction of the dike, followed by a smaller black cow with a white patch on its head. The rest of the cattle went on grazing unconcernedly.

We urged the cows on with frequent slaps and shouts towards a wooden gate in the dike. I dragged the gate open and the cows lumbered across the culvert, and headed for the cottage. Mairi helped me to close the gate for the hinges were broken, and we sat on the dike, watching the cows go home.

I leaned back, propping myself up on one elbow, feeling the sun hot on my face. From where I lay, the dark cone-shaped peak seemed to looking down at me.

'What is that hill called?' I asked her.

Mairi jumped down and turned round, her elbows on the dike, and her small, brown face cupped in her hands.

'Which one?' she asked.

'The one like a cone with the hollow below it,' I said.

She squinted up at it.

'That's Sgurr a' Mhadaidh Ruaidh.'

'It sounds good when you say it like that,' I said, teasing her.

'But it is just as good in English,' she replied seriously.

'It can't be,' I smiled.

'It is,' she insisted. She straightened up and glanced again at the towering peak. 'It is the Hill of the Red Fox.'

Chapter 8

THE Hill of the Red Fox! I felt the impact of the words like a blow in the face. I looked up at the towering peak, inclining over the dark hollow. So that was the Hill of the Red Fox, no more than a few hours' walk from Achmore, and I had been wondering how I would find it. I could hardly believe that the hill I was gazing at could be the one named on the torn page from the diary. The message had been thrust into my hand in such strange circumstances that the whole incident had acquired a dream-like quality. That it was real, as real as the girl on the dike beside me, was something I could not readily grasp.

I floundered in a host of wild surmises. How had the man with the scar known I was going to Achmore? What had he hidden at the Hill of the Red Fox? What would I do if the man with the brilliant blue eyes suddenly appeared on the scene? Did the man with the scar intend to contact me again, and if so, would he take me into his confidence?

Each line of thought opened up a dozen possibilities, every one more bewildering than the last. Chance seemed to have thrust me into a labyrinth from which there was no escape, and I wished desperately that I had someone to confide in.

All these thoughts raced through my mind in the space of a few seconds, and I was startled when Mairi cried: 'Race you back to the house.'

She sped swiftly across the close-cropped grass, her pigtails streaming out behind her. I scrambled to my feet and started forward.

'Mairi! Stop!' I cried. 'Wait for me.'

She did not give me even a backward glance, and I raced after her. When I neared the cottage, I saw the reason why my cries had gone unheeded. Murdo Beaton was standing outside the cottage, his hands in the pockets of his faded blue denim jacket. Mairi was not to be seen, and I supposed she had darted inside the house.

As I drew near him, I slowed to a walk. There was a dull flush on his face, and he kept digging the heel of his tackety boot into the soft turf. I knew he was angry, but my mind was in such a turmoil that, if he had not spoken first, I believe I would have blurted out the whole story to him.

'Where have you been?' he snapped.

'Out the back,' I answered, 'on the dike.'

'I heard you calling Mairi,' he said suspiciously. 'Let the girl be. Time enough for fooling around when the work is done, and there is always work in this place.' He half turned, and added ungraciously: 'Come on in. Breakfast has been ready this while back.'

I followed him into the kitchen, deriding myself for being so foolish as to think I could confide in him. If treasure were hidden at the Hill of the Red Fox, the last man to inform would be Murdo Beaton of the long face and the shifty eyes.

The kitchen table had been moved against the bench, and I joined Mairi on the bench. She did not look at me, but sat with her hands in her lap, her head down. The old woman sat at the end of the table, and I noticed for the first time how her fingers were swollen and twisted with rheumatism.

Murdo Beaton took his place at the head of the table, and took off his cap. He ran both his hands through his wispy red hair, cleared his throat, and said a long grace in Gaelic.

I glanced furtively at Mairi. Her head was bowed and her eyes tightly closed. The cailleach's eyes were open, and I could hear her mumbling the words of the grace to herself. Murdo Beaton had his forehead bowed on his clasped hands, and he spoke slowly and with great deliberation.

He had finished the grace, and sat back in his chair and cleared his throat, before Mairi opened her eyes and took up her spoon.

How I enjoyed that first breakfast in Achmore. I was hungry

after the tramp across the moor in the keen morning air, and not even the shock of the discovery of the Hill of the Red Fox could blunt my appetite.

We had bowls of brose with fresh cream, and newly-baked girdle scones with home-made butter, and cups of strong, sweet tea. I was too hungry to notice the lack of conversation, and it was such an honest hunger that conversation would have interfered with the serious business of eating.

Murdo Beaton ate rapidly, stuffing spoonful after spoonful of brose into his mouth without pause. The spoon had no sooner reached his mouth than it was dipping down again to the bowl, and his mouth moved forward to meet it on its upward journey. He finished first, and leaned back, gazing at the ceiling, picking idly at his teeth with a matchstick.

When we had all finished, he clasped his hands and bent forward again, and delivered another long grace. I noticed that he had snatched up his cap and left the room before Mairi opened her eyes.

She looked at his empty chair, and stood up and started to gather the empty dishes. When she reached across for my bowl, she said softly: 'Don't be letting him know you went for the cows with me.'

She saw my eyes on the old woman, and added: 'The cailleach's deaf.'

I nodded, and she went on gathering the dishes as if nothing had passed between us.

Murdo Beaton was milking the big black cow when I went outside. I lay down on the grass in the hot sun, watching him.

He was crouched down on his heels, holding a small tin pail under the cow's udder with his left hand. His right hand worked steadily at one teat at a time, and the milk spurted into the pail, rising in a creamy froth. When the pail was full he tipped it into a bucket by his side and went on milking.

When he had milked both cows, he called to Mairi, and she came running out carrying two old pails. He tipped a quantity of milk into each one of them, and she went off towards the byre.

I got up to follow her, and he said sharply: 'Let her be, I want no fooling with the calves.' He saw the hot flush spreading over my cheeks, and added, in a more reasonable tone: 'If it is work you are after, bide a while. You can help with the peats.'

I lay down again on the grass, my hands behind my head. Murdo Beaton waited until Mairi had reappeared with the empty pails, and he said something to her in Gaelic, as she went into the house.

I watched him go into the byre and presently he came out again with a calf, jumping and bucking wildly on its tethering rope. He drove the tethering stake into the ground with his heel, and the calf rushed madly round and round, kicking its hind legs up in the air. He brought out the other calf and tethered it, and it made the same mad rush. I was afraid it would break its neck when it suddenly reached the end of its tether and was slewed round by the taut rope and jerked off its feet.

Murdo Beaton whistled the dog, Caileag, and she sprang up from the open cottage door and raced down the croft to where the cows had wandered. Snapping and barking around their heels, she worked them up to the house. I watched man and dog and beasts go through the gate to the common grazing, thinking what a peaceful picture they made. When I looked at the calves again they had stopped their wild racing and were grazing placidly.

Without being really aware of it, my eyes kept swinging round to the Hill of the Red Fox. The white wisp of cloud had vanished, and the black peak was clearly defined against the clear blue of the sky. I thought for a moment of writing to my mother, and telling her everything that had happened, but I could hear Aunt Evelyn saying: 'Stuff and nonsense! Mysterious messages in trains, indeed! Haven't I always told you the child reads too many books?'

No, there was no help to be expected from that quarter, I

told myself. I was sure Mairi would help me, but what could she do? And if I told Mairi there was always a danger that her father would get to hear of it.

I picked a handful of daisies from the grass and started stripping the white petals. How did the man with the scar know that I would be sure to see the Hill of the Red Fox? I was certain I had never seen him until that fateful moment at Corpach when he darted into the compartment. I went over in my mind everything that had happened from the time he had opened the door.

He had stood for a moment, wiping the sweat from his face, before crossing the carriage and standing over me. I remembered how he had glanced at my suitcase, and tucked the address label under the case so that it was hidden from view. The address label! Why hadn't I thought of it before. The man with the scar had seen the address label on my case and known that I was travelling to Achmore.

It seemed simple enough looking back on it, but his mind must have worked at lightning speed to have comprehended the significance of my address and hidden it from his pursuer in the space of a few seconds. I felt a certain admiration for the man with the scar, no matter what he had done. What cool courage and resource he had shown, for all the agitation betrayed by his clenching hands.

I remembered how he had written in his diary after the train left Glenfinnan. He must have known there was a tunnel on the line, and decided to pass me a message under cover of darkness. I recalled how he had stepped into the corridor as soon as the train drew out of the tunnel. I could see now that he had drawn his pursuer away from the carriage in case I betrayed the fact that he had communicated with me.

But I was still no nearer a solution to the message. HUNT AT THE HILL OF THE RED FOX. Hunt for what? Once again I looked at the black, jutting peak above the dark hollow. What could be hidden on that remote hill? I determined to find out if any ships had been wrecked off the coast during the war.

Perhaps a cargo of bullion had been hidden on the hill. But I could not understand what MI5 had got to do with it, unless it could be the registration number of a ship.

When Murdo Beaton came back he was leading a brown mare. He harnessed her to the cart that was standing outside the byre, its long shafts sticking high in the air, and tossed a large creel into the cart. Then he called to Mairi, and she ran out of the house to join him. He took hold of the bridle and urged the horse down the croft.

I felt a stab of disappointment, thinking he had forgotten me, but he called back: 'Well, boy, if it is work you are after you had best be moving.'

I scrambled to my feet and ran down the croft, trotting along beside the big wooden wheels of the cart.

We worked at the long, straight peat cutting I had first seen on my way to Achmore. The dry peats were stacked in small heaps, and Mairi and I filled sacks from these heaps. Murdo Beaton filled the big creel, working alongside us. When the creel was full we held it for him, balanced on the edge of the peat face, and he dropped down to the bottom of the cutting and took the weight of the creel on his back. There was a strong rope threaded through the back of the creel with the two ends hanging loose. He caught up these ends and drew them tight across his chest, bracing himself to take the full weight of the loaded creel. Then he would start forward across the uneven turfs at the bottom of the bog, plodding doggedly on until he reached the fence at the foot of the croft.

Mairi and I followed him, carrying our sacks. The mare was tethered to a fencing stob, and we scrambled over the fence and loaded the peats into the cart.

When the cart was full we followed it up the brae to the cottage, and the peats were dumped at the end of the house. Mairi said she and the cailleach would make a stack when all the peats had been shifted from the bog.

We worked without a pause all afternoon, and my shirt stuck to my back with sweat. My back started to ache and the muscles stiffened in the backs of my legs. My hands became raw and tender from handling hundreds of dry, rough peats, and every time I emptied my sack into the cart a cloud of fine peat dust was wafted into my eyes, making them smart and sting.

I could never have carried on had it not been for Mairi. For all her slight body, she was far stronger than I, and she worked unceasingly. Except for her hair clinging damply to her forehead, and her flushed face, she showed no signs of tiring. I gritted my teeth and urged my aching body to further efforts. If a girl could stand up to the work, I could not lie down and admit defeat.

Not that Murdo Beaton spared himself. For every small sack carried by us he shifted two great creels of peat, and I realized the strength there must be in that long, gangling body. He never took off his fisherman's jersey, or even his denim jacket, but the sweat trickled steadily down his face through the black of the peat dust.

From where we worked, I could see all the crofts of Achmore spread out on the hillside. The men were busy hoeing the potatoes, and what had once been patches of uniform green merged into a clean pattern. I could see the straight green lines of the shaws with the black earth between as each man cleaned his potato patch.

Once, when I looked up, I saw that the men had left their work and had gathered in a small group. They were looking down at us, and talking together.

Murdo Beaton straightened up and wiped the sweat from his brow with a grimy hand. His face hardened when he saw the little group on the hillside.

'There's the men of Achmore for you,' he said bitterly. 'Blethering away like a lot of old sweetie-wives, and grumbling when honest, hardworking folk do better than themselves.'

He bent to his work with redoubled energy, and I saw the spreading stain of sweat across the back of his jacket and under the armpits. I tried in vain to brush the midges from my face, and stooped wearily to my task.

In the early evening, after we had unloaded the cart, we went into the cottage for a strupag of bread and cheese and scones and tea.

When Murdo Beaton rose to lead the way to the door, he said: 'If you are tired, boy, you can stay where you are.'

'No, I'm fine,' I said, seeing Mairi springing lightly to her feet, and I forced my unwilling legs to carry me out to the croft.

The sun was lost behind a haze, but the closeness in the air was worse than the fiercest heat of the sun. The bog seemed to be swarming with midges. They were in my hair, around my face and neck, biting my legs, and the more I slapped and scratched and waved, the worse they became. They were almost unbearable. I would stoop to gather an armful of peats, only to drop them again so that I could free my hands to scrub furiously at my face and neck in an effort to stop the terrible itching. By the time I had stooped again for the peats the itching was as bad as ever.

I thought with each sack I filled that this one must surely be the last I can will my weary body to carry, and each time we climbed the brae to the house I rested more heavily on the back of the cart. Somehow or other, I carried on, but in the end I was picking up peats without being conscious of the movement of my body.

When we unloaded the cart for the last time, and Murdo Beaton said: 'That is enough for one day. It is time we were taking potatoes,' I could have flung myself down on the cool grass and lain there until sleep came.

He led the horse down to the byre, and Mairi thrust a towel and soap into my hands, and said quickly: 'Take a wash in the tub; it will be good for you.'

At the end of the house a spring gushed out of the limestone rock into a tub below. The water was carried away by a side drain into the main drain running down the croft.

I took off my shirt and vest and washed the sweat and dust off my face and body. When I had dried myself I walked stiffly into the kitchen and sat down to dinner.

After soup, there was meat and potatoes. The potatoes were piled high in an enormous dish in the centre of the table, and we helped ourselves. Mindful of my uncertainty of the previous night, I watched Murdo Beaton hold up one on a fork, and peel it deftly with quick strokes of his knife, before I followed suit.

When the long grace was over, I excused myself and went to my room. I was going to write to my mother, and I thought I would undress first and get into bed. I can remember pulling back the blankets and swinging stiffly into bed, but no more.

I must have been asleep before my head touched the pillow.

Chapter 9

M Y limbs were stiff and sore when I awoke the next morning. I thought I would never be able to stoop to lift a peat from the ground, but the stiffness soon passed. After I had filled the first two sacks, I was surprised to find that I was working more swiftly than before and carrying the loaded sack with greater ease.

The sun blazed down from the same cloudless sky, and it was a relief each time the cart was loaded and we followed it up the brae, away from the heat of the bog to the cooler air of the hillside.

By late afternoon, we had cleared over half the peats from the bog, and the cailleach started laying out peats to make a foundation for the stack.

Mairi and I were filling our sacks from the same heap, and Murdo Beaton was working a little way in front of us, when I first noticed the men coming down the brae from the crofts at Achmore. There were six of them, and they walked in a straight line, bunched closely together.

Mairi went on filling her sack until she noticed that I had stopped. She glanced up and saw the marching men, and her eyes went to her father's bent back but he never even looked up.

The men crossed the fence at the bottom of the crofts and made their way over the bog towards us. Murdo Beaton straightened up, and I knew he had seen them, but he went on filling his creel with peats.

Neither Mairi nor I moved, and the six men carried on past Murdo Beaton without a word. He went on working, and they stopped in front of Mairi and me.

The man in the centre of the group stepped forward, his hand outstretched. He was a short, stocky man, and I took him to be the oldest of the five for his hair was white and he had a bushy white moustache. His face was ruddy and smiling, and he looked at me from keen blue eyes beneath eyebrows as white as his hair.

'Ceud mile failte agus slainte mhath, Alasdair,' he cried, shaking my hand vigorously. Before I could speak he went on: 'There you have it in the old tongue, my boy.' And he repeated solemnly in English: 'A hundred thousand welcomes and good health, Alasdair.'

'Why, thank you,' I stammered.

He made a sound like tut-tut, spitting it out between clenched teeth.

'There is always a welcome at our firesides for the son of Alasdair Dubh, an duine bochd. I am Hector MacLeod and these are the men of Achmore come to welcome you home. We waited for you to come to us but if the mountain will not come to Mahomet, then Mahomet must go to the mountain.' He laughed hugely, and urged his companions forward.

One by one, they shook me firmly by the hand.

Calum Stewart, a big, shy man with a bright red face. Lachlan MacLeod, dark and lean, with a grip like steel. Donald Alec MacDonald, another big man with piercing grey eyes. Iain Ban MacDonald, the tallest of them all, his cap perched on top of a mop of fair hair. Roderick MacPherson, a small dark man with twinkling eyes, who said: 'Don't be after thinking the bodach is the only one with the Gaelic, Alasdair. Failte do'n duthaich. Welcome to the country, boy.'

They stood around me, smiling and joking, and teasing Mairi in the Gaelic to judge from her blushes and giggles.

All the time, Murdo Beaton went on working steadily, never looking up.

It was only when Hector MacLeod turned to him, and said: 'Murdo Ruadh, the peats can go to pot for a day. We must make a ceilidh with Alasdair Beag,' that he straightened up.

His small, pale eyes flickered over the group, lighting on me for a second and then moving away again.

'You are welcome to take the boy,' he said in a flat, expressionless voice. 'It is his own doing that he is working at all. But myself is for lifting these peats, and lift them I will.'

I did not want to leave Mairi to carry on unaided, and I protested that I must finish the work, but they pooh-poohed the idea.

Hector MacLeod seized my arm in his.

'Man alive,' he cried, 'what would your father be saying if we did not make a ceilidh this day?' and they marched me off across the bog, not heeding my protests.

We were clambering over the fence, when Hector MacLeod said: 'And how do you like this place, eh?'

I saw his shrewd blue eyes on my face.

'Fine,' I said.

He laughed and slapped his thigh, and turned to Calum Stewart who was on my other side.

'The boy is a Cameron, right enough,' he declared. 'I mind the day we took Alasdair Dubh to Glasgow. He was only twelve at the time and we took him on the trams and the buses and fed him ice-cream and took him out at night to see the lights of the city. When we got back home we took him to his father, and his father asked him what he thought of the big city. Well I mind the day. We sat round in a circle waiting for him to speak about the wonders of the city. And all he said was "Fine."'

He laughed again, and Calum Stewart smiled a friendly smile.

We made straight for the house on the croft adjoining my own. It was a big stone house with a slated roof.

Hector MacLeod led the way into the kitchen, shouting 'Peigi! Morag!'

A plump, smiling woman with gleaming black hair coiled in a bun on the back of her head came into the room, followed by a younger woman.

'This is my wife, Peigi,' said Hector MacLeod, 'a grand woman with a girdle-pan, but an awful blether forby.'

'Ist, ist,' said his wife.

She shook hands warmly with me, and said: 'Never you mind the bodach, Alasdair. 'Tis himself is the blether. We are right pleased to have you with us.'

66

Her daughter Morag shook hands with me smiling, and I was made to sit on a chair in front of the fire. Hector MacLeod leaned back in an old rocking-chair and the men sat on the long wooden bench behind me.

The kitchen was big and airy. The walls were lined with tongued and grooved boarding painted cream and the floor was covered with linoleum. An old brown dresser stood against the wall, opposite the window, and the sunlight glinted on its sparkling delf. There was an easy chair on one side of the gleaming black range and a table under the window.

The men lighted their pipes, and Iain Ban MacDonald said: 'Surely you never came all the way from London by yourself, Alasdair?'

I liked the easy way they used my name, as if they had known me all my life.

'My mother took me to Glasgow, but I came on from there by myself,' I said.

'Well, well,' exclaimed Calum Stewart, between draws on his pipe. 'You are a hardy.'

'How is your mother?' asked Lachlan MacLeod. 'Fine I remember her, although it must be all of ten years since she was in this place.'

'She's well,' I said, thinking how pleased she would be to know that this dark silent man had remembered her.

Roderick MacPherson said: 'I saw you at the peats yesterday. I am thinking it is your back would be knowing all about it before the day was done.'

'I was a bit stiff,' I admitted ruefully. 'But I'm better today.'

'You did too much altogether,' declared Calum Stewart. 'You will be after killing yourself.'

'Or I will be after killing the Red One,' said Donald Alec MacDonald quietly.

I looked at him quickly but there was no laughter in his piercing grey eyes and nobody laughed.

Hector MacLeod frowned and flashed him a warning glance. There was an awkward silence and suddenly everyone started talking at once. I had the feeling that they were too polite to embarrass me by dwelling on Murdo Beaton, but it was plain to see that he was not welcome in Achmore.

Mrs MacLeod and Morag spread a spotless white cloth on the table, and amid much good-humoured banter, we all sat in to tea.

Hector MacLeod presided at the head of the table, throwing out a word here and there whenever the conversation showed signs of flagging, and nodding his white head appreciatively at the best of the sallies. I noticed how cunningly he drew everybody into the talk, and they all had something to say except Lachlan MacLeod. That dark, silent man never spoke a single word, but his was a friendly silence, broken by his slow smile and the warmth of his eyes.

I had never before talked to men like these. They treated me as an equal and listened to me as attentively as they did to white-haired Hector MacLeod. I remembered Aunt Evelyn's scathing: 'Small boys should be seen and not heard,' whenever I offended her by speaking out of turn. There was none of that in Hector MacLeod's kitchen. Indeed I was encouraged to speak, when I would have preferred to sit quietly listening to the men.

It was after tea, and the women were clearing away the dishes, when Hector MacLeod said: 'Duncan Mor should be here this night.'

'Aye, right enough,' they all echoed. 'Duncan Mor should be here.'

'Who is Duncan Mor?' I asked.

They all looked at Hector MacLeod and he rocked back in his chair and drew thoughtfully on his pipe before replying.

'Duncan Mor was your father's best friend,' he said slowly. 'They were aye together, the pair o' them, although Duncan was a wheen older than your father. They were the biggest men in a township o' big men, and Duncan Mor stood a full head taller than your father.

'He was the first mate on the *Empire Rose* and a sorry man,

I'm thinking, that he did not go down with Alasdair Dubh. Ach well, that's the way o' the world.'

He sighed heavily and drew on his pipe.

'How did it happen!' I asked eagerly. 'How was he saved?'

'The *Empire Rose* was well out in the Atlantic and a dirty sou'wester was blowing up. It was New Year's Day. The torpedo caught her amidships and she settled quickly in the stern listing hard to port. They couldn't clear the starboard boats at all. Duncan Mor was ordered to take the first boat and they managed away right enough. Your father's boat never got clear. It capsized and they were all lost.'

'It was a bad day for us when the *Empire Rose* went down,' said Donald Alec MacDonald, 'but I doubt no man felt it as bad as Duncan Mor, an duine bochd.'

'Where does he stay?' I asked.

'He has a croft by the river at Mealt,' replied Hector Mac-Leod. 'Mind you, boy, the same man would have been over to see you this while back if himself had been free to call.'

'But he must know I would want to see him,' I said.

'Oh, he would know, right enough,' acknowledged Hector MacLeod. He hesitated, leaning forward and tapping out the bowl of his pipe into the fire. I could see he was debating with himself, and suddenly he burst out: 'Ach, why should I be quiet. You will find out for yourself soon enough. There is bad blood, boy, between Duncan Mor and the Red Fellow.'

The laughter had died from the room, and the atmosphere had become strained. I was going to say something when Hector MacLeod said quickly: 'Did you ever hear a port-a-beul, Alasdair?'

'No,' I said, wondering what it could be.

'Come on Ruairidh,' they all cried, and I had the feeling they were glad of something to distract my attention from Murdo Beaton.

Roderick MacPherson sang a port-a-beul, the old mouth music.

He sang it at great speed, his feet tapping out the rhythm, and his hands slapping down on his thighs. It must have been very funny, apart from the comical faces he made, for the men kept breaking out in great gusts of laughter. Hector MacLeod had to cry. 'Ist! Ist!' to quieten them.

When it was over, we all clapped loudly, and Roderick sang another port-a-beul. It was even faster than the first, and such was the lilt in the air that Iain Ban sprang to his feet and danced a wild reel round the kitchen. He collapsed on the bench, laughing and panting, and Hector MacLeod wiped his eyes, and cried, 'Good for you, boys!'

There were more jokes and laughter and happy talk, and I did not feel the time passing at all. But the men exclaimed that the cows would not wait milking any longer and said they must go.

They clustered at the door, saying how much they had enjoyed the ceilidh.

Roderick MacPherson's twinkling eyes met mine, and he smiled and said: 'We will take you fishing tomorrow night, Alasdair, so don't be killing yourself at the peats.'

Then they were gone, clattering across the lobby in their heavy boots and calling: 'Oidhche mhath, Alasdair, oidhche mhath, Eachann.'

Hector MacLeod walked with me to the edge of his croft, and stood for a while in silence with his hand on my shoulder.

His last words were: 'Don't be making a stranger of yourself, Alasdair. You will always find an open door in this place.'

I crossed the drain and walked slowly towards the thatched cottage. It was after eleven o'clock but the brief Hebridean night had not yet fallen. I did not even glance up at the dark peat of the Hill of the Red Fox for my mind was full of my new-found friends.

Murdo Beaton was alone in the kitchen, looking at a newspaper. It was folded into a small square, and he held it at arm's length, squinting at it longsightedly, the way men do who are not accustomed to reading.

'It is time you were in bed, boy,' he said briefly, glancing up at me.

I stood inside the door, and he turned again to the newspaper in his hand.

'Well, good night,' I ventured.

He did not speak or look up, so perhaps he had not heard me. I closed the door quietly and went to bed.

I woke up in the night knowing dimly that something had disturbed me. The luminous hands on the dial of my watch pointed to two o'clock. I lay quite still, listening intently, and I heard the murmur of men's voices. The sound seemed to be coming from the direction of my window and I realized they must be standing outside the door of the cottage.

Some time passed before I grasped the fact that they were speaking English, and I listened with renewed interest, for I knew that the men of the township spoke Gaelic amongst themselves. I caught the words LOCHAILORT and SILENCED and MIDNIGHT SATURDAY before the voices faded and were still.

There was the sound of a door scraping shut. Then silence. Then stealthy footsteps slowly approaching my room. I lay perfectly still, hardly daring to breathe, but the footsteps stopped outside my door. There was a silence in which every sound of the night became magnified a hundredfold. I heard every rustle of the wind in the rowan trees outside the house, and the scurrying run of a mouse across the floor, before the footsteps retreated from my door. I heard the creak of the kitchen door and then silence again.

I started to breathe once more, like a swimmer who has been under water for a long time. The wind still shook the branches of the trees, but there was no longer a lurking menace in the rustling of the leaves. The rapid beating of my heart gradually stilled. It was as if all the nerves of my body had been stretched taut and were slowly relaxing again.

I went over in my mind the fragments of conversation I had heard. Perhaps it was because I was tired and afraid, I don't know, but it was a long time before I recalled the name of the place where the man with the scar had leapt off the train.

With a sudden stab of fear, I realized it was Lochailort.

Chapter 10

AT the sound of that one word, Lochailort, I knew that my suspicion of Murdo Beaton had been justified. Lochailort, to me, meant the man with the scar leaping desperately off the train and his pursuer racing down the corridor to the swinging door. It was the start of the trail to the Hill of the Red Fox.

The voice I had heard was not the voice of Murdo Beaton; it was the voice of a stranger. Someone had stood outside the house with him and spoken the word Lochailort. Someone who was so anxious to avoid being seen that he had waited until two in the morning before making his furtive approach. But who could it have been? Who? Who? Who? The question hammered insistently at my brain.

Of one thing I was certain: it could not have been the man with the brilliant blue eyes. He was unaware of my destination and ignorant of the fact that I carried a message from the man with the scar.

I recalled again the fragments of conversation I had heard. LOCHAILORT. SILENCED. MIDNIGHT SATURDAY.

The sudden impact of the frightening truth stunned me. I felt my heartbeats quicken and the palms of my hands grew moist with sweat. I heard a sudden noise and started up fearfully in bed, straining my eyes to penetrate the darkness of the room. But it was only a sudden gust of wind rustling the leaves of the rowan trees, and I sank back on the pillow breathing hard.

I wondered how I could have been so stupid as to have overlooked the obvious truth for so long. The message I carried in my wallet must have been intended for Murdo Beaton! There could be no other explanation of the stranger's secret visit to the cottage.

I saw in my mind's eye the address label on my case, penned

in Aunt Evelyn's bold capitals. MASTER ALASDAIR CAMERON, C/O MR MURDO BEATON, ACHMORE, SKYE. The man with the scar was the only person on the train to have seen that label. He had seen Murdo Beaton's name, as well as my own, and that was why he had given me the message, thinking I would pass it on to him. M15 was doubtless the code number he used; he would not be likely to put his own name on an open message.

My thoughts raced wildly. If the man with the scar had come to Achmore himself, he must have succeeded in shaking off his pursuer, and Murdo Beaton would know that I had failed to deliver the message.

LOCHAILORT. SILENCED. MIDNIGHT SATURDAY. The words buzzed in my head like a swarm of angry bees. SILENCED. Who was to be silenced? My blood chilled. They must know that I still had the message; that the secret of the Hill of the Red Fox was shared with me. If anybody had to be silenced, it was me. I could imagine the man with the scar saying softly: 'The boy must be silenced. Midnight Saturday will do.' And Murdo Beaton nodding his long head.

I had read many adventure stories, and I used to play a game, imagining myself to be the hero facing dreadful perils with cool courage. But this was no game, and now that I knew my life to be in danger I was afraid. None of the heroes in my stories was ever afraid. Sword in hand, they fought off half a score of attackers with a smile on their lips. But this was different. A whispered word, spoken in the darkness of the night, could be far more frightening than a dozen sword blades.

I lay awake for a long time listening wide-eyed to all the sounds of the night. I heard a cock crow, and the first red rays of the rising sun were lighting the sky before I slept.

My fears receded in the bright light of day, amid the sight and sounds of the everyday life of the croft. There was nothing sinister about Murdo Beaton in his blue denim jacket and tattered khaki trousers. I watched him closely, but he seemed the same as before; surly and morose, no doubt, but there was nothing threatening about him.

I scoffed at myself for having been so foolish. It was like the night terrors I had known as a small child; they vanished with the coming of day.

We worked all afternoon at the peats, and by tea-time the last load had been carted from the bog.

After tea, I watched Murdo Beaton and the cailleach building the stack. They built up the sides first, setting the peats at an angle so that they interlocked. Each layer of peats was placed further in, to give an inward slope to the wall, so that the finished stack would be weatherproof. Mairi and I helped them by selecting peats of a uniform size for the outer walls, and the stack slowly began to take shape.

I heard a man's voice calling me, and I knew it would be Roderick MacPherson ready for the fishing.

'Do you mind if I go fishing?' I asked Murdo Beaton.

'Away you go, boy,' he said, never looking up from his work. Perhaps it was my imagination, but he seemed glad to be rid of me.

When I topped the rise, I saw Roderick MacPherson, and I ran across the crofts to join him. He was carrying a long cane rod over his shoulder and attached to the rod was a neatly wound line.

He smiled at my eager face, and said: 'It is a good night for the fishing, a bhalaich. See the clouds gathering. You should take home a good fry tonight.'

'But where are the others?' I asked, as we set off down the croft.

'Lachlan and Iain Ban went to the shop,' he replied. 'They will meet us at the shore.'

We crossed the fence at the bottom of the crofts and made our way over the bog to the plank bridge across the burn. The air was full of the scent of heather and bog myrtle and the ground was coloured by patches of blue veronica. We startled a brown hare, and it went leaping off across the moor in a zigzagging run.

When we crossed the main road I thought of the night I had stood there, miserable and alone, my case in my hand. It did not seem possible that it could be the same road, or the same me.

What I had thought, looking down from Achmore, to be the cliff edge was not the cliff at all but a high escarpment. We followed a track down the escarpment and tramped across a narrow glen. Roderick pointed out the lonely ruins of a cottar's house, and we followed a swift flowing burn past a dipping fank. We stopped for a while at the fank, and I was shown the sheep pens and the narrow walled path to the dipper.

From the fank, a narrow path wound round an overhanging rock and dipped sharply to the shore. Lachlan MacLeod and Iain Ban were sitting on a rock, smoking their pipes, and they greeted me cheerily.

The boat was lying under the shelter of the cliff face, firmly anchored by the strong ropes which were lashed to massive boulders. It was at least thirty yards, across rough shingle, to the water's edge, and I wondered how we would ever get the boat launched.

Iain Ban saw the dismay on my face.

'Wait you, a bhalaich,' he smiled. 'You'll see.'

The men untied the ropes and Roderick collected an armful of small round logs from a nearby stack. He placed one under the bows of the boat, and spread out the rest at intervals of a few yards, leading down to the sea. Roderick and Iain Ban took up position on one side, and I joined Lachlan MacLeod on the other side of the boat.

They shouted together: 'One . . . two . . . HUP!' and at the last cry strained forward dragging the boat over the line of rollers.

'Why do you leave her so far from the water?' I asked, when we were resting before starting the next heave.

'This is a bad shore,' Roderick explained patiently. 'There is a terrible surf wi' a gale o' north wind. If she wasn't well clear she would be battered to pieces.'

Iain Ban clambered into the bow, and Lachlan MacLeod took the oars. I sat in the stern, and Roderick pulled up the rolled tops of his thigh boots and waded out, pushing us clear of the shore. Then he climbed into the stern alongside me, and Lachlan pulled out to sea.

I looked up at the towering cliffs descending sheer into the water. The sea washed into the dark openings of several caves, and I watched the gulls swooping down to their nesting places in the clefts of rock. Lachlan MacLeod pointed out an eider-duck, and I watched her wing her way to her nest low on the cliff face.

A solitary house was perched on the cliff top where it jutted out to sea, and the croft lay below on an incredibly steep slope. A man was working on the croft, hoeing potatoes, and he seemed to be clinging to the hillside like a fly to a wall.

Roderick unfastened his line, and I saw that he had eight hooks, set one below the other. They all carried a different coloured fly. He cast the line into the water, and sat holding the rod loosely between his knees.

Iain Ban passed me a rod with the line uncoupled.

'But it's only got one hook,' I said.

'Just as well,' laughed Iain Ban, 'or it is yourself would be after getting mixed up in the hooks and not the fish.'

Roderick showed me how to grip the rod, and he told me to swing it in as soon as I felt a tug on the line. At that moment he swung in his own line and landed five gleaming fish in the stern. I almost dropped my rod in the excitement of seeing them threshing wildly about my feet. There were four sparkling mackerel and a smaller fish I had not seen before.

Roderick unhooked them deftly and tossed them back into the well of the boat. When he picked up the small fish, I asked him its name.

'That's a saithe,' he said, 'the nickname for the men of Raasay.' He grinned. 'Mind you, Alasdair, you would need to be as big as Duncan Mor before you dared call them that.'

I felt a tug on my line and almost overbalanced as I swept the rod up into the air. I saw the gleam of silver on the end of the line, but the long rod was difficult to handle, and the fish wriggled off the hook before I could guide it into the boat.

76

'Hard luck,' said Iain Ban, busily unhooking six big mackerel.

But almost at once there was another tug on my line, and Roderick safely guided a saithe into the boat at my feet. I tried to unhook it, but it slithered through my fingers.

'Take my rod,' said Roderick.

We exchanged rods, and he bent down to unhook the saithe. I felt a tremendous tug on his line, and heaved it clear of the water. In a fever of excitement, I swung the rod round and landed a heap of threshing fish in the stern. There were six mackerel and a much larger fish, rather like a saithe.

'Good for you, Alasdair!' cried Lachlan MacLeod, and I was pleased indeed to be praised by that dark, silent man.

'You have got a lythe,' said Roderick, unhooking the big fish and looking appreciatively at its bronze-flecked back. 'One day we will go to Holm Island and Bearrreraig. That's a rare place for lythe – the real big fellows. We need rubber eels to bait those boys.'

We fished steadily, catching mainly mackerel and saithe. Sometimes the fish rose constantly to our flies; at other times our lines trailed in the water with never a tug. Then Lachlan MacLeod would swing the boat round with a few powerful strokes, and head back for the patch of water where we had struck the last shoal.

Once he rowed far out from shore, and I saw a break in the cliff face, and a sheltered bay by the gorge below Achmore Lodge. Iain Ban pointed out the Kilt Rock to the north. It rose from the sea like a giant kilt spread out over a flat surface, and a waterfall dashed over its top to the sea far below.

It was growing dusk, the long dusk of a Hebridean high summer, and Rona rose like a black shadow from the still waters of the Sound. When we spoke our voices seemed to carry loudly over the water, but we were all silent when Lachlan MacLeod finally pulled for the shore.

I leaned over the side, trailing one hand in the water, listening to the rhythmic splash of the oars. Roderick filled his pipe and I heard the spurt of a match and saw the spent matchstick go bobbing away on the tide. Then there was silence again, except for the cry of a gull and the steady creak of the rowlocks as Lachlan bent to the oars. I had often wondered why my father had gone to sea, but it was at that moment, I think, that I realized why.

Iain Ban started to whistle a catchy reel, and I said suddenly, speaking as soon as the thought flashed into my mind: 'Were any ships wrecked off the coast during the war?'

Roderick shook his head. 'No, it was quiet enough here,' he said. 'They hardly knew there was a war on.'

'What about the plane crash?' said Iain Ban.

Roderick laughed. 'We were all away at sea,' he explained, 'but there was some excitement right enough. A plane crashed on Sgurr a' Mhadaidh Ruaidh.'

'The Hill of the Red Fox,' I murmured, half to myself.

'Aye, that's it,' he said.

'It is a wonder the Red Fellow didn't tell you about it,' said Iain Ban. 'He was the first to get to the crash.'

'What was it carrying?' I asked, trying to keep the tremor out of my voice.

'Och, I don't rightly know,' said Roderick carelessly. 'Just the crew, I suppose. At any rate, they were all killed.'

The boat grounded on the shingle, and Iain Ban leapt out and hauled the bows clear of the water. We hauled her up on the wooden rollers until she was under the shelter of the over-hanging cliffs, but all the time I was thinking of the aircraft that had crashed on Sgurr a' Mhadaidh Ruaidh. Murdo Beaton had been the first man to get to the scene of the disaster. What had he found there? Perhaps the answer to that was the key to the riddle of the Hill of the Red Fox.

Iain Ban was tossing the fish out of the boat into four heaps. He looked across at me and said: 'Tired, Alasdair?'

'No, I was just thinking,' I said.

Roderick walked in front of the fish, and turned his back on them. Iain Ban pointed to one of the heaps, and said; 'Who?'

'Lachlan,' said Roderick.

78

He pointed again.

'Alasdair,' said Roderick.

Once more Iain Ban pointed.

'Myself,' said Roderick, and when he turned, smiling, they were busy stringing the fish.

There was nobody in the kitchen when I got back to the cottage. I dumped the fish down on the table, wishing that Mairi could have seen me come in with my catch. The room looked cosy in the dim light cast by the paraffin lamp, and I sat down on the bench. I was tired after the stiff climb from the shore, and I stretched out full length with my feet resting on the arm of the bench. Murdo Beaton's blue denim jacket was hanging over the arm of the bench and, in moving, I knocked it to the floor. I bent down to pick it up, and as I did so a folded newspaper dropped out of the side pocket.

It was the first newspaper I had seen since coming to Skye, and I picked it up and glanced at it. It was dated 1 July, the day after I had arrived at Achmore, and it was folded in such a way that a small paragraph under a single black heading caught my eye immediately. I read it quickly.

UNKNOWN MAN FOUND SHOT

The body of an unidentified man was found near Lochailort late last night. He had been shot in the back. According to a police statement, the man was between thirty and thirty-five years of age and of medium build. He was wearing a light fawn raincoat and a dark grey suit. There was a distinctive scar on the back of his left hand, stretching from the knuckle joint of the little finger to the wrist.

I carried the paper over to the lamp and read the last line again. I remembered only too well that clenching hand with the vivid red scar.

My head reeled. If the man with the scar was dead, who was the stranger who had visited the cottage in the middle of the night?

Hardly knowing what I was doing, I replaced the newspaper in the jacket pocket, and hurried into the safety of my bedroom.

Chapter 11

I SAT on top of the green mound of Cnoc an t-Sithein, wondering what to do.

It was midday, and the sun blazed down from a Mediterranean sky. Murdo Beaton had left for the hill with Caileag loping along at his heels, and Mairi and the cailleach were working at the peat stack.

All morning I had felt the need to get away by myself to try to sort out my tangled thoughts. After Murdo Beaton had left, saying he was going to take stock of the lambs, I slipped away.

The township cows and stirks were grazing all around me, and I watched a bunch of ewes with their lambs moving up and down by the drain under the dike. They had wandered down from the hill, and were trying to find a break in the dike in an attempt to regain the sweeter pasture of the crofts.

I was searching as desperately as the sheep, not for a gap in a dike, but for a way out of my encircling troubles. Everything had seemed crystal clear until I read the paragraph in the folded newspaper. Now I was back where I had started, but the mystery had taken on a more sinister aspect with the death of the man with the scar.

He was the man who had been silenced, there could be no doubt about that. And whoever had shot him must be working in league with Murdo Beaton. What would the murderer do if he discovered that I carried a message from the man with the scar? Despite the heat of the sun I could not repress a shiver. Anyone desperate enough to commit murder would not shrink from it a second time in order to achieve his ends.

I had struggled on alone for too long; my only thought now was to whom should I tell my tale. I thought of Hector MacLeod, but he was an old man, and this was no undertaking for old men.

I remembered what he had told me about Duncan Mor. Big Duncan. Even Roderick MacPherson's laughing eyes sobered with respect when he spoke of him. Well then, Duncan Mor it should be, I decided. Any action was better than tormenting myself with my own troubled thoughts.

I scrambled to my feet and tramped quickly over the moor in the direction of the river. The moor resembled an enormous basin, and when the ground dipped I lost sight of the river, but I carried on steadily until I came to a high wire fence. I crawled under the fence, crossed a rough cart track leading to the hill, and came up against a broad earthen dike. The crofts of Mealt lay beyond, sloping gently to the river.

When I clambered up on top of the dike, I saw Duncan Mor's house at once. It was a stone-built bungalow with a slated roof, facing east, and built close to the river bank. There was a walled garden in front of the house, and a man was sitting on the wall watching me. A big black and white collie started to bark furiously, and I heard the man say: 'Quiet, Glen.'

I ran quickly down the croft and stopped a few feet from him. He slid off the wall and stood looking down at me. I had a sudden strange feeling, foolish as it may seem, that we had met before.

We stood there looking at one another, and I grew uneasy, waiting for him to speak. If I scowled – and he maintained I did – it was to cover my shyness at his silence.

He was easily the biggest man I had ever seen, but he was even taller than he looked for the great breadth of his shoulders took something from his height. He was wearing blue denim trousers supported by a broad leather belt, and I noticed the narrowness of his waist and the flatness of his stomach. The sleeves of his open-necked shirt were folded above the elbow, and whenever he moved his arm to brush away a fly, I could see the easy play of muscles beneath the brown skin. I knew that his eyes were on my own painfully thin arms, and I scowled harder than ever, and gazed stubbornly at my feet, determined not to be the first to speak.

'Aye, you are a Cameron, right enough,' he said at last, 'a dour looking black beggar like your father before you, and like as not ye're as thrawn as he was.'

He had a deep, booming voice. The words seemed to rise from the depths of his diaphragm, gather volume in the great barrel of his chest, and be flung out on the air.

I took a deep breath and hoped he had not noticed the nervous clenching of my hands.

'Thrawn or not,' I said, 'my name is Alasdair Cameron, and I am told you were a friend of my father's.'

'A dhuine dhuine,' he cried. 'I saw Alasdair Dubh in the dark scowl of you, and I growled, to see if the London life had taken the Hielan' blood from you, and you stood your ground like a man.'

He stepped forward and gripped my shoulders, and I was forced to look in his eyes. They were grey eyes, set wide apart, and I noticed with a start of surprise that his hair was grey too, lying close to his head in tight curls. His body was the body of a young man, and for all his grey hair there was something about his face that would never age like the face of other men.

'Aye, I was your father's friend,' he said, 'and it is the hard task you have before you to live up to that brave man.'

No man had ever spoken to me like that before. Sometimes, usually on Remembrance Day, Aunt Evelyn would dab her eyes and say something about 'your poor brave father', and although I knew it was wrong of me, I felt embarrassed, and made some excuse to leave the room. On such days, my mother stayed in her room all day, and she never said anything at all. But it was different the way Duncan Mor spoke, looking me straight in the eye, and speaking the words in his loud, ringing voice.

I felt his strong fingers probing my shoulders.

'The good Hielan' bone is there,' he went on, 'and if the bone is right the flesh and muscle will come in the Lord's good time. It is wonderful what hill air and sun, on top of a bowl o' brose in the morning, will do for a man. Sit you down, Alasdair Beag. It is high time you and me had a crack together.'

We sat with our backs to the garden wall, watching the lazy flow of the river to the sea. Achmore Lodge was hidden from view, but I could see the break in the cliffs where the river tumbled down the gorge to the sea.

I heard the sound of a car and looked up with surprise. A Land Rover was jolting over the rough track to the hill. The driver was wearing dark glasses, and a white haired man sat beside him. Two other men in tweeds were in the back.

'That's a party from the Lodge,' said Duncan Mor. 'The fellow with the white hair is Major Cassell and the other two will be guests I suppose. They will be after trying the loch for trout.' He chuckled. 'It would scunner you to see some of those lads from the south, Alasdair. Many's the time I've seen them wi' gear costing a small fortune; hollow glass rods, Ambidex Reels, nylon lines, cast pouches and boxes o' flies, and some o' them there not fit to catch a cold, let alone a good brown trout.'

I laughed with him, and asked who Major Cassell was.

'Major Cassell has taken the Lodge,' Duncan Mor replied. 'A naturalist, but a nice enough man by all accounts. I'm told he thinks nothing of sitting up all night on the rocks just to watch a bird nesting. Still, it takes all sorts to make a world, and he does no harm, poor man.'

'Is he the landlord?' I asked.

'Well, in the old days it was always the laird who stayed at the Lodge,' he answered, 'but the Board of Agriculture's your landlord today. St Andrew's House, Edinburgh. Believe me, there's some thrawn beggars in the Board, but mind you, the crofter is far better off than he was in the old days.'

Duncan Mor went on to talk of sheep and cattle, and fishing in the hill lochs and poaching salmon on wet dark nights. He told me of the feats of strength of my grandfather, in the days when there was no road from Portree, and everything had to be brought in by boat to Rudha nam Braithrean; of how he had once carried a boll of meal on his back all the way up the steep cliff from Rudha nam Braithrean to Achmore without pausing to rest on the way.

He had me laughing and talking, with no thought that a short time ago we had been strangers, and when he said quietly: 'What has the Red Fellow been up to?' it was not like disclosing confidences to a stranger.

'But how did you know?' I stammered.

'There was black trouble in the face of you before you spoke a word,' he answered, 'and if there is trouble in Achmore look no further than that sly fox of a Murdo Ruadh.'

There was one question, above all others, I had to ask.

'Was he a friend of my father's?' I wanted to know.

'A Thighearna bheannaichte,' Duncan Mor exclaimed. 'Murdo Ruadh a friend of Alasdair Dubh! If the big black fellow were here this day he would take Murdo Ruadh by his long neck, and throw him out of Achmore.' He brooded in silence for a while, then added: 'Not that I am against Mistress Cameron. She was not to know the man at all, at all.'

'But what has my mother got to do with it?' I asked.

'Well, it was herself gave him the croft,' he replied, 'and him always grumbling about the big rent he was paying. Mind you, I know the fly tongue of the man, and I know Mistress Cameron would not be the one to be charging a big rent.'

'But he has never paid any rent,' I said hotly.

Duncan Mor sat bolt upright.

'Murdo Ruadh has never paid any rent?' he repeated.

I shook my head.

'Then how did he get the croft?'

'He wrote a letter to my mother after she had gone back to London,' I explained, 'and said he was a good friend of my father's and my father had told him he could have the croft as long as we were away.'

Duncan Mor sprang to his feet, his great fists knotting. A hot flush crimsoned the brown of his cheeks, and I could see the working of a vein in his forehead. I thought he was going to burst a blood vessel. Never had I seen a man so angry.

Without a word, he started off across the croft. I ran after him and caught his arm.

'Where are you going?' I cried.

'Where do you think I am going?' he retorted savagely. 'I am going to get my hands on that long cratur and break every bone in his miserable body.'

I knew it was no idle boast, as I watched the muscles bunching on his powerful forearm when he ground his fist into the palm of his hand.

'But there is more to it than the croft,' I said wildly. 'A man has been murdered and there is something hidden on the Hill of the Red Fox and if they find that I've got the message. . . .'

I broke off to draw breath, and my excitement had the effect of cooling him down. He put an arm round my shoulder and led me back to the wall and we sat down again.

'A story should start at the beginning, Alasdair Beag,' said Duncan Mor calmly. 'Now then, let me be hearing it.'

I told him everything that had happened from the time I had first seen the man with the scar clutching the bar outside the window of my compartment, to the whispered conversation I had overheard. He listened in silence, slicing a coil of thick, black tobacco with quick, dexterous strokes of his knife, shredding the tobacco in his hands, and filling his pipe.

I told him how I had thought that the message must have been intended for Murdo Beaton, and that the man outside the cottage was the man with the scar. I did not disguise the fears I had known, thinking that they intended to silence me, and I described my consternation at finding the newspaper and reading that the man with the scar had been murdered.

When I had finished, I was surprised – and, to be truthful, annoyed – to see that Duncan Mor was smiling.

He took his pipe from his mouth, and said: 'And you have kept all this to yourself all this time?'

'Yes,' I said, trying to conceal my dismay at his cool reception of my story.

'You were afraid that something might happen to you?'
he went on.

'Yes,' I admitted.

'But you never showed the message to another living soul?'

'No.'

'How old are you, a bhalaich?' he asked.

'Nearly thirteen,' I said.

Duncan Mor sat forward, resting his chin on his hands, wrapped in a brooding silence.

After a while, he took out a large khaki handkerchief and blew his nose several times.

Not looking at me at all, he said: 'My, what would I give to have the big black fellow here this day.'

'You believe me, don't you?' I said sharply.

His big brown hand covered mine for a moment, and he said: 'Surely, I believe you, Alasdair Beag, but you are too like your father, an duine bochd.' He smiled, showing even white teeth. 'You must give me time to get used to being an old man, and not a boy any longer.'

'Well, what are we to do?' I demanded. 'Who do you think was the man who came to see Murdo Beaton?'

Duncan Mor stroked his chin.

'Likely enough, it would be the fellow with the bright blue eyes. It follows, do you see? Remember the words you heard – Lochailort and Silenced. Well, the bold fellow pulled the communication cord and got off the train near Lochailort, and I don't doubt but that he silenced your man with the scar. Then he came to the house to tell Murdo Ruadh.'

'But how would he know his way to Achmore and why didn't he try to question me?' I said.

'Think,' said Duncan Mor quietly. 'If the man with the scar hid the address label on your case, the other fellow would have no idea where you were bound for. But like as not Murdo Ruadh has been mixed up with him since a while back. Aye, I'll warrant it is not the first time that he has had a crack with Blue Eyes.'

'But how do you know?' I insisted.

'Och, I've known for a while back that the Red Fellow was up to his long neck in some dark doings,' he answered guardedly.

'But what can it be?' I asked.

'I don't rightly know,' he said, tapping his pipe stem against clenched teeth.

I thought of the rest of the conversation I had overheard.

'What about midnight Saturday?' I said. 'It's Saturday today. What do you think they are going to do?'

Duncan Mor's grey eyes regarded me steadily.

'Whatever happens this night,' he said slowly, 'don't be thinking ye're going to be stravaiging around the countryside, because you're not. And why this Saturday? Blue Eyes might have arranged to meet the Red Fellow next Saturday.'

I knew he was putting me off, and I said quickly: 'You know well enough that if anything happens it will be tonight.'

'Maybe I do,' he answered, and his eyes were steel hard when he said: 'This is no idle ploy, Alasdair, mark that well. One man has died already. The less you know about this business the better for you. Myself will keep an eye open tonight, and you can see me on Monday.'

'Perhaps we should go to the police,' I said, knowing the truth of his words.

'Well, aye, we could go to the polis,' assented Duncan Mor, 'but I am not for the polis as long as Murdo Ruadh is in this. You see, Alasdair Beag, it is a habit in this place to steer clear of the polis where our own men are concerned. We kept our own law before the English brought their law to the Highlands, and it is the old law that will try Murdo Ruadh in the end.'

I told him of the aircraft that had crashed on Sgurr a' Mhadaidh Ruaidh during the war, and how Murdo Beaton had been the first man to reach the scene of the crash. When I said that the aircraft could have been carrying bullion I got the impression that he was not really listening. His grey eyes had a faraway expression and he kept tapping his teeth with the stem of his pipe.

87

When he spoke, it was not of the aircraft at all.

'That number on the message,' he said slowly. 'Think now. Are you sure that it was M 15?'

'Positive,' I said readily. 'It was a capital M and a figure one and a figure five.'

'All the same, I would like to be seeing it,' said Duncan Mor. 'Bring it over with you when you come on Monday.'

I said I would, and he walked with me as far as the dike.

Before I left him, he said: 'When you get back to Achmore, Alasdair, be sure to tell Murdo Ruadh you met me today.'

'But why?' I asked, surprised.

'Well, we have two foxes to deal with,' he said slowly. 'One o' them is the Hill of the Red Fox and the other is that long red fox at Achmore. A harmless enough cratur the fox, Alasdair, until it is cornered. Then it can be dangerous. So if the Red Fellow should think to turn on you, I doubt himself will think again when he knows you and I have had a crack together.'

I saw the look in Duncan Mor's steely grey eyes. It was a look that would have quelled stouter hearts than Murdo Beaton's.

Chapter 12

I WAS cheered and heartened by my meeting with Duncan Mor, although I could not help feeling disappointed by his refusal to consider my suggestion about the crashed aircraft. I was certain he was holding something back from me, but it could be, I reflected, that he was unwilling to acknowledge the fact that I had stumbled upon the truth in case I unwittingly betrayed my knowledge to Murdo Beaton. He had told me it was dangerous to know too much, and if he had made no comment on the crashed aircraft it showed how close I was to the truth.

The cailleach was reading the *Oban Times*. She had spread the long sheets across the table and was peering at the print through a large magnifying glass. Mairi told me it was the only paper her father allowed in the house, and I wondered from whom he had obtained the *Daily Express* that had fallen from his pocket when I knocked his jacket off the bench. Perhaps Blue Eyes, as Duncan Mor called him, had given it to him.

I helped Mairi to feed the hens, scattering handfuls of grain on the grass, and laughing at their frantic foraging. They would start up at each fresh handful of grain and rush towards it, leaving untouched the corn already spread on the grass.

'I saw Duncan Mor today,' I said.

Mairi was about to cast a handful of grain, and she checked herself, her hand poised in mid-air still clutching the grain.

'Don't be telling himself,' she said quickly.

'Why not?' I asked.

She let the grain trickle slowly to the ground between her slightly opened fingers, and picked another handful out of the pail before she replied.

'He doesn't like Duncan Mor,' she said slowly. 'He wouldn't be pleased if he knew you were seeing him.'

'Do you like him?' I said.

'Who? Duncan Mor?'

I nodded.

'Everybody likes Duncan Mor,' she said guardedly.

'But do you like him?' I insisted.

She glanced back at the house.

'I like him better than anyone in Achmore,' she said fiercely.

The surprise must have shown on my face, because she went on: 'You should have seen him last Hallowe'en at the guising. He was dressed up as an old cailleach. I saw him over at Hector MacLeod's, and he made me laugh so much that I got the hiccups, and Roderick MacPherson dropped a cold key down my back to try and stop me hiccupping.'

'I'll bet your father didn't know you were there,' I said, 'or the cailleach.'

She tossed her dark head, sending her pigtails whirling.

'I don't care,' she said defiantly, 'but, anyway, the cailleach wouldn't tell him. She tells me all sorts of things that he doesn't know about.'

'But she is his mother,' I stammered. 'It . . . it doesn't seem right.'

'Well, she doesn't like him,' said Mairi flatly. 'She is getting old right enough, and she talks to herself and she is deaf, but she doesn't miss much for all that. She tells me stories of long ago. She told me Duncan Mor was going to marry my mother until himself told a lot of lies and put an end to it, and that is why Duncan Mor hates him.'

I could not understand Mairi. She had never seen a train or a railway station or a city street, but there were times when she spoke like a grown-up and seemed much older than I. She went down to the main road and bought the groceries off Lipton's van, and worked at the peats and the potatoes, and fed the calves and herded the cows, and did many things that I could not have done. She had a small, serious face, and did not laugh easily, no matter how much I teased her. There was always a watchful look in her eyes, as if she were waiting to hear a footstep behind her, so that she would be ready to shut the smile off her face and dart away to take up some workaday task.

Caileag suddenly appeared, sniffing at the scattered grain, and Mairi picked up the pail and darted off to the house. When I looked round, Murdo Beaton was standing in front of the cottage.

After tea, when Mairi and the cailleach were clearing the dishes, I said: 'I was talking to Duncan Mor today.'

I tried to speak casually but my voice sounded unnaturally loud. Mairi straightened up suddenly and dropped a cup. It smashed on the floor, and Murdo Beaton spoke to her sharply in Gaelic. I wondered if he had heard me, for he went on picking his teeth with a matchstick, his eyes on his mud-stained tackety boots. At length, he laid the match on the table but his eyes were still on his boots.

'Well, well, so you were talking to Duncan Mor, eh?' he said. 'A great talker, Duncan Mor MacDonald, but the Mac-Donalds had aye an active tongue in their heads. Look you at Duncan Mor. He has the souming for six cows and their followers, and forty sheep and a horse forby. And what does he keep? I will tell you, boy. He keeps one old rag of a cross Ayrshire cow and a handful of sheep, the most o' them cast ewes that should have been cleared long since.

'Mind you, the same fellow will not go hungry – not Duncan Mor MacDonald. See you, there is many a way to turn a shilling in this world forby the honest way o' the poor crofter struggling with his sheep and cattle and a few acres o' barren soil. There is salmon in the river and the same salmon fetches big money in Portree. But whose salmon, boy? Aye, that iss the question. Whose salmon?'

His long index finger prodded me in the ribs.

'It iss Major Cassell's salmon. Think of the poor Major paying a big rent for the Lodge and the fishing, and the bold Duncan Mor creeping down to the falls on a dark night to net the pool. Some poor folk must spend all their days in labour, but not Duncan Mor MacDonald. The big fellow can use his big tongue in idle gossip, and wait for the rain to make a flood on the river, so that he can net the Major's salmon. Oh, a fine man, I grant you, with the smooth tongue of the MacDonalds on him and all their false pride. But wait you, boy, if you are spared, you will see the day when Duncan Mor MacDonald is humbled in the dust, even as it says in the Good Book.'

I had never before heard him say more than an odd word or two, and I realized that I must have touched him on the raw to have provoked such an outburst. He had started by speaking softly, but his voice rose steadily and the colour crept into his sallow cheeks. By the time he reached the last sentence, he spat it out with such concentrated venom that I became aware, for the first time, of the depth of the enmity between himself and Duncan Mor.

'Well, I like him, anyway,' I said stubbornly.

Murdo Beaton's hands gripped the chair between his legs, and I knew he was trying to control himself.

'I have warned you, boy,' he said flatly. 'I will say no more.'

'Duncan Mor was a friend of my father's,' I persisted.

'There are good friends and bad,' was all he said.

He got up and pulled on his cap.

When he had reached the door, he turned and said: 'You come and go as you please, boy, but tomorrow is the Sabbath and as long as I am in this house the Sabbath Day will be kept holy. See that you are in your bed early for the door closes in this house long before twelve o'clock on a Saturday night.'

And with that he was gone, leaving me wondering if there was any connexion between the whispered words 'midnight Saturday' and his insistence on my being indoors early. Not that it was really early, I had to admit. Indeed, it was far later than my normal bedtime at home, but nobody here went to bed early, young or old.

Mairi leaned across the table, her eyes wide.

'My, he was wild,' she whispered. 'You are a daft beggar, Alasdair Cameron, after I told you not to say anything.'

But there was a new respect in her look, and for once I felt older than her and strangely proud.

I sat on the side of the bed, chewing the end of my pen, and trying to think of something to say to my mother. I had sent her a postcard after I arrived, but her first letter remained unanswered.

I wrote:

Dear Mother and Aunt Evelyn,

Thanks for the letter. I am fine and having a good time. They have two cows here and two calves and a brown mare. I help Mairi to feed the hens. She says a lot of them are clucking, and when they are clucking they sit on the nest all day and don't lay any eggs. Some of the cluckers she puts inside an old creel and hangs it up with a sack tied over the top. After they have been in the creel for a few days they don't cluck any more.

I met Duncan Mor MacDonald today. He was first mate on the Empire Rose *and he says I am like my father. He is the biggest man I have ever known and I like him a lot. He is going to take me fishing.*

I wondered if I should tell her what he had told me about Murdo Beaton, and how he had secured the croft by a trick, but I decided against it. My mother would be worried and there was no knowing what she might do. It never even occurred to me to tell her about the mystery of the Hill of the Red Fox. I wondered if every boy felt like me. Here was I, writing to my mother, and keeping back all the things that really mattered. Was I so different from other boys, or did everybody behave like that? It was strange how you could love someone like your mother, and yet always keep a part of yourself locked away, so that it was easier to talk to Duncan Mor than to her.

I went on:

I have been out fishing already. Roderick MacPherson and two other men took me out in a boat and we caught lots of mackerel and saithe. I was the only one to catch a lythe. One of the men was Lachlan MacLeod and he asked to be remembered to you. He is a nice man.

It has been very hot here, but it is not like a hot day in London. The air is lovely and fresh up at Achmore, it is almost like being in an aeroplane.

There did not seem to be much more to add, so I signed it, 'Love Alasdair'.

I read the letter through, and as I did not want to appear to be too happy away from them, I added: 'P.S. – I am missing you both.'

I had taken off my sandals and was pulling off a stocking, when I remembered the whispered conversation I had overheard. Midnight Saturday! And Murdo Beaton had been insistent that I should be indoors early! Duncan Mor had said that he would keep an eye open, but how could he possibly watch Murdo Beaton's movements? I drew back the blankets and slipped into bed fully dressed. At least I could see what Murdo Beaton did. He had said that nobody left the house late on a Saturday night, so if he went out it must mean that he was keeping his midnight assignation.

There was a wind rising. It came in sudden, sharp gusts that shook the branches of the rowan trees, and I heard a wild flurry of leaves and then silence until the next gust came. From far down the croft came the harsh croak of a corncrake; on and on and on with never a break. It made my throat feel sore listening to it. It was like the steady drip of a tap; at first no more than a background noise but steadily thrusting its way into your consciousness to the exclusion of all else. I started to count, saying to myself, when I have counted sixty it will have stopped. I went on from sixty to a hundred, and then two hundred, but the steady croaking went on and on. I dozed off to sleep with the sound of it loud in my ears.

Had it not been for a dog's angry barking, I would never have heard the door opening. The sound of the dog barking in the distance awakened me, and I struggled up in bed and glanced at my watch. It was half past eleven. At that moment, I heard the scrape of the front door as it was opened and pulled carefully shut again. I leapt out of bed and pulled on my wellingtons.

Tiptoeing across the room, I opened the door and eased my way into the lobby. I opened the front door a little and peered through the crack. The sky had darkened but it was still clear enough to see to the bottom of the croft, and I saw the long figure of Murdo Beaton hurrying past the byre. I waited until the byre hid him from view, then I opened the door wide and stepped outside. A sudden gust of wind drove a spattering of rain into my face, and I stepped back and snatched my raincoat from the nail on the lobby wall. Closing the door quietly behind me, I ran down to the byre.

In the shelter of the byre, I struggled into my coat and watched Murdo Beaton. He was walking fast with his head down and he never once glanced back. When he disappeared over the dike at the bottom of the croft, I ran after him.

I wondered what I would do if he suddenly turned back and I met him face to face, but I steadily put the thought from my mind and carried on. When I reached the dike, I was panting hard, and I leaned against it and peered cautiously over the top.

I thought I had lost him, but then I made out his stooping figure cutting across the bog in the direction of Achmore Lodge. He was moving faster than I had realized, and I clambered over the dike and ran after him, ready to fling myself flat at the first sign of him turning his head.

After I had covered a few hundred yards the ground sloped sharply to the burn, and I sprinted along, bent almost double. I was so intent on keeping my quarry within sight that I was careless of my footing, and I pitched forward heavily on my face. When I picked myself up again there was no sign of Murdo Beaton.

I moved on more cautiously, following the line of an old peat cutting, and I could hear the swift flowing waters of the burn before I spotted him again. He was on the other side of the burn, still moving rapidly in the direction of Achmore Lodge.

By good fortune I must have kept to his path because I reached the burn at a point where four large, flat stepping stones made its crossing a simple matter. Taking care to keep well down, I pressed on behind him.

Before he reached the Lodge he veered left and cut across the main road. By the time I had reached the road, I had lost sight of him again and I stood for a moment not knowing which way to go. I plunged across the road and came on to a narrow winding track. I raced on and almost gave myself away when I rounded a bend, where the track dropped steeply, and saw him directly below me. I fell flat on my face in the wet bracken by the side of the track, and watched him carefully until he vanished around an outcropping of rock. I scrambled to my feet and followed him slowly.

The track wound round the top of a disused quarry and came out on what seemed to be the face of the cliff. There was no sign of Murdo Beaton and I advanced slowly, wondering what could have happened to him. I reached the edge of the cliff and lay flat on my stomach looking down.

I was looking down into the gorge where the Mealt river entered the sea. The roar of the falls was loud in my ears, and looking back I saw the bridge over the river on the main road and the long white waterfall crashing down into the gorge.

There was a sheltered bay where the river met the sea, and the narrow crescent of sand gleamed whitely against the dark waters of the Sound. A long, low building stood on the far river bank and behind it there was a square of tall poles hung with nets. A boat lay at her moorings a little way from shore, lifting and dropping against the wash of the incoming swell, and I saw a tiny dinghy drawn up on the shore in front of the building. Of Murdo Beaton there was no sign. He had vanished.

I inched forward cautiously until I was hanging over the grass-covered cliff face. It seemed to be a sheer drop to the gorge far below, and I was on the point of retreating along the track, when I saw him. He was half-way down the cliff, but from where I was lying it did not seem possible for any man to make his way down that sheer face to the bottom of the gorge.

I watched him closely. Sometimes he disappeared from view under an outcropping rock, only to reappear again lower down. I slowly realized that there must be a narrow path winding down the face of the cliff to the gorge below. I lost sight of him again for a long time, and when at last he came into view he was walking rapidly down the opposite bank of the river towards the long, low building.

I wondered how he had crossed the river. There must be a bridge farther back, hidden from view.

Two men emerged from the shadow of the building to meet him. I edged back from the cliff face in case one of them should look up and spot my white face against the dark line of the cliff.

Some insect was crawling up my leg and I rolled over on my side and bent forward to brush it away. As I did so, I looked back along the track. My heart gave one sickening leap and seemed to contract. I looked round wildly but I had my back to the cliff and there was no escape.

I stared fixedly in front of me, unable to move. A man was coming towards me, bent almost double, and running swiftly.

Chapter 13

THE man reached me as I scrambled to my feet, and flung himself on me. I was thrown to the ground with a force that knocked the wind from my body, and before I could cry out a hand was clapped over my mouth. I struggled wildly, but my arms were pinned to the ground by the weight of the man's body, and I knew that further resistance was hopeless. I let my body go limp, but the hand across my mouth never slackened.

A voice hissed in my ear: 'Of all the thrawn beggars!'

I looked up, wide-eyed, into the angry face of Duncan Mor. He was wearing a long black oilskin coat and a sou'wester pulled down over his eyes. The sou'wester had hidden his face when he came charging towards me with his head down, and his figure had been concealed by the long coat.

He took his hand from my mouth, and I gasped for breath.

'I should skelp the stuffing out o' ye,' he declared.

'The stuffing's out of me already,' I said weakly.

'Never the fear o' it,' he hissed. 'It would take a bigger dunt than yon to knock some sense into that thick black skull.' But for all his angry tone, he patted my shoulder, and added softly: 'I had to do it, a bhalaich. Another second and you were for shouting your head off.'

'But how did you know I was here?' I whispered.

'I didn't,' he said grimly. 'Was I not after telling you I would be keeping my eyes open this night?'

'I know, but I heard Murdo Beaton leave the house,' I said, 'and I thought it would be a good idea to follow him.'

'Fine I could see you had the thrawn streak of the Camerons in you,' exclaimed Duncan Mor.

'But . . .' I began.

'Ist, ist,' he hissed, and motioned me to follow him.

Side by side, we crawled forward until we were lying full length on the edge of the cliff, looking down to the tiny bay far below. The three men were standing on the shore, gazing out to sea. From our vantage point, they looked like toy figures dwarfed by the immense perpendicular slopes of the sides of the gorge.

The wind was rising steadily. It came in sudden gusts, sweeping across the gorge and slashing the rain into my face. With each gust, I sheltered my face in the crook of my arm until the lull came. It was more sheltered down in the bay, but I noticed that the boat was tossing at her moorings, and the dark surface of the Sound was broken by white-topped waves.

Suddenly an intermittent light flashed from far out in the Sound. One of the men on the shore raised something to his shoulder, and an answering series of lights flashed across the water.

'Is it morse?' I whispered.

Duncan Mor's lips were within an inch of my ear when he answered.

'Aye,' he murmured. 'The fellow down below is signalling with an Aldis Lamp.'

The three men ran back to the dinghy and dragged it down to the river. The tallest of the three took up the oars and rowed out to the moored boat. When the dinghy came alongside the boat he shipped his oars and leaned over and grasped the gunwale while the other two sprang aboard. The oarsman clambered after them, and I saw him stoop in the stern of the boat and fasten the dinghy's painter. Another man freed the mooring rope, and the tall man took up the oars and pulled out to sea with long, steady strokes. As the boat left the shelter of the bay, and met the full force of the wind, I could see her pitching and tossing. A white cloud of spray broke over her bows, drenching the oarsman, but he never faltered and the boat moved steadily out to sea.

'The Red Fellow is at the oars,' said Duncan Mor, 'and a dirty trip he is in for by the looks o' things.'

'Do you think they'll sink?' I asked. 'It's not a very big boat.'

'If it was yourself at the oars you would be thinking it was big enough,' said Duncan Mor. 'Mind you, a coble is on the slow side, and difficult to handle, but it will stand an awful hammering.'

Dark rainclouds were scudding across the sky, and the boat had dwindled to a tiny speck in the distance. It would soon be lost to sight in the gathering darkness of the night, and I felt able to speak freely.

'What is the building down there?' I asked, pointing to the long, low building by the river bank.

'The salmon fishermen's bothy,' said Duncan Mor. 'You can see one of their nets there, spread out on the drying poles. A seal made an awful mess of it, and the boys will be after patching it on Monday.'

He pointed out the marker buoys in the bay, and described how the bag nets were laid to catch the incoming salmon as they tried to make their way up the river.

'A fine dry spring, wi' a steady breeze o' north wind, and there is good fishing here,' he said. 'I have seen the time when they cleared over a hundred salmon a day, and most o' them twelve pounders at that.' He chuckled. 'Mind you, there is always a few manage to get by the nets and reach the pool under the falls. Many a good salmon I lifted from the pool, Alasdair.'

'Whom do they belong to?' I asked, thinking of Murdo Beaton's outburst about salmon poaching.

'Whoever has the Lodge takes over the fishing,' he replied. 'I would say that the fish in the nets yonder' – he pointed down to the bay – 'belong to Major Cassell. The Major, poor man, paid for the nets and he pays for the men to work the fishing. But the fish in the river, well now, that is another story as the other man said.'

'But aren't they Major Cassell's fish just the same?' I persisted.

'Well, I never rightly asked them,' he said jokingly. 'But if there was no rainwater from the hill there would be no river, and I doubt if Major Cassell could claim title to the rains from the heavens. No, no, Alasdair, the Lord put the fish in the river and they are there for the taking.'

I looked down at the bothy, with its white stone walls capped by a black roof of tarred felt.

'What would happen if the fishermen should wake up?' I said.

Duncan Mor laughed.

'The bothy is empty,' he answered. 'The salmon fishermen come down every morning and leave in the afternoon. This place has the name of being haunted and they would rather tramp miles to work than stay the night. One of those boys comes all the way over the moor from Garos. Mind you, it is a gey funny ghost if you ask me.'

'But somebody might see the signalling lights,' I said.

'Never the fear o' it,' he scoffed. 'All good folk are in their beds long since. It is the Sabbath the morn.'

'Who do you think are the other two in the coble?' I asked.

'Whoever they are, they can be thankful the Red Fellow is at the oars,' said Duncan Mor. 'It is no easy work to bring a boat back to this shore on a night like this.'

The rain was falling steadily and dark clouds hung low over the Sound. The black roof of the bothy merged into the shadows, and only the white crescent of the sandy beach remained clearly defined. I strained my eyes, peering across the darkening water, but there was no sign of the coble.

The rain dripped down the collar of my coat, wetting my neck, and I shivered, feeling chilled. Even as I watched, the Sound was blotted out in darkness and rain, and all I could see was the wash of the waves on the shore.

Suddenly Duncan Mor cocked his head.

'Ist!' he hissed.

I could hear the roar of the falls, and the soughing of the wind in the gorge, and something else. It was a low, humming noise, and it came from the darkness of the Sound. After a while it faded, and there was only the ceaseless pounding of the falls and the eerie moan of the wind.

We lay perfectly still for a long time until I began to get pins and needles in my foot, and I wished I could get up and stretch my chilled limbs and stamp my feet. I was going to ask Duncan Mor if it was safe to move, when I heard the creak of rowlocks. There was silence again, then I heard the low murmur of voices over the water, and saw the dark shape of the dinghy nose up the river. It drew in to the bank in front of the bothy, and two shadowy figures leapt out and hauled it up the river bank.

A few seconds must have elapsed, although it seemed like minutes, before I realized the significance of what I had seen. THREE MEN HAD GONE OUT IN THE BOAT BUT ONLY TWO HAD RETURNED.

I almost cried out aloud in astonishment, and I looked at Duncan Mor, but he motioned me to be silent. When I looked down again, the two men could not be seen. Then I saw the sudden faint flare of a match, sheltered by cupped hands, and the glowing point of a cigarette end. The men must have moved to the shelter of the bothy.

After a while, a red point arched through the air and vanished in the river. Two shadowy forms emerged from the end of the bothy, and made off up the river bank.

Duncan Mor signed to me to follow him, and he crawled along the track on all fours. I followed him awkwardly, surprised at the stiffness in my legs. When we were clear of the gorge, he straightened up and I walked by his side.

We walked rapidly, and in silence, and stopped at the main road. Duncan Mor glanced round.

'You need all your time,' he said sharply, 'or the Red Fellow will be on your heels. Do you think you can manage?'

'I think so,' I said doubtfully.

The night had darkened and the formless blackness of the moor lay all around. I was filled with misgivings, but I dare not acknowledge that I was afraid of losing my way.

'If you can't manage,' he said, 'I will come with you, but I would rather be on the heels of the fellow with Murdo Ruadh.'

If it had not been for me he would have been unhindered, so I said recklessly, 'I'll manage.'

'Right, then,' he said swiftly. He flung out his arm. 'Away you go in that direction, and you will strike the stepping stones over the burn wi' no bother. Keep straight on and you will come out at the foot of the croft. If you make your way up the croft by the drain you can't go wrong. Oidhche mhath mata.'

I plunged across the road in the direction of his pointing finger, and when I thought I was out of sight, I started to run. I stumbled over the uneven ground, never looking to my right or left, fearful of losing my way. The wet coat, flapping around my legs, hindered me, and I got a stitch in my side, but I gritted my teeth and carried on.

I stopped just in time, or I would have pitched headlong into the burn, and I walked cautiously along the bank looking for the stepping stones. The bank sloped steeply down to the burn, and it did not look like the place where I had crossed when following Murdo Beaton. I retraced my steps, anxiety mounting, and I was about to risk plunging across the burn in my wellingtons, when I saw the stepping stones.

I stepped across, congratulating myself on my good fortune. It was not as difficult as I had expected. The worst part was over now that I had crossed the burn. All I had to do was to reach the dike and make my way up the croft to the safety of the house.

I ran on, buffeted by the wind and the rain, and slowed down by the rising ground and the burning pain in my side. I caught my foot in a tuft of heather and crashed heavily to the ground. Without looking where I was going, I picked myself up and stumbled on. I blundered into a patch of soft bog, and before I could check myself I had sunk in up to my knees. I struggled desperately to free myself, but I could get no purchase to lever my legs clear of the suction of the bog.

It was the darkness that terrified me. If only I could see where I was, and what I was doing, but I was trapped in the blackness of the night. I struggled frantically, but I felt myself sinking deeper. Gathering my strength in a final despairing effort, I lunged forward and fell face downwards into the wet slime of the bog.

I lay there panting, gasping in great breaths of air. When I had rested, I struggled to my feet and heaved desperately, trying to lift my right foot clear of the bog. There was a squelching, sucking sound and I thought I was free, but my foot came out of my wellington and I staggered and almost overbalanced a second time. The shock of the icy water of the bog on my stockinged foot made me catch my breath, and I groped around for my wellington and pulled it clear of the bog. I pushed my foot into it and stepped back, at the same time drawing my left foot clear.

Once I was on firm ground, I made a wide detour of the soft patch of bog. Half-walking, half-running, I staggered on.

I expected to strike the dike at any time, but the ground seemed to be sloping away in front of me. I dug my nails into the palms of my hands to try to relieve the awful burning pain in my side, and ran on, sucking in quick breaths of air.

By the time I reached the burn, I had slowed to a stumbling walk. I stood on the bank, rocking on my heels, gazing stupidly at the dark rushing water. I drew the back of my hand across my eyes trying to brush away the rain and the sweat, and work out what had happened. It was the dike I should be facing, not the burn. The burn lay in the opposite direction to Achmore. Gradually it dawned on me that from the time I crossed the stepping stones I must have wandered round in a wide arc. Had it not been for the burn I would have stumbled on blindly until I reached the road.

I turned round and forced my aching legs to carry me forward. With my heart pounding madly, I stumbled on into the blackness of the night. I don't know how many times I fell. It seemed that I was forever picking myself up and staggering on, when all I wanted to do was to lie still in the wet heather and gasp my fill of the cool night air.

When I reached the dike, I sagged across it, almost sobbing from exhaustion. I had never thought I would manage to find it, and now that the solid bank supported me I could hardly summon sufficient strength to clamber over it. The pain in my side seemed to be constricting my stomach, but I dug my hands into the bank and crawled painfully over the dike. I almost fell into the drain below, but I managed to pull myself clear and crawl on to the firm ground of the croft.

The going was easier now, and I staggered on, bent almost double, up the steep brae. I no longer felt the wind or the rain; I was incapable of feeling anything except the knife turning in my side. My legs were not now moving of their own accord; I had to force them forward for each individual step.

I pulled up short against the dark bulk of a house and, dulled as my senses were, I felt a shock of horror when I realized that it was not the familiar thatched cottage. I thought I had blundered into some nightmarish land, where everything was strange, and all the familiar landmarks had vanished. I groped my way round the house, wondering where I could be. Then I blundered into the rain-butt under the drainpipe and knew it was Hector MacLeod's.

I ran blindly across the croft, stumbling over the drain, and topped the rise above the cottage. I wondered what I would do if Murdo Beaton had reached the house before me, but it was like someone else thinking, and I was at the door of the cottage with my hand on the knob. There could be no turning back now, I realized dully.

I opened the door cautiously, trying to breathe steadily, and shut it carefully behind me. I leaned against it feeling sick and dizzy. No sound came from the house. I peeled off my coat and hung it on the nail, and tiptoed across the lobby to my room.

There was still no sound as I flung off my clothes and crawled into bed. Oh, the blessed ease and comfort of those rough, grey blankets and that hard chaff mattress! I closed my eyes, listening to the wild hammering of my heart. The burning pain in my side eased to a dull ache.

How long I lay there before I heard the scrape of the door opening, I don't know. Perhaps it was no more than a few minutes.

Murdo Beaton's voice called: 'Have you been out, boy?'

Like a fool I cried: 'No,' and I had no sooner spoken than I could have bitten off my tongue.

It was almost three o'clock. What would he think, when he heard me answer him readily at a time when I should have been asleep for hours?

I heard the spurt of a lighted match and then – it seemed hours later – footsteps moving across the lobby to the kitchen.

I thought of my raincoat hanging in the lobby, dripping wet and plastered with mud and slime, and I was sick with the knowledge of my own folly.

Chapter 14

I DREADED meeting Murdo Beaton for I could not think of a reasonable excuse to account for the mudstains on my coat, and I was sure he would question me. I was glad it was Sunday. Mairi had told me that they all stayed in bed until after midday on the Sabbath and I had the whole morning in which to concoct a tale. I racked my brains, but no matter how hard I tried I could not think of an excuse likely to deceive him.

It was nearly one o'clock when I plucked up courage to creep into the kitchen. Murdo Beaton was sitting on a chair in the far corner of the room with the big family Bible resting on his knees. Mairi was preparing the breakfast things. He glanced up as I came into the kitchen, and I fought down a sudden desire to turn tail and run and walked self-consciously to the bench and sat down.

I steeled myself for the expected onslaught, but it never came. The silence was worse than all my imaginings, and I found myself wishing he would speak so that I could get it over and done with. I shot him a quick, sideways glance and saw that he was immersed in the Bible. His eyes were intent on the printed page, and his lips moved soundlessly.

Mairi took a tray in to the cailleach, and when she came back he shut the Bible and we sat in to breakfast.

The grace was even longer than usual, but apart from that it was like any other breakfast. If he was suspicious of me, he did not show it, and he even unbent so far as to remark on the fine weather, which was something I had never before heard from him.

After breakfast, he went out and brought home the cows himself and milked them. I went down to the byre to see if there were any eggs, and when I came back Mairi had changed into her Sunday best. When I saw Murdo Beaton again he was wearing a blue serge suit and a stiff white collar.

I wondered if he would take me to church with Mairi, and as if reading my thoughts, he said: 'You had best stay at home, boy. The service is in Gaelic.' At the door, he turned, and added: 'No playing outside, mind. Remember this is the Sabbath Day.'

In the evening they went to another church service – the meeting, as he called it. When they got back, and had changed into their working clothes, Mairi went out to fetch home the cows for milking. I sat sullenly on the bench, determined to endure the silence of the kitchen, rather than ask him for permission to go.

He looked across at me, and said: 'You had best go with her, boy. It is not good to be staying indoors all day.'

I was surprised by his consideration, and stammered my thanks and raced after Mairi.

I caught up with her just past the dike, and she glanced round in surprise.

'Does he know you are here?' she said.

'He told me to come with you,' I replied, feeling suddenly alive again after the long, dull day indoors.

'Well, well,' was all she said, and I could understand her surprise.

She giggled suddenly, and said in a whisper: 'Where did you go last night?'

'What do you mean?' I countered, trying to hide my confusion.

'You went out after my father,' she said. 'I heard you.'

I did not know what to say, and I stammered stupidly: 'Did your hear your father go out?'

She nodded. 'And I heard you, too.'

'Well, I went to see what he was doing,' I said defensively.

I expected her to be angry with me, or to show some surprise, but I never believed she would laugh.

When she had finished laughing, she said: 'I could have told you, if only you had asked me.'

I stopped and faced her, and echoed incredulously: 'You could have told me?'

There was a tiny streamlet trickling through the moor at our feet, and she did a little skip and hopped over it, and turned and looked at me.

'Yes, I could have told you,' she said. 'He went down to the salmon fishing station, didn't he?'

My heart gave a sickening leap, and I might have blurted out the whole story there and then if I had not been so dazed.

All I said was: 'How do you know?'

'Och, I heard him twice before, going out late on a Saturday night,' she said, carelessly. 'The second time it happened I was a wee bit frightened, so I ran after him and asked him where he was going. He said a wind was springing up, and he would need to take in the coble because the salmon fishermen would not be out until Monday morning.'

'Oh, I see,' I said slowly.

So there had been other Saturday nights when Murdo Beaton had rowed out into the darkness of the Sound! I had wondered how Duncan Mor had suddenly appeared on the scene and now I knew why. He had known all along that the midnight meeting would take place at the salmon fishing station, and he had gone straight to the gorge knowing that Murdo Beaton would be there.

I remembered how Murdo Beaton had urged me to accompany Mairi, and I wondered if he had coached her to tell me this tale. For all he knew, I might not have succeeded in following him to the gorge, and her story might be intended to lull my suspicions. I glanced sharply at her. She was humming a snatch of song, and her dark eyes looked straight into mine, and I was sure there was no deceit in her smile.

'Race you to Cnoc an t-Sithein,' I cried, and we ran madly shoulder to shoulder and collapsed in a laughing heap at the foot of the green mound.

I was glad when Monday came, and I was free to go to see Duncan Mor. I stood in the doorway of the cottage, looking around. Murdo Beaton was working well down the croft hoeing the potatoes, and Mairi had gone to feed the hens. I was about to race up the croft when I remembered that Duncan Mor wanted to see the mysterious message.

I hurried into my room and took my wallet from my jacket and thrust it into my trouser-pocket. Nobody saw me, as I left the house and ran up the croft to the dike.

Duncan Mor was sitting on the river bank with a flat red tin by his side. It was filled with fishing hooks.

I sat down beside him, and said: 'What are you doing?'

He glanced up, as if I had been with him all the time, and said: 'Just sorting out a few flies.'

The hooks did not seem big enough to hold a fish, and I said so.

'Wait you,' he laughed, holding a tiny hook between his thumb and forefinger, 'the same fellow will land you a fine brown trout. Peter Ross never failed me yet.'

'Who is Peter Ross?' I asked curiously.

'Yon's Peter Ross,' he answered, stroking the teal wing of the fly on the hook. 'A fancy name to be sure, but there are fancier ones than him.' He picked up the tin and shook it. 'Why, there is Teal and Silver and Black Spider and Grenwell's Glory and Royal Coachman, and this black lad here with the red tail is known as Bloody Butcher.'

He snapped the lid shut, and I saw that the laughter had gone from his eyes.

'Let's be seeing your message,' he said quietly.

I took out my wallet, surprised to find that my hands were trembling. I had folded the message into a small square, and hidden it inside a book of stamps, and thrust the stamp book back into the back of the wallet. At first I could not find it, and I had a sudden fear that I had lost it, but it was only hidden behind my mother's letter. I took out the stamp book and shook it open, but nothing dropped out. I turned over each page, but the folded slip of paper was not to be seen. In desperation, I emptied my wallet, scattering the contents on the grass, but the message had vanished.

'I doubt the Red Fellow was there before you,' said Duncan Mor slowly, 'unless it dropped out of your wallet.'

'But it couldn't have,' I protested. 'It was folded up inside that book of stamps and I haven't taken my wallet out of the house since I came to Achmore.'

'Ach, well, you know well enough what was written on it,' he said quickly, seeing my crestfallen face.

'Indeed, I do,' I cried. 'I can see it before me now, just exactly as it was written.'

Duncan Mor's grey eyes looked at me reflectively.

'Would that be what the lawyers would call a considered statement?' he asked.

I thought for a moment that he was teasing me, but his face was serious.

'I mean, can you really remember how it was written?' he went on.

'I'm sure I can,' I said eagerly. 'I read it hundreds of times and I know just how it was written.'

Duncan Mor handed me a crumpled notebook and a pencil.

'On you go,' he urged. 'Take your time and write it down.'

I held the notebook on my knee, and wrote carefully in block capital letters: 'HUNT AT THE HILL OF THE RED FOX MI5.'

Duncan Mor watched me, and when I had finished he said quickly: 'Are you sure the MI5 was written like that: a capital M and a single stroke and a figure five?'

'Certain,' I said, puzzled.

I could not understand what he was driving at, and his next words did not make it any clearer.

'Then how d'you know it was meant to be a one?' he demanded.

'What else could it have been?' I retorted.

'It might well have been an I,' he said thoughtfully. 'Well yes, it might have been MI5.'

'MI5?' I echoed. 'But it doesn't make sense.'

Duncan Mor regarded me gravely.

'Oh, there is sense in it, right enough,' he said. 'It could be a sort of signature, did you but know what signature to look for. You see, Alasdair, there is a special branch of the Military Intelligence at the War Office whose job it is to keep an eye on all the enemies of this country.'

'You mean spies?' I interjected.

'Aye, spies, and maybe others who are more dangerous than spies,' he said slowly. 'Well, then, this special branch of the War Office works very much on the quiet. People don't talk about it, and even if a man's best friend were an agent he would never tell him so. All that folk know about it is that it is called MI5.'

'Then you mean the man with the scar may have been a secret service agent of ours?' I gasped.

'I mean just that,' he said deliberately, 'and I would lay all the tea in China to a plate o' salt herring an' tatties that I am right.'

I jumped to my feet.

'Then we must go to the police,' I cried.

Duncan Mor sighed.

'The polis, is it?' he said. 'Right you are, a bhalaich, we go to the polis. We tell them the man with the scar gave you a message. Good enough. The polis – mind you, they are an awful suspicious crowd – the polis ask to see the message.' He spread out his hands. 'We haven't got it.'

'Yes, but I can remember it,' I said hotly. 'Every single word.'

'Aye, but it is evidence the polis are after,' he countered. 'Where's your evidence, Alasdair?'

'I saw the man with the scar jump off the train,' I cried, 'and I saw the other man pull the communication cord and go after him.'

'Aye, you saw him jump off the train,' agreed Duncan Mor, 'but who else saw him?'

'Nobody else saw him,' I said. 'But several people saw the other man jump out. I heard them talking to the guard.'

'But you were the only one to see the man with the scar jump off,' insisted Duncan Mor. 'I can imagine fine what the polis would say. They would say you talk about a message you can't produce and a man, that nobody else saw, jumping off a train.'

'But you were with me on the cliff,' I protested. 'We both saw Murdo Beaton take two men out in the coble, and only one of them came back with him.'

'Right enough, Alasdair,' he agreed, 'so the polis ask Murdo Beaton and he denies that he was out on Saturday night. Well then, it is the Red Fellow's word against ours, so the polis decide to investigate. They are great lads at investigating, the polis. They go to the big man in the district to find out about us. They go to Major Cassell. Now, the Red Fellow has done many a job for the Major; sometimes he goes with a party from the Lodge as their ghillie. Good enough. So the Major tells the polis that Murdo Ruadh is a fine, upstanding man, but that Duncan Mor MacDonald has the name of being a black rogue of a poacher. No, no, a bhalaich, it won't do. We must bide a while on our own until we are better fixed.'

'I see that,' I admitted glumly, sitting down again. 'But if only we knew what it was all about. What happened to the man in the boat, and who was the other man with Murdo Beaton, and what has the Hill of the Red Fox got to do with it?'

Duncan Mor rose to his feet, and I noticed how swiftly and easily he moved for a man of his size.

'You are the boy for the questions, Alasdair Beag,' he said, smiling. 'But I am thinking it is safer not to know the answers to some o' them.'

'But we've just got to find the answers,' I said.

'We will find them, never fear,' he assured me, 'but see how fine and clear the hills are looking, and just a wee blow of wind from the sou'east. On your feet, a bhalaich, and we will see if Peter Ross will be after lifting you a fine brown trout from the loch.'

Duncan Mor took me up into the foothills to lonely Loch Liuravay. We tramped along a track by the river, until the river swung away to the south, then cut across rough country with the heather chest high in places. I had not realized how high we had climbed until I looked back and saw the whole of the Mealt valley spread out before me. I could see the five white houses at Achmore, and the green crofts of Maligar and Marishadder, and the blue peaks of the Quiraing.

Loch Liuravay lay at the foot of the Hill of the Red Fox, and I gazed up at the towering peak, and told Duncan Mor we should be searching it instead of wasting our time fishing.

But he only laughed, and said: 'Time enough for that, Alasdair, when you have the spring o' the heather in your legs, and you can stride the hill wi' the best o' them. If I am spared and well, I will be after putting legs on you fit to tackle Sgurr a' Mhadaidh Ruaidh.'

Duncan Mor laid down his split cane rod and fitted a cast with three flies to his line. I looked across the still, silent waters of the loch, and I felt sure that no man-made ripple had ever broken its dark surface. The hill rose sheer out of the water, casting a shadow over the loch, and there was an eerie silence about the place. If only the silent loch could speak and tell us the secret of the Hill of the Red Fox. I looked up at the black forbidding face of the hill, and shivered. One man had died already trying to find that secret.

Duncan Mor started at the south end of the loch and worked his way north. I admired the deft way he made his cast, so that the fly alighted gently on the water, making no more than a faint ripple. The fish were not rising and he had covered half the loch before I saw him land a speckled brown trout. Two more rose to the fly in quick succession, but he had worked his way to the north end before he hooked another one.

He laid his rod aside and slipped the fish into a small canvas bag.

'Well, Peter Ross didn't do so badly, eh?' he said. 'It is a fine meal of fresh trout for you and me when we reach the house.'

We sat down in the heather and he lit his pipe and puffed at it contentedly. I stretched out in the heather with my hands clasped behind my head, gazing up at the towering peak of Sgurr a' Mhadaidh Ruaidh. How I longed to be able to climb that dark peak – treasure or no treasure – and gaze out across the Minch to the blue hills of the Outer Isles. If only Duncan Mor would lead me to the summit. It never even occurred to me, at that time, that I might climb the Hill of the Red Fox alone.

I rolled over on my side, and said suddenly: 'How do you suppose people can work in offices all day long when . . . when . . .'

'When they could be lying in the heather wi' a few fresh trout in their bag?' laughed Duncan Mor. 'Aye, it is strange, right enough, but it is a strange, strange world, a bhalaich. See you, it is the fellows in the black jackets and the striped pants that make the big noise in this world. Myself now, I could shout my big head off, but who would take any notice of me – a poor loon of a crofter?

'Oh, I can hook a trout, right enough,' he hastened to add, seeing that I was about to speak, and guessing what was in my mind, 'and plough a fair furrow, and build a stack and shear a sheep, and the work of the hands is good work, but it counts for little in the eyes of the world. The Lord Himself was born in a byre, but you will never see the great ones of the world with dung on their boots.'

He looked down at me, and went on slowly: 'This may seem a good enough life to you, Alasdair, but if ye're wanting to make a big noise in the world it is the striped pants you'll be needing.'

I saw his keen grey eyes flicker past my face to the hills above, and he bent forward and knocked out his pipe on the heel of his boot, and said quietly: 'Don't look surprised, but maybe we are more important than I think. Take your time about it, but glance over at that hill beyond the end o' the loch.'

I counted twenty slowly, then glanced up at the hill.

'That's enough,' he said sharply. 'What did you see?'

'I didn't see anything,' I said, puzzled. 'Only something flashing in the sun about half-way up.'

'Aye, something flashing in the sun,' said Duncan Mor grimly. He rose to his feet. 'We had best be going. Some fellow up there has the glasses trained on us!'

Chapter 15

UNTIL I was ten, my mother and I used to spend the summer holidays with an aunt of hers who lived in Tunbridge Wells. Then her aunt died, and the trips to Kent stopped, and we stayed in London during the holidays.

I don't remember much about Tunbridge Wells, except eating cream cakes in tea-rooms that smelled of furniture polish, but the memory of the long, empty days I spent in the town remains clear in my mind. There was never anything for me to do and the days seemed to be interminable. Every night when I went to bed I would count the number of days to the end of the holiday. I looked upon each day as a gate; an old, rusty gate that creaked open slowly, inch by inch, on protesting hinges. There seemed to be an endless succession of such gates, barring our way to the station and the train back to London.

But it was different in Achmore. It was over a fortnight from the day Duncan Mor took me to Loch Liuravay to the time of the clipping, but it seemed to me no more than one long summer's day. The day of the clipping is a day I can never forget, so I have made no mistake about the time.

I think the time passed so quickly because there were no minutes and hours, no days and weeks; only sunshine and cloud and rain and wind. There was some talk, but more friendly silence, and much laughter; and all the sounds and smells of the hills and moors. It seemed as if it must go on forever, but I had forgotten that forever belongs to Peter Pan and the nursery. And I forgot the brooding bulk of the Hill of the Red Fox, looking down on dark Loch Liuravay.

Every morning I ran across the moor to the house by the river, and Duncan Mor took me for long tramps into the foothills. Sometimes the sun was shining, but there were days when the wind tore down from the hills, flinging the rain into our faces. It made no difference. Wet or fine, we tramped the moors, and I could feel the spring coming into my step and the hardening of my calf muscles.

Sometimes after a few days of rain, a bluish mist drifted in from the sea and hung about the hollows of the hills, so that there was absolute stillness in the air and the world seemed to have stopped turning. Then the mist would lift for a moment, and the long purple shape of Rona would emerge, seeming to float in the air, and the peak of a hill would loom up, black as ink, and surprisingly close.

Once, in a fit of remorse, I asked Murdo Beaton if I should stay on the croft and help him, but he urged me to go, and seemed glad to be rid of me. But whenever I was in the cottage with him I knew that his pale, restless eyes alighted on me the moment my back was turned. He never looked at me directly, but I was certain that he was watching me all the time.

One day Duncan Mor took me into the hills south of Loch Cuithir. We scrambled up a rough scree, and he led the way along a narrow ledge around the shoulder of the hill. Two rabbits started up in front of us and went bounding down the hillside until they were lost among the reddish brown boulders at the foot of the hill. There was bare rock all around, furrowed with the course of the winter rains, and pitted with the scars of ages.

Somehow or other, two stunted rowan trees had managed to grow on the ledge and a tiny stream trickled down the hillside from a cleft in the rock behind them. Duncan Mor pushed the trees aside, and I saw that they covered a deep fissure in the rock. He squeezed his way in and motioned me to follow.

The opening in the rock widened into a cave, and I shivered in the dank air. When my eyes grew accustomed to the gloom, I saw that we were standing inside a gigantic hollow in the heart of the hill. A spring bubbled out of the rock and coursed across the sloping floor to the entrance of the cave. I dabbed my fingers in the water and drew them away quickly. It was icy cold.

'Alasdair Dubh knew this place,' said Duncan Mor, 'and not another man in Skye, save myself.'

I wasn't really listening, for I was looking at a big black pot lying on its side in the far corner of the cave. There was a length of twisted copper pipe behind the pot and a heap of mildewed peats.

Duncan Mor laughed his great, booming laugh, and the echo came back eerily from the roof of the cavern.

'This is where the old bodachs made the white whisky,' he said. 'There is not a finer still in the whole of the West, barring one I came across over Gairloch way. You can light a fire here and no man will see your smoke, and no man can say where it goes.'

His words echoed round the cave, and I cupped my hands to my mouth and called: 'Alasdair Cameron.'

Back came the echo: 'Alasdair Cameron.'

'You would never feel the time long in this place,' laughed Duncan Mor. 'There is always a voice to keep you company.'

I shivered.

'My, but it's cold,' I said.

'Aye, it is cold, right enough,' he admitted, 'but many a poor hunted cratur made for this place in olden times. The cold never worried a man with the law on his heels. Besides, you could lie up fine and snug. Give me a rabbit from the hill, and a trout from the loch, an' a puckle o' meal, and all o' the men o' the western world would tramp the tackets off their boots looking for me.'

'Well, I wouldn't fancy it,' I said, never knowing that one day I would be recalling his words with a sob of relief.

Sometimes I sat on the wall outside Duncan Mor's house and practised on the feadan, as the chanter is called in the Gaelic, for he said he would make a piper of me. He would lean on his crossed arms, his pipe in his mouth, guiding me over the fingering exercises.

One day I got hopelessly mixed up and I threw the chanter aside in disgust.

Duncan Mor puffed thoughtfully at his pipe for a minute or two, then he said slowly: 'How long have you been at the learning?'

I thought for a moment, and said: 'Seven days. This is my seventh day and I'm no better than the day I started.'

He laughed and laughed until the tears ran down his cheeks.

'Oh, Alasdair Beag, Alasdair Beag,' he sighed, wiping his eyes. 'Have you not heard the old saying? To the making of a piper go seven years of his own learning and seven generations before. Mind you, at the end of his seven years one born to it will stand a chance of making good, but not before, a bhalaich, not before.'

I laughed and picked up the chanter and tried again.

That was the way of Duncan Mor.

Another day, when we were in the foothills, he pointed out the rabbit runs and showed me how to set snares.

'You could be doing wi' a good breeze o' north wind for this job,' he explained, 'so that your snare goes back with the grass, then the poor fool of a rabbit will never see it.'

'But why a north wind?' I asked.

'Well, in the autumn and winter a north wind will bring showers o' hail,' he explained, 'and the night you get the hail is the night you will do well at the snaring. Once the hail showers start, the rabbits make off for shelter, and they are so daft to get to their holes that they have never a thought for the wee snare dangling over their run.'

We had a spell of sultry weather, and Duncan Mor looked up at the hot, leaden sky, and said: 'The first fine day there is a breeze o' wind we will need to make a shot at the clipping. This is bad for the maggot, and bad enough for the sheep without the maggot when you think o' the poor craturs labouring around under the weight of their winter fleece.'

'But why not do it right away?' I wanted to know. 'Why wait for a wind?'

'Think o' those poor craturs being rounded up by the dogs,'

retorted Duncan Mor. 'And herded all the way up to the hill fank for the clipping. Supposing there wasn't a breeze o' wind to cool the air, they would be near dead before they got the length o' the fank. Aye, and others forby the sheep would be suffering.' He grinned. 'For it's hot work at the clipping.'

We started early one morning, when the grass was heavy with dew, and a cool breeze came down from the Quiraing. Every man in the township turned out, and all the dogs milled around, barking and snapping and eager for work.

We fanned out in a wide semi-circle, sweeping the ground systematically; the dogs working the sheep in a solid phalanx towards the hill fank.

Glen suddenly shot off at a tangent, making for five ewes and their lambs who stood in a frightened bunch on a near-by hillock. Duncan Mor shouted and whistled him back to the gathering.

'Why are you leaving them?' I asked, seeing other ewes and lambs in the flock.

'We'll not be shearing the milk ewes for another fortnight or so,' he answered. 'The rise in the wool comes later on them. The ewes and lambs we have got here' – he pointed to the solid mass of sheep the dogs were herding – 'were mixed up with the wild ewes and hoggs and wedders. When we get to the fank we will let them away again.'

After much shouting and waving by the men, and excited barking and snapping on the part of the dogs, the sheep were safely penned in the fank. The fank, which was built of dry-stone walls, had been dug out of the hillside, so that the ground outside was level with the tops of the walls. A rushing burn tumbled down the green hillside alongside the fank, and the brown hills, coloured with shelvings of green, rose in a sheer wall to the south and west.

The dogs settled down around the walls of the fank, red tongues lolling and panting heavily. Although their work was done, they sat in a watchful circle ready to head off any sheep that might succeed in scrambling out of the fank.

I was given the job of guarding the gate to the fank, a few pieces of flimsy wood lashed together with pieces of stack rope. When the men came for their sheep, I held the gate open for them, blocking the opening with my body until they had passed out again.

Every man's sheep had a different keel mark. Duncan Mor's sheep had a red keel mark across their ribs, and Hector MacLeod's carried a blue keel on the back of their necks. In addition to the keel mark, which was really for identifying sheep easily at a distance, they all had a distinctive ear mark. Murdo Beaton's sheep had a deep V cut in the right quarter of their left ear, and all Iain Ban's sheep could be identified by the slit in the top quarter of their right ear.

Murdo Beaton was the first to start clipping. He dragged a struggling hogg from the fank, and tied its forelegs to one of its hindlegs. With the sheep lying on its side, he started clipping its belly working up to the shoulder and neck with swift strokes of the shears, then clipping down to the tail. Then he swung the hogg over to her other side, and I watched the brownish fleece being peeled away, revealing the dazzlingly white body of the newly shorn sheep. I looked at the spotless white hogg, and the dirty fleece, in amazement. A few minutes ago the fleece had looked perfectly normal, but now it appeared filthy, and I wondered how it was possible to produce hanks of clean wool from it.

Murdo Beaton dabbed some Stockholm tar on the places he had nicked with the shears, and painted his keel mark on the flawless white of the hogg's back. Then he untied the rope, and the sheep struggled to her feet and trotted away, looking around uncertainly at her fellows in the fank.

Murdo Beaton deftly rolled the fleece, twisting the tail out to bind it in a compact roll, and I opened the gate for him while he selected another sheep.

As the clipping went on, I noticed that he was withdrawn from the rest of the men. He never joined in their banter, and I never once saw him speak or laugh. But I had to admire his speed at the shearing. From the moment he took up the shears until he set the sheep free, he never took more than six minutes. None of the other men were so quick, but they would often pause to laugh at some sally of Duncan Mor's, and Roderick MacPherson had them all laughing when he compared the faces of the sheep with the women of the township.

All afternoon and early evening the work of clipping went on, and the laughter died out as they settled down to work. There was the steady snip-snip of the shears, the low murmur of conversation, the bleating of sheep, and behind it all, the murmur of the water of the burn as it flowed down to the river. The sheep in the fank gradually thinned out, and the mounds of fleeces grew steadily in size.

Duncan Mor had clipped all his sheep, and he started to help Hector MacLeod. Murdo Beaton had finished too, and he was packing his wool into a bag. When he had pressed the last fleece into the bag, he fastened the neck, and slung the bag across his shoulders. I watched him moving swiftly down the hillside to the track beyond Loch Cuithir where Mairi was waiting with the horse and cart. Hector MacLeod painted his blue keel mark across the neck of a shorn hogg and released her. He wiped the sweat from his brow, and looked across at Duncan Mor who was clipping another of his sheep.

'Well, Duncan,' he said wearily, 'we are near the last o' them now, and no thanks to Murdo Ruadh. Myself and Lachlan clipped the cailleach's sheep when himself was away from home, but he has no word of that now.'

Lachlan MacLeod nodded his dark head and said shortly: 'What do you expect of the Red Fellow?'

'Allow the Red One,' said Duncan Mor. 'The same fellow would not spare a minute if it was not going to put a penny in his pocket.'

'Ach, we know him well enough,' commented Iain Ban. 'He is past changing now.'

'Aye, as Domhnull-nam-Faochag said when he was asked why he did not leave off gathering the whelks and take an easier job with the Hydro; 'tis difficult to straighten the twist of an old stick,' remarked Iain Ban.

There was general laughter, and the men bent to their task and clipped the remainder of the sheep. When the wool was packed, I put the shears and the tins of marking fluid into a sack, and we made our way down the hillside.

The wool was loaded into Hector MacLeod's cart, and the rest of us walked on ahead while he led the horse by the bridle.

Roderick MacPherson whistled a catchy reel, and Calum Stewart told of a man in Raasay who could poach salmon with a length of rabbit snare wire fastened to a long stick.

'Mind you, there is an awful knack in it,' he said. 'I could never manage it myself.'

'Give me three hooks tied back to back, and a stout length of line, and you can keep your rabbit wire,' declared Donald Alec MacDonald.

Duncan Mor nodded, and Iain Ban said: 'Many a good salmon was lifted with the torch and gaff.'

'True enough,' assented Duncan Mor. 'There are more ways of lifting a salmon than there are days in the week.'

The conversation went from salmon to piping and from piping to the price of wool and from wool prices to a hill drainage scheme for the township that the Department of Agriculture was considering.

I was so busy listening to the conversation that I did not realize we had reached Duncan Mor's croft. He shouldered his bag of wool effortlessly, and bade us a cheery good night.

When we reached Achmore, Hector MacLeod wanted me to go in with him, but I owed my mother a letter and I wanted to catch Willie The Post with it in the morning, so I went straight to the cottage. I don't know when I got the idea that I would give Mairi a fright; it was just one of the things one does on the spur of the moment. At any rate, I stopped in front of the kitchen window, and leaned forward and flattened my face against the glass.

There was no sign of Mairi, but Murdo Beaton was sitting at

the table with his back to the window. There was a tin box at his elbow over half full of pound notes, and spread across the kitchen table, in neat bundles, was more money than I had ever seen before. As I watched, he slipped the elastic band from one of the bundles and started to count the notes carefully.

I don't know how long I stood there, but I was just going to tiptoe away when he glanced over his shoulder and saw my face at the window.

Chapter 16

WE looked at each other for a long time, and for once his eyes did not waver from mine. Suddenly he swung round, scooped up the money from the table, and thrust it into the tin box. I walked the few paces to the door, and tried the handle, but it was locked.

I waited fearfully outside the cottage, wishing that I had never thought to play a silly joke on Mairi. Now he would think I had been spying on him, and he was bound to be furious. I wondered where all the money had come from. There must have been hundreds of notes in the tin box. Murdo Beaton walked about in rags, and had pleaded poverty from the first day I met him, but he had more money in the house than I had ever seen before, and I had often watched Aunt Evelyn checking the week's takings.

I heard the key grate in the lock and my heart skipped a beat. The door was flung open, and Murdo Beaton beckoned me inside. He followed me into the kitchen and closed the door behind him. I stood in front of the fire, very much on the defensive. He had his back to the door. His cheeks were flushed and a muscle in his cheek started to twitch.

Before I realized what was happening, he sprang across the room and seized me by my shirt front.

'Who sent you to spy on me?' he hissed.

'I wasn't spying on you,' I said indignantly. 'I was playing a joke on Mairi.'

'A fine tale,' he snarled, 'with Mairi and the cailleach away at the meeting.' He shook me violently, and his bony knuckles dug into my chest. 'The truth now. Who told you to spy on me?'

'I wasn't spying on you,' I repeated. 'I was going to give Mairi a fright. I didn't know she was out.'

'You know well enough that herself and the cailleach go down to the meeting every Wednesday night,' he insisted.

'I'd forgotten,' I said. 'I didn't even know it was Wednesday today. Besides, if I had known you were counting your money I wouldn't have looked in the window.'

At the mention of money, his colour deepened, and he raised his right fist. I thought he was going to strike me, but he let his arm fall to his side and released his hold on my shirt. I glanced at the table but there was no sign of the tin box.

'I am sorry, boy,' he said slowly, 'but I was wild when I saw you at the window. As for the money, it is not yourself I would be hiding it from, not at all, at all. But there are other folks in this place who would like to be knowing what I have managed to put by me; folk who would squander their last penny and waste their time in idle talk about those who know the value of thrift.' He pulled at his long upper lip, and added: 'Not that there was much in the box, but what is there was earned by the sweat of my brow.'

He watched me closely, doubtless to see the effect of his words, but I looked down at my feet and did not speak.

'Well, well, this is a fine chance for you and me to have a crack together, Alasdair,' he said, with some show of heartiness. 'The cailleach and Mairi are away so the men must fend for themselves, eh? Sit you down, boy. The tatties are ready and there is cold mackerel in the press. A fine fish the mackerel. I always say there is just the one thing between cold mackerel and cold salmon, Alasdair. Do you know what that is: I'll tell you. The price, Alasdair, the price. There is salmon going from here to London by the ton; aye, by the ton, boy. And fetching big money. Fools in the city wi' more money than sense paying over ten shillings a pound for it. Think o' that, Alasdair. Over ten shillings the pound! But you and me are not so foolish, eh? No ten shillings the pound for Alasdair Cameron and Murdo Beaton. Indeed, no. We take the mackerel – the poor man's salmon – and what does it cost us?' He snapped his fingers. 'Not that, boy. Not a penny piece, Alasdair. And a fine meal it makes us.'

It was the first time I had ever heard him use my name, and I could not understand his sudden friendliness. All the time he was straining the potatoes and putting out the fish and making the tea, he chattered away unceasingly. When he sat in to table, he made no attempt to say the grace, but pushed the potatoes over to me and urged me to help myself.

'Take plenty of tatties, Alasdair,' he said. 'You will be hungry after the long day at the fank and there is nothing like tatties to build a person up. These are Kerr's Pink. A grand tattie. Fine and dry. I don't believe you would get the like o' these in London, Alasdair.'

'No,' I said, eating my food without really tasting it, and wondering what he was driving at.

'Aye, I thought not,' he went on. 'It is a fair disgrace the way poor people are robbed in the cities, paying good money for nothing but trash – just trash. Mind you, there is not the equal of these tatties in this place. I took home the seed from Dingwall, Alasdair, and a pretty penny it cost me between freight and everything, but I believe it was worth it for all that.' He pushed the dish across to me. 'Take more, boy. Take more. We must feed you up so that your mother will never recognize you, eh?'

I mumbled something about having had plenty, but he carried on as if he had never heard me, and all the time he was talking he was forking up great mouthfuls of potatoes and fish.

'Mind, you,' he rattled on, 'I see an awful difference in you already. You have fairly put on beef since you came to Achmore. The place is agreeing with you, boy. I believe you are liking it fine here, Alasdair.'

'Yes, I like it fine,' I said eagerly.

Murdo Beaton pushed his empty plate away and tipped back his chair, hooking one foot round the leg of the table.

'I believe you will be after coming here every year,' he said.

I swallowed a mouthful of strong, sweet tea and nodded.

'Duncan Mor says he will take me up to the top of the Storr next year,' I said.

The words were out of my mouth before I remembered the enmity between the two of them, but he did not seem at all concerned.

'Well, well, that is very good of the big fellow,' he said, 'very good indeed.' He must have seen my look of surprise because he added quickly: 'Oh, I have had my quarrels with Duncan Mor, but he is a good enough man at heart.'

I was so pleased to hear him speak well of Big Duncan that I could have forgiven him for all his surly conduct of the past few weeks. Perhaps, after all, I had misjudged him. Perhaps there was some simple explanation of the midnight meeting at the salmon fishing station, and the boat that had returned to the bay without one of its passengers. I was going to ask him outright, and I only succeeded in checking myself in the nick of time. If he thought I had been spying on him counting his money, it would not do to admit that I had followed him across the moor to the gorge.

'I'm glad you spoke well of Duncan Mor,' I said impulsively. 'I'll tell him so when I see him again.'

'Oh, but I was never the man to bear a grudge,' said Murdo Beaton. 'You see, Alasdair, some folk have a smooth tongue in their heads, but not me. I was aye slow to express myself, and it has given me the name of being a dour sort o' beggar. You thought I was a dour sort o' man now, did you not?'

He thrust his long nose across the table, and his pale blue eyes were fixed squarely on my face. There was a wild gleam in his eyes, as if he were trying to contain some inner excitement, but I scoffed at myself for letting my imagination play tricks on me. There was nothing in the kitchen to excite him; only the two of us, on either side of the table, talking together. No wonder it was the first time I had noticed the strange light in his eyes; he had never before looked at me directly.

Murdo Beaton repeated his question: 'You thought I was a dour sort of man, did you not?'

'Well, yes, I suppose so,' I admitted, a little shamefaced to have been exposed by his frankness.

'Ach, well, there's more than yourself made the same mistake, Alasdair,' he said mildly. 'Mind you, I was sort of reserved when you first came to Achmore. I thought to myself, here's a smart boy from the city who will be after thinking the heather is growing out o' my ears.' He shook his head. 'I was wrong, right enough, and I always believe in admitting when I am wrong, which is more than I could say for a few in this place. Oh, I see my mistake now. I should have been frank and open with you from the start, Alasdair, because you are a boy after my own heart. You and I are going to get on fine together.'

'Well, I'm pleased to hear it,' I said, 'but I thought you didn't want Mairi to talk to me.'

'Not at all,' he declared. 'Right enough, I said something to Mairi just after you came, but that was for the benefit of the cailleach. She is an old, old woman, Alasdair. She was never even the length o' Kyle, and she has the notion that there is nothing good about city folk. The cailleach is too old to argue with; you must just say something to please her, and then that is the end of it.'

'I know what you mean,' I said. 'My mother had an aunt in Tunbridge Wells, and she didn't approve of the pictures, so my mother didn't dare tell her when we had been to a matinée.'

'Isn't that just what I am saying myself,' Murdo Beaton maintained. 'Old folk get all sorts of queer ideas into their heads, but it is not right to argue with them.'

'I suppose Mairi will soon be back,' I said, thinking how pleased she would be to see me on such friendly terms with her father.

'Ach, I told the cailleach to make a ceilidh at Willie The Post's,' he said. 'Willie's mother and herself are first cousins. Never you mind, Alasdair, what do you say to a spot of fishing off the rocks ?'

'Fine,' I said eagerly, 'if you don't think it will be too dark.'

'Not at all,' he asserted. 'There is a wee bit of mist over the sea, but it is just a grand night for the rocks.'

I put on my raincoat and wellingtons and followed him to the byre where he took down his long cane rod from the rafters.

'Aren't you going to the meeting about the Hill Drainage Scheme?' I asked. 'I heard the men talking about it. They said it was to be held at Hector MacLeod's house.'

'Well, no, Alasdair,' he said thoughtfully. 'It's not my place to go. You are the tenant here, so I can't speak for this croft. I am just here with your permission.'

I felt a secret glow of pride at his words, but I thought it better not to say anything. Still chatting freely, he led the way down the croft and over the moor to the rocks.

The tide was coming in and running strongly. Murdo Beaton walked out on a big black rock, rather like an enormous table, that was almost awash.

He handed me the rod and said: 'Cast your fly to one side and take it quickly through the water, but mind your step here. The tide is flowing fast and it is easy enough to get cut off on these rocks.'

He did not need to warn me for I did not like the place. It was almost dark, and the ebb tide seemed to suck greedily at my legs as it washed back off the rock. Then the next wave foamed in to shore, breaking over the rock, and washing hard against my legs. There was something gloomy about the black rock and the mournful cries of the gulls and the sucking and surging of the sea in the rocks.

I made a couple of half-hearted casts and, much to my surprise, I caught a small saithe.

'Well done, Alasdair,' cried Murdo Beaton, and he hurried forward to unhook the fish for me.

The tide had risen swiftly and the whole of the rock was now underwater. I was afraid of losing my footing on the slippery surface.

'I think we had better get back,' I said doubtfully.

'Aye, the tide is rising fast,' he agreed.

We made our way across the submerged rock to the shore, and I was relieved when my feet touched dry ground again. The mist was drifting in from the sea, and the overhanging cliff was no more than a black shadow in the fading light.

'Give me the rod,' said Murdo Beaton. 'It would never do to be going back wi' one wee cuddie.'

He took the rod and worked his way out on a rock that was not yet under water, and started to fish. Every time he had a catch he unhooked the fish and tossed it ashore to me. I watched him anxiously, fearing he might lose his footing and be swept away, for the water was almost up to his knees. But he fished on without the slightest concern until I had over a dozen small fish strung on the line at my feet.

At last he scrambled over the rocks to me, and said: 'Ach well, Alasdair, I doubt we left it a bit late. Still, there is a good fry in that lot, and the wee cuddies are the tastiest o' the lot.'

He led the way up the cliff with the long rod slung over his shoulder, and I carried the fish. A smirr of rain had started to fall and when I looked back the sea was blotted out.

We had crossed the main road when he stopped suddenly and faced me.

'Dash it!' he exclaimed. 'I promised Major Cassell I would take a look at the bothy last thing to see if the door was properly secured. The Major went down himself last night and found it unlocked, and there is a queer penny worth o' gear stored there.' He hesitated for a moment, then added: 'If you are tired, away you go to the house.'

I wondered if he was making an excuse to be rid of me, and all my old suspicions flooded back into my mind.

'I'm not a bit tired,' I said. 'I'll come with you.'

However, he seemed to be quite pleased to have me with him and he set off along the track he had taken the night I followed him.

When we reached the top of the gorge, he stopped and said: 'Maybe you won't be thinking much of this place, Alasdair, when you get back to the city life. Maybe we will never see you again.'

'No, indeed,' I said. 'I just don't know how I'll manage to stick it in London for a whole year until the summer holidays are here again.'

'So that's the way of it,' he said softly, and carried on again before I had a chance to speak.

A narrow path, no more than a foot wide, wound round the side of the cliff face. Had he not been leading the way, I would never have found it in the dark.

Suddenly, he stumbled and let out a cry of pain. I was walking cautiously several yards behind him and when I reached him he was lying on the narrow path writhing in pain.

'What happened?' I cried.

'Ricked my ankle,' he muttered through clenched teeth. 'I doubt I can never put this foot to the ground.'

He struggled to his feet, and put both hands on my shoulders.

'Help me up the path,' he gasped. 'I'll try to hop along behind you as best I can.'

When we got to the top of the gorge, he sank to the ground, holding his ankle in both hands.

'Maybe the pain will ease off in a while,' he said. 'As long as I can just crawl down and take a look at the door of the bothy. If it were anyone but the Major I would never attempt it this night, but the poor man is depending on me and I promised him I would see that the place is locked up.'

He tried to get to his feet, but groaned in pain when he felt his weight on his damaged ankle.

'You'll never manage it,' I said. 'I had better go for you.'

'Were you ever down there before?' he asked.

'No, but surely it's not all that difficult,' I said.

'Not at all,' he said. 'Just follow the track; that is all you need do. You will come to a bridge. Cross the bridge, and the bothy is about fifty yards down the river bank. Mind you, Alasdair, it is myself that is thankful, for my conscience would never let me rest until I had seen to the bothy, supposing I had to crawl down on my hands and knees.'

I set off cautiously along the track, digging my feet hard into the ground to make sure that I did not lose my footing. I was reminded of a game of snakes and ladders, because one moment I was going in one direction, then the track would wind round sharply and I would be groping my way along in the opposite direction.

The mist had drifted in from the sea, so that I could not see the river and the bay below or even the waterfall. As I made my way down the roar of the falls became louder, but all I could see was the dim outline of the gorge towering high above me, and a few feet of the path ahead. I was half dazed by the noise of the falls, and I felt sure I would lose my footing and crash down to the foaming torrent of the river far below, and I wished I had not been so foolhardy as to volunteer for the job.

The loose earth of the track gave way to bare rock, and I almost slipped and fell. I steadied myself and strained my eyes trying to see what lay ahead. I felt the wall of the cliff-face rising vertically above me, and the track appeared to be a narrow ledge cut in the rock. It fell sharply away in front of me and I edged forward slowly until I came up against two iron bars about eighteen inches apart that forked out at an upward angle over the river. They were bound with rough rope, making a sort of cat-walk to the narrow plank bridge that loomed up out of the mist and darkness of the night.

I crawled up the cat-walk on my hands and knees, and made my way on to the bridge. I stood up slowly and took two uncertain steps forward and then my nerve failed me. I stood quite still, knowing that I could move neither forward nor backwards, and I felt my head reel.

The roar of the falls was deafening, and I could hear the surge and splash of the river against the rocks far below. I knew with a sudden, terrifying clarity that the only thing between me and the river was a narrow greasy plank with no handrail.

I blinked the rain out of my eyes and tried to keep a grip on my senses. One false move and I was over the side, and my cries would be drowned in the roar of the falls. In any event, Murdo Beaton was helpless and in no condition to come to my aid. I felt my head swimming, and I knew I must force my limbs into some sort of action before a fit of giddiness overtook me and I toppled off the narrow bridge.

My first thought was to crawl back the way I had come, but I knew I could never turn round on that greasy plank. I tried to make myself believe that I was standing on a kerbstone and running along it, as I had so often done in London, without slipping once. I dug my teeth into my lower lip until I felt the salt taste of blood, and started to inch forward along the bridge.

I shall never forget the terror of that walk across the bridge. It was the noise of the falls and the darkness and the sense of not knowing what lay below that was the worst of all. I kept looking down at my feet until I remembered that the best way to keep one's balance was to look straight ahead. I forced my eyes up and stepped on gingerly.

I have no very clear recollection of what happened. I know that I put one foot out and found no solid plank to support me, and I tried to draw back and lost my balance. I seemed to fall very slowly, and I clawed desperately for a support. My fingers closed round an iron bar, and I felt a searing pain in my armpits as the downward motion of my body was checked.

I hung on desperately, but my hands were cold and numb and the rounded iron bar offered no purchase. Slowly, so slowly that I wondered for a moment if I was imagining it, I felt my hands slipping off the bar. I can recall thinking stupidly what a relief it would be to have the awful strain taken off my arms.

Chapter 17

A VICE-LIKE grip fastened around my wrists and I was hoisted high in the air and thrown across a broad back. I lay there limply, head downwards, utterly spent. What was happening to me had assumed the vague, nightmarish outlines of a bad dream. I could only lie still and hope that I would wake up in the morning in the snug safety of my bed.

I was not really conscious of being carried over the bridge and taken behind the shelter of a rock on the other side of the river. All I know is that I was set down as gently as a baby and supported by a strong arm.

'It is me,' a voice whispered. 'Duncan Mor. Are you hurt, Alasdair?'

I heard somebody say: 'No, I'm fine,' and realized dimly that it must be my own voice. It seemed to be coming from a long way off.

'Don't speak. Rest a while,' counselled Duncan Mor, and his arm tightened around my shoulders.

I closed my eyes, thankful for his support. My arms felt as if they had been dragged out of their sockets, but the searing pain had subsided to a dull ache. The roar of the falls was not so loud as it had been on the bridge, and I heard the sound of a dislodged stone tumbling down the hillside.

It was then that I heard the footsteps – quick footsteps – running down the track to the bridge, and the creak of the bridge as a man's weight descended on it. It must be Murdo Beaton, I decided, coming to see what had happened to me, and I was about to call to him when Duncan Mor clapped a hand over my mouth. I often wonder what would have happened if he had not acted so swiftly.

'Ist!' he hissed in my ear.

The beam of a torch stabbed the darkness, playing on the rushing waters of the river, and we crouched down behind the rock. After a while, the torch went out and there was the sound of hurried footsteps on the track. It seemed an age until Duncan Mor sat up and took his hand from my mouth.

'Well then, what happened?' he said grimly.

I told him how I had looked in at the window of the cottage, thinking to frighten Mairi, and seen Murdo Beaton counting his money at the table; of his anger when he saw me, and his sudden friendliness, culminating in the offer to take me fishing.

'I know he took you down to the rocks, but when I saw the pair of you heading back for Achmore, I thought you would be safe enough,' said Duncan Mor. 'Why did you come down here with him?'

I told him Murdo Beaton had forgotten to see if the bothy was locked up for the night, and how he had sprained his ankle and I had volunteered to look at the bothy for him.

I had been through so much that night that I thought I could be startled no longer, but the force of Duncan Mor's reaction to my words jolted me upright in stark surprise.

'I will break that long cratur in pieces,' he vowed, and the words were somehow more deadly because they were spoken in a whisper instead of his usual booming tones. 'I will have the black heart of him out of his miserable body supposing I have to tear it out with my bare hands.'

'But he wasn't to blame,' I stammered, still too dazed to comprehend the significance of the quick footsteps I had heard. 'I fell off the bridge.'

But he swept on, unheeding, and I was glad of the darkness that I could not see the terrible anger on his face. It was enough to hear it in his voice.

'The Red One had you on the rocks, never thinking that I was up on the cliff watching his every move,' he raged. 'The bold fellow was standing behind you. One push in the back and you were away. But no. That would have been murder by his own hand, and Murdo Ruadh would never stain his conscience with murder. So he takes you to the gorge with a tale about seeing the bothy. A chruthaidhear, the slyness of the man! Nine seasons Neil Ross has been at the salmon fishing, and not once did he fail to lock up the bothy. But any tale is good enough if it will drag you here. Aye, the Red One would never smirch his conscience by pushing you off the rocks. Not him. But he would fox a sprained ankle, so that he could keep well clear of you, and send you down here. Aye, he lay up there on the grass knowing he was sending you to your death.'

'But it is all a mistake,' I cried. 'I tell you, I slipped and fell.'

Duncan Mor picked me up in his arms like a baby and clambered over the rocks to the bridge. When we were in the centre of the bridge he set me down, holding me close to him with his left arm. He fumbled in his pocket for matches and struck one.

The flare of the match lit the darkness around us and I felt my stomach heave in a spasm of nausea. Part of the bridge was missing! I gazed blankly at the rushing waters of the river far below, and the match sputtered and went out. But the darkness could not hide the picture in my mind. The bridge was built on two horizontal iron bars. The bars were covered with wooden planks about a foot wide and two feet across, and four of those planks were missing.

Without a word, Duncan Mor picked me up and made his sure-footed way back to the river bank.

When we were behind the shelter of the rock, he said: 'Now do you see? Those planks have been missing this while back. It is safe enough for a man who knows the place, but what chance had you creeping along in the darkness?'

I tried to speak, but my lips moved without any words coming out. I was ashamed to find I was trembling uncontrollably.

Duncan Mor patted my shoulder.

'You are feeling the shock, a bhalaich, and no wonder,' he said. 'But wait you. When I lay hands on the Red Fellow he will wish it was himself had fallen off the bridge.'

'But why should he want to kill me?' I burst out.

It had been an adventure before, but now I was frightened and unsure of myself.

'I told you it could be dangerous to know too much, but I thought you would be safe enough for all that,' he said slowly. 'I doubt there is more than the Red Fellow had a hand in this business. He would be afraid to make a move by himself, but if somebody big enough suggested to Murdo Ruadh that you would be better out of the way, the same fellow would take the hint quickly enough. And if you were out of the way, Alasdair, there would be nobody left to take the croft at Achmore from him. Aye, that would be the way of it. The Red Fellow would be helping himself in more ways than one.'

'If he tried once and failed,' I suggested nervously, 'he might try again.'

'You stay with me from this night on,' said Duncan Mor shortly. 'Murdo Ruadh will need to be watching his own skin.'

He fell silent and I sensed he was thinking hard.

At length he said slowly, half to himself: 'It's queer they didn't try to put me out of the way, too.'

'Perhaps Murdo Beaton tried to kill me because I saw him with all that money,' I suggested.

'You may be sure he wouldn't be pleased,' said Duncan Mor dryly, 'but tonight's work was planned a while back I'm thinking. See you, Alasdair, the fly fellow picks a night when all the men in the place are indoors at a meeting, and the cailleach and Mairi are away at the kirk. There is nobody about to see him take you to the rocks, and he could go creeping back and say he had never laid eyes on you. Fine I know the man.'

'But YOU saw him,' I pointed out.

'Aye, I saw him right enough,' he agreed. 'But I was the only man in the place not at the meeting, and I saw him because I was looking for him.'

'I don't understand,' I faltered.

'You mind the day you found the message had been stolen from your wallet,' said Duncan Mor in his deep, commanding voice, 'and I told you a fox could be a dangerous sort of cratur when it was cornered?'

'Of course I remember it,' I said.

I could never forget that day. It was the first day I had tramped through the heather with him. It was the day he had taken me to Loch Liuravay and we had eaten a supper together of brown trout.

'Ever since that day,' he went on slowly, 'the Red Fellow has not taken a step outside the house between nightfall and sunrise without me seeing him.'

'But . . . but how?' I stammered.

'I was on the hill behind the house,' he said simply, 'flat to the ground. It is easy enough if you have ever stalked deer.'

I thought of nights when the wind had swept across the open crofts, driving the rain before it in swirling, maddened gusts. I thought of him lying in the wet grass, cold and numbed, waiting until the morning sun crimsoned the Ross-shire hills before he crept stiffly away. I knew perfectly well that it was myself he had been watching, not Murdo Beaton, and I did not know what to say.

'That was how I saw the pair o' you leave the house tonight,' he continued. 'I followed you, but when you came up from the rocks I only waited to see you cross the road for I thought you would be safe enough seeing you were heading back to Achmore. Then I made straight for this place.'

'But how did you know I would be crossing the bridge?' I asked.

'Never the thought I had of you being on the bridge,' he said grimly. 'Good life, Alasdair, if I had known you would be after crossing the bridge it is myself would have been standing at the other side. No, no, if it wasn't for a broken gasket on Alec Nicolson's lorry it was you for the river, boy.'

I thought he was joking, but he went on to explain.

'I had some salmon for Alec Nicolson and he was going to

collect them last night but the lorry broke down. Willie The Post told me Alec would be along late tonight, and when I saw you on your way back to Achmore I came down to get the salmon. I heard your cries when you fell and made for the bridge. I'm telling you, another minute and it was you away.'

I shuddered again at the thought of the terror I had known on the bridge, and I said quickly: 'Well, the lorry did me a good turn, anyway.'

'That's the spirit,' approved Duncan Mor. He stood up and his voice was brisk: 'Think no more of it, Alasdair. It was a hard knock you had there but that is the way o' the world. Many a bad time your father had, but I never saw him down in the mouth. He always used to say, "Never mind, Duncan, we never died a winter yet".'

I stood up alongside him, feeling stiff and sore. He took my arm in his and led me along the river bank. The towering walls of the gorge loomed up on either side, and I felt I would never breathe freely again until I had escaped from the dark prison of the gorge.

We had been walking on smooth grass, but the grass gave way to rocks and Duncan Mor guided me over them. When I looked up again, we were standing almost directly under the falls. I could see the creamy surge of the river as it raced over the black rocks above and cascaded down to the pool in front of us. The noise was tremendous; a ceaseless pounding of the ear-drums as thousands of gallons of water crashed into the pool.

Duncan Mor bent over a hole in the ground and drew out a large sack. There was a neatly rolled net on the rock beside me, and he wedged it into the hole and shouted something at me.

The noise of the falls was deafening and he had to put his lips close to my ear and shout before I heard him say: 'Up you get, Alasdair.'

I was sitting on a big, flat rock, and I did not think it possible that one man could move it. But Duncan Mor swung it around as easily as if it had been a kitchen chair, until it was covering his hiding place.

He stooped down and swung the sack on his back, and I was glad that I was compelled to shout, so that the tremor in my voice was not apparent.

'Do we have to cross the bridge?' I yelled.

'No, there is a path on this side that will bring us out on the road,' he bellowed, 'but it is not for your legs tonight.'

Before I could protest he bent his knees and scooped me up over his left shoulder, as easily as if I had been a bag of thistle-down. With the heavy bag of fish on one shoulder and me on the other he started the arduous climb out of the gorge.

It was a country of strong men, and I had grown accustomed to seeing hundred-weight bags being lifted from ground to shoulder level with no apparent effort, but I am sure that no other man in Achmore could have done what Duncan Mor did. I knew the weight of the fish, because I had tried to lift the sack and could not move it from the ground, but he carried me as well, and at the same time climbed up the steep, twisting track in the darkness.

We came out on the main road close to the bridge over the river, and I slid to the ground. Duncan Mor hid the sack in the deep bracken by the roadside and took out his pipe.

I was the first to hear the sound of a vehicle, and when I told him he drew me down into the cover of the bracken.

'Maybe it isn't Alec at all,' he said softly, 'and it would look bad if we were seen here at this time o' night.'

I saw the dim lights of a vehicle as it passed the drive leading to Achmore Lodge and came down the brae to the bridge.

'It is Alec, right enough,' said Duncan Mor. 'He has only his sidelights on.'

He stood up, and the lorry drew in to the side of the road. No time was wasted. The driver jumped out of the cab and hurried round to Duncan Mor. I heard a few whispered words in Gaelic, then the driver opened the cab door on the nearside and slid the seat forward. There was a hinged panel under the seat and he opened it, revealing a deep compartment. Duncan Mor lifted the bag of salmon into the hidden chamber, and the driver closed the panel and replaced the seat.

I watched the red tail-lamp of the lorry disappearing into the distance, and realized for the first time how tired I was. Duncan Mor put his hand on my shoulder and we moved off along the road. When we had crossed the bridge we left the road and took the short cut alongside the river to his house.

We had almost reached the house, when I said: 'What are we going to do now?'

'We must wait and see for a day or two,' said Duncan Mor slowly. 'This is a queer, queer business, and we must be sure we make the right move.'

'You know a lot more about it than you've told me,' I said, and I could not keep the resentment out of my voice.

'Maybe I do, Alasdair,' was all he said.

'Then why don't you go to the police?' I demanded.

Duncan Mor stopped and faced me.

'It is no good me going to the polis,' he said firmly. 'I may know more than you, Alasdair, but most of it is guesswork. If I wore a gold chain on my waistcoat they would listen to me, but they would never take heed of any wild story from the likes o' me. No, no, you are safe enough if you accuse a tinker of lifting a hen, but it is another story, as the other man said, when it is the lads with gold chains on their waistcoats you are after.'

We walked on in silence and I followed him into the house. The bed of red peats in the fireplace cast a dim, cosy glow about the room. Glen met us at the door, and he was growling, but I did not notice the man in the chair until he stood up.

The buttons of his jacket caught the light and sparkled, and I saw that he was wearing the uniform of the Inverness-shire Constabulary.

Duncan Mor's late night visitor was a policeman.

Chapter 18

IF Duncan Mor was surprised, he did not show it. He walked over to the fireplace and wedged some fresh peats on the red embers of the dying fire and lit the lamp. When the mantle had heated he turned up the wick, and I screwed up my eyes against the bright light.

The policeman remained standing.

He cleared his throat, and said: 'You are Duncan Mac-Donald?'

'Aye, that's me,' said Duncan Mor.

He was sitting on the corner of the kitchen table, calmly filling his pipe, but I noticed that his eyes were wary.

'You are the tenant of number four Mealt?'

Duncan Mor was lighting his pipe and he looked at the policeman over the flaming match and nodded.

I was standing with my back to the door, and I saw the policeman looking at me curiously. I glanced down and saw that I had a nasty cut on my right knee. The blood had congealed and the skin around the cut was puffy and discoloured. I must have struck my knee against the iron bar of the bridge support, but in the shock of the fall I had not felt it.

'What happened to the boy?' asked the policeman.

'He had an accident,' said Duncan Mor shortly.

Without another word, he went into the scullery and came back with a basin of water and a roll of bandage. He cleaned and bathed my leg and bandaged it, and sat me down in the old easy-chair by the fire. I sat on the edge of the chair, scraping my nails along the frayed moquette of the arms, and watched the policeman. Duncan Mor resumed his seat on the table. His pipe had gone out and he lit it again. He seemed quite unconcerned.

The policeman was studying a thick black notebook. He shut it deliberately and snapped the elastic band in place and put it back in his tunic pocket. I wished he would speak. The silence was nerve racking. I did not know then that he intended it to be.

Finally, he said: 'Can you give an account of your movements between nine and ten o'clock on Tuesday night?'

'Why should I?' said Duncan Mor calmly.

The policeman's lips tightened.

'I should warn you,' he said coldly, 'that a serious charge has been preferred against you. You can do yourself no good by refusing to answer questions.'

'What is the charge?' said Duncan Mor.

The policeman cleared his throat. 'The charge is theft,' he said. 'A considerable sum of money was stolen from Achmore Lodge on the night of Tuesday last, and I have reason to believe that you are responsible for the theft.'

I started forward in my chair. Theft! The very idea was ridiculous. As if Duncan Mor would steal from Achmore Lodge or from anywhere else for that matter. But there was a terrible finality in the policeman's words, and I had a sudden feeling of helplessness at the thought that all the power of the law was against us.

'Well, well,' said Duncan Mor slowly. 'Theft, eh? I doubt you are in for a hard job before you can manage to prove that.'

'Where were you at nine o'clock on Tuesday night?' asked the policeman.

'I had just finished milking the cow, and I was sitting in the kitchen reading a piece in the *People's Journal* about our police force,' answered Duncan Mor. 'It seems that the police are costing an awful amount of money, and little wonder too, if they can afford to be chasing backwards and forwards from Portree on daft errands like this. Just you tell me who accused me o' thievin' and I will save you a job. I would break him in two and hand you the pieces.'

'You were in the house at nine o'clock on Tuesday night?' persisted the policeman. 'Yes or no?'

144

'Yes.'

'Did you have a caller from the Lodge?'

'Aye, that poor truaghan of a gamekeeper,' said Duncan Mor. 'The poor cratur's so fat he could hardly waddle in the door. But don't be thinking he was here laying down the law. Oh, no. It was Duncan this and Duncan that and Duncan would you be so kind as to accompany me to the Lodge. I am telling you, I have seen some gamekeepers in my day but never the equal o' yon fellow.'

'So you had a visit from Mr Judge, the gamekeeper?'

'Yes.'

'What time would that be?'

'About nine o'clock.'

'Why did he want you to go to the Lodge?'

Duncan Mor scratched his head.

'Well, he hummed and hawed for a while, and then he told me the Major would like a word with me.'

'Did he say why the Major wanted to speak to you?'

'Yes, he told me the Major was after getting worried about the way his salmon were disappearing from the pool.'

'But you wouldn't know anything about that?' said the policeman sarcastically.

'I'm not paid to look after the Major's salmon,' retorted Duncan Mor coolly. 'That is the gamekeeper's job. I told him so.'

'And what did he say?'

'Oh, he said he wasn't accusing me of poaching salmon, but he thought it would be better for me to have a friendly chat with the Major, as the poor man was terrible worried about the poaching.'

'So you accompanied Mr Judge to the Lodge?'

'Yes.'

'What time did you arrive there?'

'About half past nine. Maybe a wee bit later than that.'

'Were you taken straight to see Major Cassell?'

'No, I wasn't,' said Duncan Mor thoughtfully. 'The keeper

showed me to the Major's study. He told me to wait while he went away and got him.'

'You were left alone in the study?'

'Aye.'

'Nobody came in while you were there, apart from Major Cassell?'

'No, but Murdo Ruadh was coming out when I went in,' said Duncan Mor, and his teeth clamped down on his pipe so hard that I thought he had bitten through the stem.

I had been listening anxiously to the quick flow of question and answer, and I sensed, rather than knew, that the policeman was gently prompting Duncan Mor towards a pit from which there would be no escape. But all my fears lifted at the mention of Murdo Beaton's name. Everything was going to be all right after all. If Murdo Beaton had been in the Lodge on Tuesday night, there could be no doubt that he had stolen the money. Had I not seen him counting the notes when I peered through the kitchen window? No wonder he had been furious and tried to kill me.

'Murdo who?' queried the policeman.

'Murdo Beaton,' replied Duncan Mor. 'He has a croft in Achmore, the next township.'

'And you actually saw this man Beaton coming out of Major Cassell's study?'

'Well, no, not coming out of the study. But he was coming away from it.'

'Did you see him shutting the study door?'

'No, but he was just a yard or two away from it.'

'Whereabouts is the study?'

Duncan Mor's keen grey eyes surveyed the policeman warily.

'I'm sure you know well enough,' he said.

I watched the policeman closely, but he showed no surprise.

'The study door is in the middle of a passage,' he said, 'and at the end of the passage is the door to the library. Right?'

'Yes.'

'So the man you saw – this man Beaton – could have been coming from the library?'

'Yes, but I would say he was coming from the study.'

'But that's just your opinion.'

'Well, yes. That is my opinion, and I don't doubt the same fellow will swear blind that he never went near the study.'

The policeman consulted his notebook again.

'When Mr Judge showed you into the study, how long were you left alone before Major Cassell came in?'

Duncan Mor considered for a moment.

'A few minutes, I reckon,' he said at length.

'Was it not nearer a quarter of an hour?'

'It might have been. I don't make a habit of timing myself when I am waiting for folk.'

'Did you see a roll top desk in the study?'

'Aye.'

'Was it open or closed?'

'I don't mind.'

'You mean to say you were in the study for fifteen minutes and you can't remember if the desk was open or closed?'

'Yes.'

'What did you do when you were in the study?'

'I just waited.'

'And looked around?'

'I suppose so.'

'But you didn't notice if the desk was open or closed?'

'No.'

The policeman studied his nails for a moment, then said suddenly: 'How many salmon fishing stations has Major Cassell got on Skye?'

I could not see the point of the question, but I was to know all too soon.

'He has five in Skye and one in Raasay,' said Duncan Mor.

'How many men do you suppose he employs on them?'

'About thirty.'

'So that with his household staff he would have a weekly wage bill for forty people?'

'I suppose so.'

'Do you know when they get paid?'

'Who? The salmon fishermen?'

'Yes.'

'They get paid on a Wednesday.'

'So you knew there would be a considerable sum of money in the house on Tuesday night?'

There was an angry glint in Duncan Mor's eyes, and he took a step forward. For a moment, I thought he was going to seize the policeman by the throat, and I started up in the chair, but he controlled himself and leaned back against the table.

'You knew there would be a considerable sum of money in the house on a Tuesday night,' persisted the policeman.

'Just bide a while,' barked Duncan Mor, and I wondered if the policeman realized how near he had been to being pitched out of the door neck and crop. 'It is one thing to know the day the men are paid, but it is another altogether to wonder where the money is coming from. I just never gave it a thought, and that is the God's honest truth.'

'What would you say if I told you there were forty five-pound notes in a drawer of the desk, as well as smaller notes and two bags of silver?'

'What do you expect me to say?' he retorted angrily. 'That I pocketed the lot and walked out? Tuts, man, there could have been a thousand pounds in the desk for all I knew or cared.'

'Where were you standing when Major Cassell came into the study?'

'I believe I had my back to the desk. Aye, I looked across at the door when I heard it open.'

'You didn't have one hand on the desk?'

'I may have done.'

'But you didn't notice if it was open or closed?'

The words flashed out, like the thrust of a rapier, but Duncan Mor remained unmoved.

'No,' he said calmly.

'What did Major Cassell say to you?'

'He told me he'd had reports that I was lifting his salmon from the pool and he told me I could expect no mercy if I was caught.'

'What did you say?'

Duncan Mor laughed. 'I told him if his gamekeeper tried using his legs for a change instead of his tongue, maybe he wouldn't have to worry so much about his salmon.'

'You were insolent to Major Cassell.'

'Not at all. I just told him what I thought.'

'You parted on bad terms?'

'Well, I wouldn't say the Major was very pleased, but it didn't put me up or down.'

'What time did you leave the Lodge?'

'I suppose it would be near ten.'

'And at ten o'clock,' said the policeman deliberately, 'Major Cassell discovered that two hundred pounds in five-pound notes was missing from his desk in the study. Do you insist that you left the Lodge without that money?'

'Certainly I insist,' declared Duncan Mor. 'I came out o' the Lodge the way I went in, and you'll never get me to say otherwise.'

'I warn you that the numbers of the notes are known. You can never hope to get away with this.'

'I'm not trying to get away with anything,' said Duncan Mor flatly. 'You can take it from me that you are wasting your time here.'

'I have reason to believe that you have the money hidden in this house,' stated the policeman.

'Well, well,' said Duncan Mor calmly, 'I suppose you thought I would come strolling back from the Lodge like a great daft loon and plant the money in the tea-caddy just so it would be easy for you to find it. Go ahead and have a look,' he went on mockingly. 'I always keep my five-pound notes there.'

He pointed to the large tin tea-caddy in the centre of the mantelpiece. There was a painting of King George V on the front of it, and the lid did not fit properly.

'If you think you can pull that old dodge on me, you are mistaken,' said the policeman curtly. He took down the tea-caddy and carried it over to the table.

'Have you any objections to me opening it?' he asked.

'Not at all,' said Duncan Mor. 'But you will find nothing there but a few bills and a form for the calf subsidy.'

The bills and the form were certainly there, but underneath them were two bundles of crisp new banknotes. The policeman spread them on the table and carefully checked the numbers with a typewritten list he produced from his pocket.

I was dumbfounded. I just sat and stared. Even Duncan Mor had lost his composure. His forehead was creased in a worried frown, and I could see his teeth biting at his lower lip.

The policeman placed the notes carefully in his tunic pocket and stood up. He could not keep the elation out of his voice.

'The numbers correspond,' he said. 'These are the notes that were stolen from Achmore Lodge. Do you still deny that you had anything to do with it?'

'Yes,' said Duncan Mor firmly.

'Then how do you account for the fact that they were hidden in this house?'

'I can't account for it,' said Duncan Mor slowly, 'but I have a good idea, and when I lay hands on the fellow responsible he will know all about it.'

'Get your coat,' said the policeman curtly. 'You will be charged and taken into custody in Portree.'

Duncan Mor looked down at his blue denim trousers. From the knees downwards they were black with rain.

'This is no way to be going to Portree,' he said, 'even supposing it is the jail I am bound for. I must just put on a decent suit and a collar and tie.'

He crossed the room and opened the door to his bedroom, and I hated to see the dejected droop of his shoulders.

'Five minutes,' said the policeman. 'No more.'

'Right,' said Duncan Mor, meekly closing the door behind him.

I was stunned by the suddenness of the blow, and Duncan Mor's resigned acceptance of it. I had expected him to rage and storm; indeed, it would not have surprised me if he had leapt on the policeman and overpowered him, but I never thought he would submit without a struggle. I looked at the policeman and wondered if I should tell him my story. But what was the use? I had no evidence, and he would think I was lying to help Duncan Mor.

The policeman lit a cigarette and paced up and down the room. He was a young man with a red face and cold blue eyes, and I did not like the evident swagger in his walk.

He caught my eyes on him, and said: 'Are you his son?'

'No, I'm staying here on holiday,' I said.

'Where are you from?'

'London.'

'Where did you hurt your knee?' he asked.

'Down the road,' I said evasively.

'Down at the pool more likely,' he retorted. 'If your parents had any sense they'd have kept you in London. There is no respect for the law here. People think they can do as they please, and I can see you'll be getting as bad as them.'

I looked down at the floor and saw the coloured label of a tobacco wrapper. It was lying in front of the bedroom door and it started to drift across the floor. The policeman saw it too, but he went on pacing up and down the room. It has always pleased me that I realized what had happened before he did. He crossed the floor twice before the meaning of the moving paper became clear to him.

When he rushed across the room and flung open the bedroom door, I was only a few paces behind him. The bedroom window was wide open and the curtains were billowing back from the wall.

The room was empty. Duncan Mor had vanished.

Chapter 19

THE policeman never moved for a full minute. He seemed to be rooted to the spot, and his red face had turned a deep crimson. I drew back a pace, when he wheeled round, and he glowered at me.

'It's the handcuffs for MacDonald when I get him,' he snapped.

I did not say anything, and he dashed out of the room leaving the door wide open behind him. I closed the door and went into the bedroom. I leaned out of the window and saw the light of the policeman's torch as he searched the byre and the stackyard. The rain had stopped and the sky was lightening in the east. I saw the policeman go up the river bank to the ruins of an old black house, and I saw his torch flashing as he circled back to the track beyond the dike.

I heard the door of his car slam and the whirr of the starter. The engine throbbed into life and his headlights lanced the darkness. I saw the car move slowly along the rough track and turn right at the main road. It was hidden from view where the road dipped sharply to the bridge, and although I watched for a long time I never saw it climb out of the hollow. I guessed that the policeman had stopped and switched out the lights. He would be making his way back on foot to watch the house in case Duncan Mor returned.

I closed the bedroom window and went out to the byre to look for Glen. The byre door was open and although I whistled and shouted, the dog never came. He must have gone off after his master.

I returned to the kitchen and sat in the chair and looked around the room. It was strange to be sitting there without Duncan Mor on the other side of the fire, but all the things he prized most were around me. It was a bare, untidy sort of room, and Aunt Evelyn would have said that it was full of lumber, but I loved it because it was such a man's room.

Duncan Mor's split cane rod lay along the back of the bench, and his twelve bore shotgun was propped up in a corner, its well-oiled barrel gleaming in the light. There was a small table under the window and it was littered with snaring wire and dozens of brass eyelets, tins of fishing hooks, two screwdrivers and a pair of pliers, a pair of binoculars and several volumes of Admiralty Charts in their faded blue covers.

There was a pail of sheep dip at one end of the bench and a pair of white rubber thigh boots propped up against the other end. Two long shepherd's crooks, with ornamental handles that Duncan Mor had carved himself, stood in the corner by the door, and several boxes of cartridges lay along the dresser top. A calendar from a seed merchant in Greenock hung on the wall above the bench, and on the opposite wall was a photograph of the crew of the *Empire Rose* with my father in the centre. Catalogues and price lists for seed oats, potatoes, fertilizers, feeding-stuffs, fishing tackle, farming implements and oilskin coats were scattered everywhere. It was not a room I could ever be lonely in.

I remembered how he had told me he never let the fire go out, and I went outside to the peat stack and selected two damp peats from the top of the stack. I flattened them down on top of the red peats, and pulled the old easy-chair closer to the fire. I turned out the lamp and curled up in the chair and shut my eyes.

Something dug into my back and I felt round the chair and pulled out a pointed wooden peg. There was a length of wire attached to it and I felt the eyelet at the other end of the wire making a noose. It was a rabbit snare. I thrust it into my pocket and closed my eyes again.

It is strange how your body can be dog-tired and yet your mind remains alert and active. All the events of the day flashed before my eyes in a series of vivid pictures. The climax could not be long delayed. Sooner or later we would have to come out into the open against Murdo Beaton, and the sooner the better if Duncan Mor was to be cleared of the charge hanging over him.

I marvelled at the cunning of Murdo Beaton. He had tried to kill me, and he intended having Duncan Mor imprisoned to get him out of the way. Duncan Mor was afraid the police would never believe him, and certainly they would never listen to him so long as they believed he was guilty of theft from the Lodge. I would have to tell my story to Major Cassell. No matter how strongly he felt about poachers, he was bound to acknowledge Duncan Mor's innocence when I explained everything to him. I would go to the Lodge first thing in the morning. Once Major Cassell heard my story, it would not be long before the secret of the Hill of the Red Fox was uncovered, and Murdo Beaton was safely behind bars.

With that reassuring thought in my mind, I drifted off to sleep.

I was stiff and cold when I awoke and I had cramp in my right leg and arm. The fire had gone out. That worried me more than my own discomfort. It was the first time the fire had gone out since Duncan Mor came home from sea. The crofter's fire never goes out, that was what he had told me, and there was something splendid about it, something heartwarming and stirring. The dead peats in the black hearth looked like a bad omen, but I laughed at myself. Mairi would say I was being as superstitious as the cailleach.

There was a pail of water in the scullery and I poured some into the basin and hurriedly swilled my face. The fire would have to wait until I got back from the Lodge. With a last glance at the cold hearth, I left the house.

At close quarters Achmore Lodge was much bigger than I had imagined. It was built of grey stone but the bleakness of the stone was lightened by the creeper covered walls. Three wide stone steps led up to a large square porch, and I climbed the steps and stood outside the door. There was an old-fashioned brass bell-pull by the side of the door and, after a moment's hesitation, I reached up and pulled it. I heard the ting-a-ling-ling of the bell echoing inside the house, and felt suddenly nervous and unsure of myself.

The door was opened by a large, egg-shaped man. His head, which was completely bald, looked like the highly polished top of an egg. He looked at me curiously and I tried to tear my eyes away from his bald head.

I gulped, and said: 'I want to see Major Cassell, please.'

'Major Cassell hasn't breakfasted yet,' said the man at the door, 'but if you will leave a message I'll see that he gets it.'

'I . . . I can't leave a message,' I stammered. 'I must see him. It's terribly important.' The man did not seem impressed, and I added desperately, 'It's a matter of life and death.'

'What's your name?' he said grudgingly.

'Alasdair Cameron,' I said eagerly. 'I don't suppose Major Cassell has heard of me, but you can tell him I'm staying with Murdo Beaton at Achmore. He knows Murdo Beaton.'

'Come in,' said the man.

I followed him into a large hall, smelling of polished oak, and he told me to wait. He was back again in a few moments, moving silently on the thickly carpeted floor.

'The Major will see you now,' he said.

I followed him across the hall and along a passage that branched off to the left. He opened a door on the right and stood aside to let me enter.

'Master Alasdair Cameron, Major,' he announced.

I had never before been ushered into a room with such awesome formality, and I walked slowly across the thick pile of the carpet, acutely conscious of my mud-stained wellingtons and bedraggled appearance.

A man rose from a chair by the fire and advanced to meet me. He was a short, stocky man with a fine head of snow-white hair and a neatly trimmed white moustache. His face was pink and shining, and he looked as if he had been scrubbed with carbolic soap.

'How do you do, Alasdair,' he said, smiling. 'Heard a great

deal about you. Means a lot. Beaton's not a talkative chap, y'know.'

He spoke in short, clipped sentences, firing out the words in staccato bursts.

I took his extended hand and he shook hands the way he spoke, firmly and briefly. He guided me to a chair and sat down again himself.

Now that the moment had come, I did not know where to start. Major Cassell regarded his neatly manicured nails, and I noted with satisfaction the thin chain of gold hanging across the brown tweed of his waistcoat.

'Murdo Beaton's up to no good,' I blurted out at last. 'I saw him with all the money and he stole the message from me that I got from the man with the scar who jumped off the train.'

'Good gracious!' exclaimed the Major. 'What's this? Trouble? Never do on an empty stomach.' He smiled broadly. 'Refuse to listen to you, my boy. Not until I've had my breakfast. Bad for the digestion. Have you had yours? I'll bet not. Suppose you rushed straight to me, eh?'

'I came straight here,' I admitted, 'and . . . and I'm jolly hungry.'

'Good oh,' he smiled. 'Food first. Business second.'

He rang the bell and told the manservant that I would be breakfasting with him.

We had porridge and cream, and bacon and egg and sausage, and lots of thickly buttered toast, and I drank three cups of tea. Major Cassell chatted pleasantly about birds and their habits, and I remembered Duncan Mor had told me he was a naturalist.

The window overlooked the drive, and I could see through the wrought-iron gates of the Lodge to the main road. On a hillock, beyond the main road, I saw the squat shape of a tinker's tent. There was a cart alongside the tent and a horse was grazing nearby.

'See you're looking at the tinks,' said Major Cassell. 'They set up camp last night. Give the beggars 'til tomorrow night.

Not away by then, I'll have the police on their tail. Tinks and poachers. Can't stand 'em. Make my blood boil.'

When we had finished breakfast, he settled back in his chair with a cigarette, but he waited until the manservant had cleared the table before he spoke.

'Now, my boy,' he said. 'What's the trouble? Must say I'm interested. Know Beaton pretty well. Always thought he was more dependable than most of the locals. However, go on. Doesn't do to make prior judgements.'

I told him everything that had happened to me right up to the attempted arrest of Duncan Mor. He listened attentively, firing a question here and there, but for the most part sitting in silence.

'So you see,' I concluded, 'Duncan Mor didn't steal your money. It was Murdo Beaton.'

'Yes, I see that,' he said thoughtfully. 'Man's an absolute scoundrel. Unprincipled.'

'Was he with you in the library on Tuesday night?' I asked.

'Who? Beaton?'

'Yes,' I said.

Major Cassell nodded. 'Wanted him to ghillie for a party. Good ghillie. Pity. Never thought the man was a rogue.'

'So there was nothing to stop him slipping into your study,' I declared triumphantly.

'Easy enough,' said the Major. 'The desk was open. Money lying there.'

'What about the Hill of the Red Fox?' I said. 'What are you going to do about it?'

The Major blinked suddenly and said: 'What was that? Didn't catch you, my boy. Thinking hard. Bad business this, y'know.'

'What are you going to do about the Hill of the Red Fox?' I repeated. 'And the man who disappeared that night in the Sound?'

'Going to do plenty,' he snapped. 'Must investigate the whole matter. Police job. Need to be careful Beaton isn't put on his guard. Don't want his accomplices to get off scot free. Hope you haven't let word slip to anyone, my boy.'

'Nobody knows anything about it,' I said eagerly, 'except Duncan Mor and myself, and he won't breathe a word to anyone. And I didn't even mention it when I was writing home.'

'Very wise,' he said approvingly. 'Never know who might see the letters. Safer to say nothing.'

I was about to speak when the door opened and a man came into the room. He was short and fat with an untidy mop of black hair and a pale face. But it was his limp I noticed most. He dragged his left leg along behind him in a sort of swinging movement from the hip.

The man was half-way across the room before he noticed me, and he stopped short and glanced at Major Cassell. The Major rose quickly and put an arm around the limping man's shoulder and steered him to the door.

'My dear fellow, I shan't be two minutes,' I heard him say before he closed the door behind him.

He did not sit down again, but stood in front of the fire looking down thoughtfully at me.

'Feel a certain responsibility for you, Alasdair,' he said at length. 'Think you had better stay at the Lodge. Safer. Never know what Beaton might get up to. Besides, you look awfully tired. Good sleep is what you're needing. Plenty of rest.'

'I am tired,' I admitted. 'I didn't get much sleep last night.'

Major Cassell rang the bell, and the man with the egg-shaped head glided silently into the room.

'Master Cameron is staying with us, Slater,' said the Major. 'Put him in the special guest room. And, Slater, see that he has everything he wants. By jove, he's an honoured guest. Understand?'

'Perfectly, sir,' said the manservant.

I stammered my thanks, but Major Cassell laughingly refused to listen and pushed me out of the room.

I followed the man Slater up two flights of stairs and along a narrow, uncarpeted passage. He unlocked a door and stepped aside to allow me to enter the room. He hovered for a moment in the doorway, and I thought he looked like Humpty-Dumpty, and tried to keep a straight face.

'Is there anything you require, sir?' he asked, his head bent forward and a little to one side in a deferential manner.

I noticed that he had become much more respectful since I had been invited to stay at the Lodge, and I wished that Aunt Evelyn had been there to hear him.

'No, thanks,' I said, and he withdrew silently, and closed the door behind him.

It was a small room with a high barred window and I supposed it must have been originally part of the nursery. But it was cheerful enough. There was an electric fire, a comfortable chair and a bedside table stacked with books and magazines. A portable radio stood on a corner shelf at the head of the bed, and the floor was so highly polished that the sheepskin rug by the bedside skidded away from under my feet when I crossed the room.

The window overlooked a courtyard at the back of the house and by standing on tiptoe I could see as far as the garage. A black saloon car was parked in front of the garage and a man in a chauffeur's uniform was busy polishing the windscreen.

I switched on the radio and sat down on the bed. Somebody was playing a cinema organ, and I listened drowsily to the music. Although I felt terribly tired, the nervous tension had relaxed, and my mind was at peace. I had the satisfaction of knowing that I had accomplished everything I had set out to do. I had proved that Duncan Mor was innocent of the theft at the Lodge, and I had got Major Cassell to set the police on the trail of Murdo Beaton. Before long the mystery of the Hill of the Red Fox would be cleared up and Murdo Beaton and his accomplices would get their just desserts.

I wondered what my mother would say when I told her of the part I had played, and I would remark to Aunt Evelyn, in a casual voice: 'Of course, Major Cassell insisted that I stay at Achmore Lodge as his guest. I had a very nice room and the servants called me sir.' Or perhaps it would sound better if I said, 'It's nice to do things for yourself again after having servants running around all over the place.'

At any rate, Aunt Evelyn could not call me a bookworm any more. Nobody could say I had not had more than my share of adventure since I came to Skye.

I had started to take off my wellingtons when the music faded and there was silence. I thought there had been a break-down, and I was just going to try to get another station when an announcer's voice said:

'This is the B.B.C. Home Service. This programme is being interrupted to broadcast the following special announce-ment from No. 10 Downing Street.

'Dr Ernst Reuter, Head of the Atomic Research Centre at Marwell, has disappeared from his home. After consultations with the Cabinet, the Prime Minister has decided that the news should be made public immediately in order that the entire nation can be alerted in an attempt to locate the missing scientist.

'Dr Reuter is the third prominent atomic scientist to have disappeared within the course of the past six months. It is believed that the other two scientists have left the country and are now in the service of a foreign power.

'All ports and airfields are being watched and it is believed that Dr Reuter has not yet succeeded in leaving the country. Dr Reuter is forty-eight years of age, heavily built, and of medium height. He has black hair and a pale complexion. Some years ago his left leg was crushed in an accident, and he walks with a pronounced limp.

'It will be recalled that a few weeks ago Dr Reuter's deputy, Mr Geoffrey Hunt, disappeared from . . .'

I never heard the rest of the announcement and I was hardly conscious of the strident notes of the cinema organ when it came back on the air. Dr Reuter's deputy, Mr Geoffrey Hunt, I repeated soundlessly to myself. Mr Geoffrey Hunt! HUNT! HUNT at the Hill of the Red Fox. GEOFFREY HUNT at the Hill of the Red Fox. So that was the meaning of the message. And like a silly bookworm I had thought of buried treasure! What a fool I had been.

My thoughts spun wildly. IT WILL BE RECALLED THAT A FEW WEEKS AGO DR REUTER'S DEPUTY, MR GEOFFREY HUNT, DISAPPEARED . . . NOW IN THE SERVICE OF A FOREIGN POWER. . . . The men in the dinghy rowing out to the coble. Two coming back. NOW IN THE SERVICE OF A FOREIGN POWER. . . . But how? Yes, yes, before the coble came back with one of the passengers missing. . . . After it disappeared into the mist and rain across the Sound, Duncan Mor had cocked his head on one side. . . . That was it. The noise. The low humming noise. What would make a low humming noise. Not a ship. A ship would be seen. But what about a submarine. Of course! A submarine. It could rise up silently out of the depths, take a man aboard, and submerge again. NOW IN THE SERVICE OF A FOREIGN POWER. . . .

Oddly enough the organ swung into the lilting refrain of the Skye Boat Song, and the words of the song crept into my mind and persistently refused to be dislodged. 'Speed bonnie boat like a bird on the wing: onward the sailors cry. Carry the lad that's born to be king, over the sea to Skye.' The organist switched to a popular tune of the moment, and the solemn words of the special announcement came hammering back into my mind.

DR ERNST REUTER, HEAD OF THE ATOMIC RESEARCH CENTRE AT MARWELL, HAS DISAPPEARED FROM HIS HOME. HE HAS BLACK HAIR AND A PALE COMPLEXION. SOME YEARS AGO HIS LEFT LEG WAS CRUSHED IN AN ACCIDENT AND HE WALKS WITH A PRONOUNCED LIMP. . . .

My head swam dizzily. Everything was suddenly frighteningly clear. I rushed across to the window and looked out. The chauffeur was leaning against the bonnet of the car, looking up at my window. His eyes were obscured by dark glasses, but I had only to look at his hands to recognize him at once. He was busy filing his nails.

Even before I ran to the door and tried it, I knew it would be locked.

Chapter 20

I LET go of the handle and leaned against the door. The door was locked and the window barred, and I had no doubt that the Lodge was well guarded. Blue Eyes, as Duncan Mor called him, was watching my window, and for all I knew another guard lurked outside the door. I was trapped.

I thought of all the books I had read in which the hero, armed with a knife or a file, made a dramatic escape from a dungeon or a fortress room in a tower. It seemed simple enough, reading about such escapes in books, and I had never stopped to think if they were really possible. But I had no knife or file, and even if I had I doubt if I could have succeeded in bursting open the door. Only a miracle could get me out of Achmore Lodge alive, and in my dejected state of mind I could not believe in the existence of miracles.

The radio was blaring out a stirring marching song and I crossed the room and switched it off. Blue Eyes was still leaning against the car, filing his nails, his eyes fixed on the window. I thought of what he had done to the man with the scar and I could not repress a sudden shiver. Duncan Mor had said it was dangerous to know too much, but I had never appreciated the dread reality of those words until now. I sat down on the bed and tried to think calmly.

A few minutes ago (or was it a few years?) I had been congratulating myself on my cleverness; even boasting of the things I would say to impress Aunt Evelyn on my return home. Would I ever be lucky enough to return home, or was I doomed to share the fate of the man with the scar? Terror seized me. I moved from the bed to the door, and from the door to the window, and back to the bed again; stumbling about in a blind panic and expecting at any moment to hear the dread sound of the key turning in the lock.

After a while, when nothing happened, I calmed down. I sat on the edge of the bed again and tried to think clearly. What galled me most of all was the fact that I had walked blindly into a trap. I had sought the aid of the very man responsible for smuggling atom scientists out of the country. I had told him everything I knew and he had solemnly assured me that the whole matter would be investigated. I squirmed at the thought of Major Cassell's flattery, and the deference of the man, Slater. How they must have laughed to themselves!

It was the thought of the humiliation I had suffered that finally dispelled the panic I had known and made me reason calmly. Duncan Mor was still free, even if he had taken to the hills. Once word reached him that I was missing, he was bound to do something about it. Perhaps he would break into Achmore Lodge and rescue me. It was a slender hope, but I seized upon it eagerly and my spirits rose.

Then doubts assailed me. How could I be sure that Duncan Mor would guess I was imprisoned in the Lodge? Did he really suspect Major Cassell? I recalled what he had said about the futility of going to the police to accuse men with gold chains on their waistcoats. Perhaps that had been a veiled reference to Major Cassell. Certainly, the Major wore a slim gold chain across the front of his waistcoat, but so did many other men. My newly won confidence gradually ebbed away, to be replaced by a feeling of blank despair.

Who would know I was missing and guess that I was being held against my will? Murdo Beaton would spread the story that I had gone fishing off the rocks and had not returned. Everybody would think I had been drowned, and Duncan Mor dare not come down from the hills because the police would be searching for him. No matter how desperate my plight, I could not depend on any help from outside.

My misery deepened. How would my mother manage on her own, when I was gone? And what agonies of remorse would poor Aunt Evelyn suffer, knowing that she alone was responsible for my holiday in Skye? She would never forgive herself.

She would never be able to pick up one of my books again, or see a photograph of me, without thinking that she had sent me to my death.

I abandoned myself to self-pity. It was Aunt Evelyn's fault; she had persuaded my mother, against her better judgement, to send me to Skye. It was the fault of the man with the scar, he ought never to have placed me in danger by giving me the message. It was Duncan Mor's fault; if he was suspicious of Major Cassell he should have warned me. Everyone was to blame but me. All I wanted was my freedom; I had no desire to harm anyone, I told myself tearfully. Even Dr Reuter could go wherever he liked, if only they would let me out.

If I had carried on for long in that vein I would have broken down and cried like a baby, but my self-respect forced me to admit that I alone was responsible for my plight. I blushed at the shameful thoughts that had passed through my mind and decided I had been thinking too much. Hopeless or no, I would try to find a way out of the room. Any action, however futile, was better than dwelling hopelessly on my plight.

I got up and examined the door. It was hung on concealed hinges and built of stout wood and the lock was on the outside. I gripped the handle with both hands and strained with all my strength, but I could make no impression on the lock. It would take a sledgehammer to burst it open.

I pulled the chair to the window and climbed up on it. The window was set into a recess in the wall and crossed by heavy iron bars at intervals of about six inches. Even if I had a file, and managed to break the glass undetected, it would be the work of weeks filing through one of the bars.

The garage doors were open, and I could see a Land Rover parked inside, but there was no sign of the black saloon. It must have started up silently and left the Lodge. The back of the garage abutted the boundary wall of the Lodge and I noticed a small green door to the left of the garage. If only I could get out of the house and through that door I would be on to the moor.

I moved the chair away from the window and sat down once more on the bed, determined to plan a way of escape. Somehow or other, I had to get out of Achmore Lodge and rejoin Duncan Mor. But whichever way my thoughts turned, and no matter how I schemed, I always came up short against the problem of the locked door and the barred window.

It was almost one o'clock when I heard footsteps approaching along the uncarpeted passage. I shrank back against the wall, watching the door fearfully. The lock must have been well oiled because I never heard the key turn. The door opened and Slater came in with a tray. I wondered how I could have laughed at his likeness to Humpty-Dumpty. I could see nothing funny about him now. His eyes were small and cold and there was a hard, vicious line to his mouth.

He put down the tray carefully on the table, and said: 'The Major thinks it would be advisable for you to rest, so I trust you have no objection to taking lunch in your room.'

He spoke in the same deferential manner as before, and backed out of the room and closed the door behind him. After a moment, I heard footsteps retreating down the passage. I realized that my legs were shaking and I sat down unsteadily on the bed. They were playing with me, like a cat toying with a mouse, and it was more frightening than the direct violence I had anticipated.

After a while, I went over to the table and tried to eat. My mouth was dry and I had difficulty in swallowing. The appearance of Slater had strained my nerves to breaking point, crumbling my resolution and inducing a state of near panic. I fought down my swiftly rising fears and thought desperately.

If I were to take all my meals in the room, then at least the door was not locked all the time. In the brief moment it was open, lay my only chance of escape. Slater was almost bound to leave the key in the lock when he came into the room and I could easily dodge past him. I could slam the door and lock him in whilst he still had the tray in his hands. It was doubtful if his cries would be heard because the room was on the second floor and at the back of the house. Even if I gained the passage there still remained many hazards to overcome before I reached the safety of the moor, but at least it was better than passively awaiting my fate.

I determined to make my bid for freedom when he returned for the tray, but it was five o'clock before I heard the sound of footsteps in the passage again.

I sat at the foot of the bed close to the door, my muscles tensed for action. Slater opened the door and moved into the room and I glanced swiftly over his shoulder, ready to take to my heels the moment he was past me. My heart sank. A tall, broad-shouldered man was standing outside the door, blocking my escape route. I realized dismally that he had probably accompanied Slater at lunch-time, but I had been too panic-stricken then to take my eyes off the manservant's face.

Slater set down the tea tray and gathered up the lunch tray. 'Dinner will be served at seven, sir,' he said smoothly.

With an ironical bow, he made his way out of the room and the door closed behind him. I heard the faint click of the lock and there was a terrible finality in the sound. It marked the shattering of all my hopes.

I ate a tiny salmon sandwich and a cake and drank a cup of tea. There was nothing to do but wait, and I stood at the window looking down into the courtyard. The wind was rising steadily. I could hear it soughing round the house, and an oil drum outside the garage suddenly overturned and went careering across the courtyard. It crashed against the wall and the cap burst off and a thin stream of oil stained the ground.

Then the rain came. It came in a sudden deluge and in a matter of minutes pools had gathered across the paved floor of the courtyard. I could hear the water pouring down the pipes outside the window, and beating against the asbestos roof of the garage.

The noise of the wind and rain drowned the approach of the black saloon. It swept silently into the courtyard, swung round in a wide sweep, and the driver reversed into the garage.

I think it was Blue Eyes who climbed out of the driving seat and four men clambered out of the back. They dashed across to the house, leaving the garage doors wide open. The doors were hooked back to the walls of the garage, or they would have been torn off with the force of the wind.

Punctually at seven o'clock I heard the familiar footsteps in the passage and Slater came into the room with the dinner tray. The broad-shouldered guard leaned against the door jamb, and Slater picked up the other tray and left the room without a word.

I had no stomach for the food and I made no attempt to eat it. I wondered if the other man stayed on guard in the passage and I tiptoed to the door and peered through the keyhole. I could not understand why I could see nothing, and it was only when I drew back from the door that I noticed the bright metal tip of the key. It had been left in the lock.

If there was no guard in the passage, and if only I could manage to extract the key, my way of escape was clear. My spirits soared, only to drop again as quickly. The solid expanse of the door lay between me and the key and I did not possess even a knife to try to poke it out of the keyhole.

I lay down on the bed and closed my eyes in a mood of hopeless resignation. If only I could go to sleep and wake up and find it had all been a bad dream. I rolled over on my side and pillowed my head in my arm. Something hard prodded me in the ribs and I sat up and felt the bed. There was nothing there. Then I remembered the rabbit snare in my pocket. I pulled it out and toyed with it, idly pushing the wooden peg through the wire noose of the snare.

It must have been fully five minutes before the idea struck me, but once it came I wasted no time. I leapt off the bed and ran to the door. I could hardly control my trembling fingers as I pulled the brass eyelet of the snare run to its fullest extent so that the wire was doubled. Then I gripped the wire between the thumb and forefinger of both hands and twisted it into a single thin rod about two inches long.

My heart was hammering madly as I bent over the lock and inserted the wire in the keyhole. I gave it a gentle, exploratory push and felt the key move back. I took out the wire and peered into the keyhole. The key had been pushed back a full quarter of an inch.

I got down on my knees and examined the base of the door. The floor of the bedroom was of bare polished wood and there was a narrow gap between the bottom of the door and the floor. It was sufficiently wide to enable the laying of a floor covering, and wide enough, I prayed, to permit the passage of the key.

I doubled the snare wire a second time, making four thicknesses of wire, and thrust it under the door. It was a tight squeeze, but I managed to pass it backwards and forwards under the door, and I was sure that the thicknesses of wire were fatter than the key.

There was now nothing to stop me poking the key out of the lock, and if I could hook it under the door I had only to unlock the door and step out into the passage. The temptation to get to work at once was almost too great to overcome, but I steeled myself to walk back to the bed.

It was too early in the evening to attempt an escape. Supposing Slater returned for the dinner tray and I met him and the guard in the passage? Supposing a man was always on guard in the passage? The latter was a risk that had to be taken, but it would be safer to wait and see if Slater returned for the key before attempting a break-out. I decided to give him until eleven o'clock before making a move, and I lay down on the bed and closed my eyes.

Sleep was out of the question, but at least with my eyes closed I could not see the door and be tempted to make an immediate move. The wind was approaching gale force and I heard the slates rattling as successive gusts made furious onslaughts on the house, and behind all the noise of the wind was the steady gurgle and flow of running water as it flooded off the roof into the drain-pipes.

I tried counting up to a thousand, and repeating all the

history dates I knew from the Battle of Hastings onwards, and saying the alphabet backwards, and going through the multiplication tables, and saying to myself, when I look at my watch it will be ten o'clock; when I look at it again it will be a quarter past ten; but no matter what I did I could not speed the passing hours. From the time I discovered the rabbit snare in my pocket, I seemed to have lived another life, much longer than the one I had known up to then.

At eleven o'clock there was still no sign of Slater, but I had a sudden foreboding that he must be on his way up to the room. I waited until half past eleven, when the room was in almost complete darkness, before I tiptoed to the door.

I inserted my wire rod into the keyhole and started to work the key out of the lock. Then I had a sudden inspiration and I blundered across to the table and felt for a book. In my haste I upset the pile of books which Slater had balanced on the edge of the table to make way for the tray, and two heavy volumes crashed to the floor before I could catch them. The noise was such that I thought everyone in the house must hear it.

I stood stock-still, in an agony of apprehension, but nothing happened. Surely if there had been a guard in the passage he would have looked in to see the cause of the noise. I listened intently, but there was only the howling of the wind and the incessant drumming of the rain to be heard. Slowly my confidence returned, and I realized that the noise of the storm must have covered the crash of the falling books, which had probably been magnified by my over-sensitive ears. My groping hands closed around a book and I opened it and ripped out a page.

I slipped the paper under the door directly beneath the keyhole and took hold of the snare again. I inserted the wire into the keyhole and pushed the key out of the lock and it fell to the floor with a dull tinkle. In a frenzy of excitement, I dropped to my knees and took hold of the corners of the paper. I eased the paper gently towards me, then felt around the bottom of the door for the key. One end of the key was protruding slightly under the door and I pulled sharply at the paper. It came away into the room, leaving the key wedged under the door.

I tried to force my fingers under the door, in an attempt to scrape the key into the room, and I broke a nail in my frantic scrabbling before I had the sense to return to the snare. I bent the wire into an arc and pushed it under the door and hooked the key into the room. I seized it with trembling hands and for a moment I wondered if I had bent it, for I could not get it to go into the keyhole. At the third attempt, however, it went in and I unlocked the door.

Now that the time had come, I felt strangely reluctant to leave the room. All sorts of fears and doubts assailed me. What if a guard lurked in the darkness of the passage after all, and was waiting for me to run into his arms? How could I hope to steal out of the house without being seen? Would they shoot me down in cold blood if they saw me trying to escape? I gritted my teeth. If Duncan Mor were in my shoes he would have been at the head of the stairs by now.

Hardly daring to breathe, I grasped the handle and opened the door.

Chapter 21

No sound or movement came from the darkness of the passage, so I took to my heels and ran. I might well have bolted straight into the arms of a waiting guard, and I was half-way down the passage before I realized how foolish I had been. I stopped short, listening anxiously. The only sound came from my own rapidly beating heart. I moved on again, this time stepping cautiously on tiptoe.

When I reached the head of the stairs I remembered that I had left the door open, but I was afraid to turn back. It was as much as I could do to move forward. The stairs were thickly carpeted and I would be unable to hear anyone mounting them until they were almost face to face with me. I could imagine Slater, at this very moment, silently crossing the hall and slowly ascending the stairs. My legs started to tremble, and I shut the picture from my mind. Summoning all my resolution, I moved swiftly down the stairs.

I did not encounter anyone. The hall lay straight ahead, dimly illuminated by the light of a hanging lantern, and I was about to race across it when I saw a passage branching off to the right. A chink of light showed under a door half-way down the passage. I hesitated for a moment, torn between the desire to make good my escape and an urge to find out as much as possible before leaving the Lodge. All my instincts urged me to carry on out of the house, but some stubborn streak of foolhardy courage, that I did not know I possessed, prompted me to tiptoe down the passage. I stood outside the door ready to flee at the first sound of movement from inside the room.

I could hear Major Cassell's voice and I bent down and peered through the keyhole. The Major's desk was directly opposite the door, and Dr Reuter was sitting in a swivel chair behind the desk. Major Cassell was bending over him, his face close to the scientist's. Dr Reuter was deathly white and he shifted uneasily in the chair. He looked badly frightened. When I saw Major Cassell's face I knew the reason why.

The Major was dressed in the same loose-fitting tweed suit he had worn that morning and his face was as pink and shining as ever. But it was not the same face. The easy smile had left his lips and his mouth was set in a thin, hard line. There was nothing jolly or hearty about him, and when he spoke his voice rasped with anger.

'Whether you like it or not, Reuter,' he said coldly, 'you leave Skye tomorrow at midnight.'

Dr Reuter leaned forward and his flabby hands gripped the carved wooden arms of the chair.

'I don't like it, Cassell,' he said nervously. 'Broadcast announcements every two hours on the radio. Every busybody in the country on the alert. A nation-wide hunt. How long do you think it will be before they trace me to Skye?'

He spoke in short, jerky sentences, and puffed continually at a cigarette.

'In the unlikely event of them tracing you, it will be too late.' said the Major smoothly. 'You will have vanished. They are still searching for Hunt, and you know where he is now.'

'I don't like it,' repeated Dr Reuter. 'Ransome got away with no trouble, but Hunt was nearly tracked down. What about the man who was on his heels?'

'Dead men tell no tales,' smiled the Major, and then, in a harsher tone: 'I have taken steps to ensure that nothing will interfere with your escape. You were to have left at midnight on Saturday, but I have radioed Commander Gregoriev bringing forward the date twenty-four hours. The submarine will surface in the Sound at midnight tomorrow.'

'I still don't like it,' said the scientist stubbornly. 'It is not too late to change our plans. If I were to turn up in Portree tomorrow my absence could be explained away as a mis-understanding. I could tell them I had decided to take a brief holiday in Skye. Say I was feeling the strain of overwork. A nervous breakdown, if you like. I had left Marwell hurriedly without leaving word. Nothing could be proved. Can't you see how it would look? All this hue and cry, and for what? A mare's nest. The authorities would look ridiculous. Later on, when things had quietened down, it would be easier for you to arrange for me to join Ransome and Hunt.'

Major Cassell listened to him in silence, studying his neatly groomed nails, a half-amused smile on his lips.

When the scientist had finished he said softly: 'My dear Ernst, I really must remind you of the penalty for high treason.' He sighed, but the mocking smile remained on his lips. 'The penalty, my friend, is death.'

He turned round and for one panic-stricken moment I thought he was about to walk to the door, but he crossed the room, passing out of my narrow circle of vision.

I heard him say: 'I'm very fond of this painting, Ernst. Duntulm Castle, the home of the MacDonalds of the Isles. The dungeons of the castle were never empty, I'm told. Many a dark secret would be revealed if those walls could speak, and it amuses me, Ernst, to think that this painting hides a secret. See how easily it swings back.'

Dr Reuter laughed nervously. 'But of course,' he said, 'I might have known. There is a wall safe behind it.'

'Exactly,' said Major Cassell. 'And in the safe is – this.'

He came back into my line of vision and I saw him put down a small metal deed box on the desk. He tapped it with his forefinger.

'There is enough evidence in this little box to hang you,' he went on in the same menacing tone. 'It is all here.' Again his forefinger tapped the lid of the deed box. 'All the secrets of our organization. How you persuaded Ransome and Hunt to join us. And are you forgetting your wife? We found her in one of Hitler's concentration camps when you thought she was dead. We have looked after her well for you all these years. But she is in Moscow, remember, and it might be unpleasant for her if you were foolish enough not to join her there.' He pushed the box aside. 'No, no, my friend, you had better think again.'

Dr Reuter shifted uneasily and the chair creaked.

'But what about the boy?' he demanded. 'He has got to be . . . to be . . .'

Major Cassell laughed. It was a laugh that made my flesh creep. 'Don't be squeamish, Reuter,' he said lightly. 'We all know that the boy has got to be silenced.'

He lit a cigarette and glanced at his watch. Taking a long, pleasurable pull, he removed the cigarette from his mouth and rolled it slowly between his thumb and forefinger.

'By the time I have finished this cigarette,' he went on, 'Master Alasdair Cameron will have ceased to bother anyone.'

I did not stop to hear any more. I crept away from the door and fled across the hall. When I reached the outer door, I flung it open and ran out into the darkness of the night.

The wind buffeted me as I stumbled down the steps to the drive and the rain lashed my face, but I was barely conscious of the fury of the storm. The Major's words were still ringing in my ears as I raced down the drive to the iron gates of the Lodge.

I wasted a full minute struggling to open the gates before I realized that they were locked. As I started to climb them the headlights of a car flashed on, cutting through the darkness and bathing every leaf and flower of the ornamental iron-work in brilliant light. I had one foot on top of the gates, and I glanced back as I drew the other foot up. The light dazzled me and in reaching forward to balance myself, I slipped and crashed down heavily on the road.

It was the fall that saved me. Even as I fell I heard the whine of a bullet passing over my head and the loud report of a rifle. I had torn the skin from my hands on the loose gravel of the road, but I hardly felt the pain. Crouching low, I dashed across the road out of the beam of the headlights and into the enveloping blackness of the night.

I glanced over my shoulder at the lighted windows of the Lodge, to get my bearings, and made off in a wide sweep in the direction of the main road. I intended to get well away from the Lodge before cutting back across the moor towards Achmore. I heard a man's voice shouting orders, and caught the words: 'To the back . . .' and then his voice was lost in the rising scream of the gale.

The wind was at my back and I ran like one possessed, stumbling over the uneven ground, falling and picking myself up again almost in the one movement. At any moment I expected to hear my pursuers pounding along behind me and the thought gave me wings. I splashed through pools and across old peat cuttings, and once I blundered into a peat stack; but I carried on doggedly. I had left my raincoat in the Lodge and I was soaked to the skin by the driving rain, but I was thankful that the wind was behind me.

When I was well away from the Lodge, I turned in the direction of Achmore. Once I had crossed the burn and the dike at the foot of the crofts, I would make for Hector MacLeod's house. Not even Major Cassell and his gang could overcome the men of Achmore.

I was running with my head down, trying to escape the worst of the driving wind and rain, and I must have gone twenty or thirty yards before I saw the lights. They were facing me across the moor, evenly spaced, in a wide arc. I stopped short, thinking with a chill of horror of all the stories I had heard of ghostly lights on the moor at night; of men who had disappeared without trace, and cattle that had vanished overnight.

The lights were moving towards me, flashing on and off. Slowly it dawned on me that what I was seeing was no ghostly vision, but the beams from five torches. So that was why I had not been followed! The Major's men must have left the Lodge by the door behind the garage and formed a cordon to prevent me breaking through to Achmore. Now they were slowly combing the moor for me, and I would be forced back against the cliffs from which there was no escape.

I watched the flashing torches coming closer and heard the shouts of the men calling to one another and I turned on my heel and ran blindly across the moor. I stumbled and almost fell in the drain by the side of the main road, then I was across the road and running madly on. In a little while I would reach the cliffs and I could retreat no farther. Partly from exhaustion, and partly from a feeling of utter hopelessness I stopped running and dropped into the wet heather. I lay on my stomach, chilled and shivering, watching the line of torches advancing slowly.

Every so often the line would halt and turn back to beat the ground more thoroughly. Once I heard the man in the centre of the line call out excitedly, and the two men on either side of him raced across to join him. I could see the light from their torches jogging up and down as they stumbled over the rough ground, little knowing that it was a false alarm and I was lying in the heather watching them. After a while, the lights thinned out again and the line moved forward once more.

It was only a matter of time before I was caught. There was no hope of hiding in the heather; they were beating the ground too thoroughly for that. Once they spotted me I was doomed. They would close in on me in an instant, and when I was captured there could be no hope of escaping a second time. Major Cassell's words were still fresh in my mind, and I knew I could expect no mercy.

The two men at either end of the arc were almost level with me. If I attempted to run to the north or south they could cut me off easily. I saw the bright beam of the torch at the southern end of the line sweep across the road. The man there must have taken up a position above the gorge. Whichever way I turned I was trapped. All I could do to delay the end was to retreat to the cliffs.

I scrambled to my feet and stumbled away from the advancing lights, my sodden trousers chafing my legs as I ran. I never saw the cart in the darkness and I blundered into it, barking my shin badly. I groped my way round the huge wooden wheel, and came up against the shadowy outline of a tinker's tent. I stood still, swaying on my feet, not knowing which way to turn. Somebody came up silently behind me and gripped my arm. I was too tired to struggle and I let him push me round the side of the tent.

My captor bent down and drew the tent flap aside, but his grip on my arm never relaxed. There was a lantern inside the tent, and in the dim light shining out of the open flap I could see that I was held by an old tinker. He was dressed in rags and his face was like an old brown nut. He called softly in Gaelic and a young man came out of the tent.

My wits started to function again, and I gasped: 'You've got to help me. They'll kill me if they catch me.'

The old man said: 'We want no trouble, boy. There is trouble enough for the likes of us without interfering with folk from the Lodge.'

So they had heard the shot, and doubtless seen the lights of the searchers on the Moor. My hopes sank.

'You had best be off,' said the young man. 'We want no part in this.'

I glanced around desperately and saw the ring of lights drawing steadily nearer. They must have reached the main road and in a few minutes they would be on me.

'But you've got to help me,' I cried.

A gust of wind shook the tent and the rain hammered incessantly on the taut canvas.

'Be off with you,' growled the young man.

The lights had crossed the main road and were coming relentlessly towards us. Perhaps it was the wave of fear that gripped me, prompting some hidden corner of my memory into action, or it may have been the freshly caught salmon I saw, half hidden under a sack inside the tent, that reminded me of the fat man who had once been a poacher and was a friend of the tinkers.

Whatever it was, I know I gasped: 'Jamie Finlayson sent me.'

Nobody spoke. Then a hand pushed me into the tent and I fell sprawling across a heap of blankets. The young man crossed swiftly to the lantern and blew it out, and I heard the wet canvas of the flap slap back into place as he left the tent.

Chapter 22

I LAY across the rough blankets listening to the drumming of the rain on the tent. My immediate reaction was one of relief that I was no longer exposed to the fury of the storm. I was too dazed to appreciate the extent of my good fortune. All I wanted to do was to lie still and rest. The chase across the moor had exhausted me, numbing my mind as well as my body. I could hardly realize that I had succeeded, at least for the time being, in eluding my pursuers.

Somewhere outside, a man cried out. I was on my feet in an instant, poised ready for flight, my tiredness forgotten. But flight was impossible. I was trapped within the narrow confines of the tent; what had been an eagerly sought shelter was now a cage. Sick at heart, I crouched down, straining my ears to catch every sound.

A sudden furious gust of wind shook the flimsy walls of the tent, and the framework rocked and creaked under the onslaught. For one dreadful moment I thought it was about to succumb to the force of the wind and leave me exposed and defenceless. Then the gust subsided and there was only the steady drumming of the rain against the taut canvas.

I heard several voices all talking at once, then a cold, commanding voice that I knew only too well, cut in and silenced the others. It was Major Cassell.

'What are you doing out at this time of night?' he demanded curtly.

It was the young tinker who replied, although I hardly recognized his voice. There was nothing belligerent about him now; indeed, his voice had such a whining, grovelling note that the little confidence I had left, vanished at the sound of it. I waited tensely for him to betray me.

'What are you doing out at this time of night?' repeated the Major, in an even sharper tone.

'We heard the shot, sir,' whined the tinker, 'and saw the lights on the moor and we were after wondering what could be the cause o' it.'

'There was no shot,' snapped the Major. 'My car back-fired. Understand?'

'Your car back-fired, sir,' he repeated obediently.

'Don't try to bluff me,' said Major Cassell angrily. 'You chaps are never inside at night; it's in the daytime you take your rest. I know you too well. At night you're prowling around to see what you can lift. It's the police for you, if you're not careful. Understand? And the old man as well.'

I could hear the whining note of complaint in the tinker's voice, although I could not make out the words.

The Major cut him short, and said curtly: 'Enough of that. I want to know if you have seen a boy running this way. I am responsible for him. He is mentally unbalanced. Understand? Not right in the head. Thinks everybody is going to harm him. It's not the first time he has run away, but I am worried about him. If he is left out on a night like this he will get his death of cold. If you can lead me to him, I'll not report you to the police this time.'

Nobody spoke for what seemed an eternity.

'Well,' said Major Cassell impatiently, 'have you seen the boy? Come on, man, there's a five-pound note for you if you help me.'

'Aye, I've seen him,' admitted the tinker.

Once more there was an ominous silence. I could picture the tinker silently pocketing the five-pound note and pointing to the tent. Still nobody spoke. There was no sound save the beating of the rain on the canvas and the rising shriek of the wind as it swept down from the hill, flung itself against the tent, and subsided angrily into a low sough, gathering strength for the next gust. It would have been a relief to my overwrought nerves if I had shouted: 'I'm here,' and put an end to the terrible suspense of my own free will. Somehow or other I controlled myself and waited tensely.

'Well, where is he?' barked the Major. 'Speak up, man.'

At least he had been unwilling to give me up, I thought, and no poor tinker could be expected to withstand the lure of a five-pound note coupled with the threat of the police. Whatever happened, it was better than waiting like this, anticipating each word as if it were the stroke of an executioner's sword. I crouched back against the wall of the tent, expecting the flap to be thrown open at any moment and the Major's men to rush in and seize me.

'I didn't want to be disappointing you, sir,' whined the tinker. 'It was myself tried to stop the boy, but he was away before I could get a right grip on him. Running like a hare he was and heading straight for the cliff. Never a chance would he have with his head down and the night so black. Aye, and bad off-shore currents too. Maybe the poor boy's body will never be washed up.'

'You are sure he went over the cliff?' queried the Major eagerly, and I noticed that he could not keep the relief out of his voice.

'Certain sure, sir,' assented the tinker. 'If I could have got a right grip on him I might have held him, but how was I to know that the poor truaghan would make for the cliff?'

Major Cassell cleared his throat. 'I'm sure you did your best, my man,' he said. 'Here. Take this.'

'Thank you, sir,' said the tinker. 'Thank you.'

The Major said something that I didn't catch and then there was silence again with only the monotonous drumming of the rain on the tent. I shivered suddenly and picked up one of the blankets and wrapped it around my legs, and sat down to wait.

I must have dozed off to sleep for when I looked up suddenly with a start the young tinker was standing in the middle of the tent with a lighted match in his hand. He lit the lamp and blew out the match and stood looking down at a silver coin in his hand. He thrust it into his pocket.

'Gentry,' he growled, making the word sound like an oath, and spat on the floor.

'Have they gone?' I asked nervously, hardly able to believe that he had stood by me.

'Aye, the most o' them,' he answered. 'But a couple of them are searching around the edge o' the cliff and another one is prowling about below the crofts at Achmore.' He looked at me thoughtfully, and said slowly: 'They must want you terrible bad, boy.'

Looking up at his dark, unshaven face I wondered how far I could trust him, and I was instantly ashamed of the thought. Had he not sheltered me from Major Cassell's men, and rejected a handsome reward, all on the strength of the name of Jamie Finlayson? But I knew it was one thing for a tinker to help the friend of a fellow poacher and quite another for him to come to the aid of the law. He would want nothing to do with the police, so I would have to be careful I didn't scare him off. If only I had Duncan Mor to guide me.

'Do you know Duncan Mor MacDonald of Mealt?' I said suddenly.

'Aye, I know the big fellow,' he said guardedly.

'He has taken to the hills,' I said. 'The police are after him.'

The tinker showed no surprise.

'I know that,' he said calmly, 'and many the long day will they spend looking for him. There is not a better man on the hill in all the western world than Duncan Mor. It is me that knows that, and it is the polis will be knowing it before they are done with the big fellow.'

There could be no doubt where his sympathy lay, so I said eagerly: 'I've got to see Duncan Mor before tomorrow night. I ...'

I stopped short. The tent flap was pulled aside and I saw the old tinker's face framed in the opening. He hissed something in Gaelic, then withdrew again, and the wet flap slapped back across the opening.

'The men are coming back from the cliff,' said the young tinker softly.

He pushed me into the far corner of the tent, and I lay flat on the grass while he threw some blankets over me.

'Be quiet,' he whispered. 'You are safe enough.'

Almost at once my throat started to tickle and I wanted to cough. I could feel the cough welling up inside me, but I fought it back and tried to breathe slowly through my nose. To make matters worse, my back started to itch, and I was sure that some insect was crawling up my leg. I clenched my fists until the nails dug into the palms of my hands, and willed myself to lie still when every fibre of my body was longing for movement.

Suddenly the blanket was yanked away from my head and shoulders. I let out a cry of surprise and sprang to my feet, but it was only the young tinker.

'They are away now,' he said quietly, 'but there is still a man on watch below Achmore and others forby for all I know. It is yourself is here for the night, boy, and maybe longer or the name of my father's son is not Seumas Stewart.'

'But I must see Duncan Mor,' I protested. 'You don't understand. It's important. I've got to see him. You don't understand, I tell you.'

'I understand well enough,' he retorted. 'You would never make the hill at all on a night like this, and what happens if you walk into the men from the Lodge? Fine they would know who had hidden you, and they would be after telling the Major. Aye, the Major with the eyes on him as cold as a hungry cat. No, no, boy, when you leave this tent it is inside a bedroll with you and into the bottom of the cart. That is all there is about it.

'But I've got to see Duncan Mor,' I cried wildly, and in my anxiety I stepped forward and clutched his ragged jacket.

He looked at me curiously, and said slowly: 'Many a thing I would do for a friend of Jamie Finlayson, but if you leave this tent, and the Major's men get you, myself and the old man are done for. We are poor folk of the road and hard enough is the life for us without the Major putting the law on us.'

I knew well enough that he was speaking the truth, but all I could do was to repeat doggedly: 'I've got to see Duncan Mor.'

The tinker took my hand from his jacket and said quietly: 'If the big fellow is to be found, it is myself will take a message to him, but time enough for that in daylight.' I made to speak, but he went on quickly: 'You are blue with the cold, boy, and shaking like a leaf. Off with those clothes and dry yourself.'

I had not realized how chilled I had become. My legs were numb and I could hardly stop my teeth chattering. I stripped off my clothes obediently, and the tinker handed me a tattered towel and I rubbed my wet body until the skin tingled and glowed.

There was an old iron stove in the centre of the tent with a crooked chimney protruding through the domed roof, and the tinker tied a string from the chimney to one of the hazel ribs of the tent and hung my wet clothes over it. Then he spread some dry hay on the ground and folded four blankets in such a way that they formed a rough sleeping bag and laid them on top of the hay.

I wriggled down between the rough blankets, certain that I would never sleep again until I had seen Duncan Mor and told him all I knew. I can remember seeing the tinker break a peat across his knee and drop it into the stove, then my eyes seemed to close of their own volition. I must have fallen asleep instantly.

I woke up once during the night and I started up and looked around fearfully, wondering where I was. The lamp was still burning and the old tinker was crouched down beside the tent flap, puffing away at a short clay pipe. There was something reassuring about his watchful figure and I turned on my side and closed my eyes again. In the morning Seumas Stewart would take a message to Duncan Mor and all would be well. But how was he to find him in all that rock-girt waste of hill country? With a sob of relief, I recalled the cave in the hill hidden by the two rowan trees. Duncan Mor was sure to be lying up in the old still. With that comforting thought in my mind, I fell into a deep, untroubled sleep.

When I awoke the flap was open and the sunlight was streaming into the tent. The gale must have spent itself during the night for the air was still. I sat up, rubbing my eyes and yawning. The old man was standing over a pot on the stove. Without a word he gathered my clothes from the makeshift line and tossed them over to me. They were dry and warm and I dressed quickly.

I was about to go out of the tent when the old man seized me by the shoulder and dragged me back.

'Stay. Stay,' he said excitedly. 'Wait for Seumas. Understand?'

His English was halting and difficult to make out, but there was no mistaking the urgency of his tone. I nodded, but he did not return to the stove until I had gone back to my bed and sat down on the blankets.

I never heard the approach of the young tinker. His shadow fell across the opening and when I looked up he was standing inside the tent. He was wearing a pair of badly fitting, thin-soled shoes, the uppers of which were split and broken, but he moved as quickly and surely as a cat. His jacket hung about his shoulders in tattered shreds and his trousers had been patched and repatched until it was hard to trace the pattern of the original cloth. Perched on the back of his head, at a jaunty angle, was an old tweed cap, and his black curly hair sprouted out from under it in all directions. His face was lean and watchful, and he reminded me of some wild animal, bold in its own fashion, but poised ready for instant flight.

'Time for food, boy,' he said, 'and then we will be after seeing about the big fellow on the hill.'

I hadn't thought to look at my watch and when I did so I saw that both hands pointed to twelve o'clock. A flood of remonstrances rose to my lips, but I bottled them down. It was my own fault that I had slept so late, and I could not deny the tinker his meal before he took the long tramp to the hill.

We ate fresh salmon with our fingers and thick slices of bread and butter and washed it all down with strong sweet tea. Nobody spoke, and I was glad of the silence because I was so hungry I did not want to waste time on words when I could be eating.

When we had finished, Seumas Stewart eyed me contemplatively.

'What do you want me to say to the big fellow?' he asked.

'Tell him to listen to the radio,' I said slowly. 'Tell him a special announcement is being broadcast every two hours. Tell him it was a submarine we heard that Saturday night in the Sound. Tell him Major Cassell is trying to get Dr Reuter away from Skye tonight.'

The tinker repeated the words over and over again, until he had memorized them, and I told him to search the hill to the south of Loch Cuithir, for I was sure that Duncan Mor would not be far from the old still.

'I will need to head south by Creag Langall,' he said, 'or they will be after seeing me from the Lodge. It will be night before I am back, but if Duncan Mor is on the hill I will find him.'

He spoke rapidly to his father in Gaelic and the old man looked at me and nodded several times and said something that brought a smile to the young tinker's face.

'My father says if you try to leave the tent he will knock you senseless,' he said.

I looked at the old man and he nodded vigorously and shook his fist at me. When I turned to speak to Seumas Stewart he was on his way out of the tent.

That day in the tinker's tent was the longest day I have ever known. The old man sat outside the open tent flap, smoking his short clay pipe, as motionless as a figure carved in bronze. From time to time he took his pipe from his mouth and spat, but that was the only movement he ever made. In the afternoon he made tea and we ate some cheese sandwiches and more salmon, then he took up his position outside the tent again. Once I thought he had fallen asleep, but when I moved across to the tent-flap his head jerked round and he motioned me back to my corner.

I thought that the hours would never pass and then, when the light faded inside the tent and it was dusk, the tempo changed. It was as if the laggard hours had slipped smoothly into step and were marching away at a rapidly quickening pace. My spirits sank. Soon it would be midnight, and at midnight Dr Reuter was due to be whisked away from Skye.

It was ten-thirty by my watch, and the old man had lit the lamp and was sitting down by the stove, when Seumas Stewart slipped into the tent in his silent, cat-like way. He closed the flap behind him and stood with his back to it.

I sprang to my feet.

'Well, did you find him?' I cried.

'Aye, I found him right enough,' he said, 'after I had near tramped my feet off circling the hill above Loch Cuithir.'

'Where was he?' I asked.

Seumas Stewart took a crumpled cigarette end from his pocket and lit it. He puffed at it for a while in silence, then said: 'Duncan Mor was coming over Bealach na Leacaich with all the men of the Long Glen behind him and not a man but was carrying a gun of some sort and himself with a face like thunder.

'"Well now," said I, "is it rabbits you are after, Duncan Mor?" "No, not rabbits, Seumas," said he, "but that weasel in the Lodge, and I will be after dragging the guts from him before this night is done." He had been hearing you were drowned, and the rage on him was something terrible. I told him you were well and safe enough in the tent.'

'Did you give him the message?' I asked, unable to contain myself any longer.

'Aye, I gave him the message,' he went on, 'and he said to me: "Tell Alasdair Beag I have heard the wireless already and this night it is the Major himself will be feeling the lash of the old law."'

'Was that all he said?' I wanted to know, unable to conceal

my disappointment at Duncan Mor's lack of appreciation for what I had done.

'No, there was more than that,' answered the young tinker, and I thought he looked at me with a new respect in his eyes. 'Duncan Mor took my arm in such a grip that I thought he would crush the muscle to jelly altogether, and he said: "I am not the man to be forgetting what you have done for me, Seumas Stewart, but your work is not yet finished this day. You will go back to your tent and you will keep Alasdair Beag there until the work of the night is done. He is a thrawn beggar and you will need to be firm with him, but you will watch over him, Seumas Stewart, or my ghost will stalk you through all eternity."'

'But where is he?' I cried. 'I must see him.'

'Duncan Mor and all the men of the Long Glen met the men of Achmore above Dun Crianan,' said the tinker. 'They made for the gorge. There was a man on watch there, but before the poor truaghan could get to his feet Duncan Mor had nearly choked the life out of him. They have smashed the coble and the dinghy and Ruairidh the Leodhasach from the Long Glen has planted something on the bridge. Then they melted away behind the rocks and into the bracken. Not a man would you see there but the gorge is alive with them, and I am thinking there is dark work on hand this night.'

I dived for the opening, but Seumas Stewart was too quick for me. He seized me around the waist and dragged me back into the tent.

'Would you have me killed?' he demanded. 'The big fellow will tear me apart – well I know it – if I let you away.'

'I don't care, I've got . . .'

My words were cut short by a low, muffled explosion, followed by a volley of shots. I saw the clay pipe slip from the old man's mouth to the ground, but he made no attempt to stoop and pick it up. All three of us stood looking at one another. A second volley of shots rang out. As Seumas Stewart ran to the door of the tent, I was hard on his heels.

Chapter 23

AFTER the noise of the explosion and the firing, there was something almost sinister about the silence that followed, as if it covered even darker deeds. Seumas Stewart's strong brown fingers closed around my arm, and we stood side by side waiting tensely. Somewhere in the distance a dog started to bark, and I could hear the lowing of a cow, but these friendly, familiar sounds seemed only to heighten the feeling of tension.

Then the firing started again, and I felt the young tinker's grip tighten on my arm. There was the harsh, ugly chatter of what sounded to me like a machine-gun, interspersed with sporadic bursts of rifle fire. Silence again, deep and impenetrable, then the sound of a dog howling. Strange how the howl of a dog at night could chill the blood more than the death-dealing chatter of a gun. I shivered.

'Eighteen years I have been on the road in Skye,' said Seumas Stewart softly, 'and never did I hear the like o' this. Think you, Alasdair Beag, of the tales that will be told of this night's work. When I am an old man they will be talking of it still, from Sleat to Trotternish. And what am I to say ? That I spent the night in my tent like an old cailleach ? Seall, Alasdair, it would shame my children's children. Come you, Duncan Mor or no Duncan Mor, we will take a look at the gorge this night.'

He set off at a swift trot, still holding me firmly by the arm. The old tinker called after us, and Seumas shouted something to him in Gaelic, but we were almost out of earshot when the old man flung back an angry rejoinder.

We trotted along the winding path that led beyond the disused quarry to the gorge. There was a thin moon overhead, partly obscured by rainclouds, and a gentle smirr of rain was drifting down. I would have stumbled and fallen many times had it not been for Seumas Stewart's supporting grip on my arm. The tinker was as nimble and sure-footed as a goat.

'No tricks now,' panted Seumas, as we neared the approach to the gorge. 'We stick together, mind. Duncan Mor Mac-Donald would have me in pieces if anything happened to you tonight, a'bhalaich.'

I was about to reply when two men suddenly sprang to their feet from the shelter of the thick bracken below the track. Something hard jabbed into my ribs, and I instinctively raised my hand as a bright light flashed into my eyes, dazzling me.

'Well, well, Alasdair Beag,' cried a familiar voice, 'so it is yourself eh? A good job for you, I'm thinking, that the big fellow is away down the gorge.'

The torch was switched off and I stood there blinking hard. It was some time before I recognized the sturdy figure of Hector MacLeod. There was another man by his side, holding a rifle at the ready, and blocking the path of Seumas Stewart. I had met him when I had been on the hill with Duncan Mor. His name was Norman Ross, and he came from the Long Glen.

'We heard the explosion,' I cried. 'What's happening?'

'Much has been happening this night,' returned Hector MacLeod soberly. 'The boys are after having broken into the county magazine in the quarry, and helped themselves to two sticks of gelignite and a length of fuse. Ruairidh the Leodhasach set a charge on the bridge. The same fellow can handle explosives. The charge was well timed, right enough. The bridge went up as Murdo Ruadh was leading the way across.' He paused and added grimly: 'That was the end o' the Red Fellow and three others forby.'

I heard the air being expelled from Seumas Stewart's lungs in a long, wondering whistle.

'There was some stramash, I can tell you,' went on Hector MacLeod. 'The rest of them dropped their guns and dived for the river. The boys shot down two of them before they got across, and Duncan Mor leapt a good fifteen feet and collared that black rogue o' a scientist. Here he is.'

He shone his torch into the bracken, and I started back when the light picked out the limp figure of Dr Reuter. The scientist was lying on his back, his hands spread out palms upwards. His face had a death-like pallor, and the blood was oozing out of a deep cut across his forehead.

'Is he dead?' I whispered.

'Never the fear o' it,' said Norman Ross. 'But I doubt it will be a while before he comes round. He was starting to ford the river when Duncan Mor landed on his back. I'm telling you that fellow has never taken such a shaking in all his days.'

He had hardly finished speaking before the ugly chatter of a quick-firing gun sounded from the depths of the gorge.

'That's no rifle,' declared Seumas Stewart.

'Yon's a Sten gun,' said Hector MacLeod. 'Three o' them got across the river to the bothy. They must have had a Sten gun hidden there, and there can be no shortage o' ammunition judging by the way they are using it.'

Seumas Stewart of the quick ears suddenly hissed a warning. He pushed me down into the bracken, at the same time flattening himself down beside me. Hector MacLeod and Norman Ross melted into the shadows. It was then that I heard the footsteps for the first time. They were heavy, dragging footsteps and they were coming slowly towards us.

'Co tha'n sud?' barked Norman Ross.

It was Roderick MacPherson of Achmore who answered.

'Thigibh an so,' he cried.

Norman Ross and Hector bounded to meet him, and Seumas Stewart and I scrambled to our feet and hurried to assist them. Hector flashed on his torch, and it was a grim sight that met our eyes. Roderick MacPherson, his clothes torn and his face streaked with sweat and dirt, was swaying on his feet with the long figure of Iain Ban MacDonald draped across his shoulder. It was only when Seumas and Hector grasped Iain Ban and lowered him to the ground, that I noticed the wound in

Roderick's leg. Norman Ross saw it, too. There was a deep gash in his left leg below the knee and the blood was still flowing freely.

But Roderick brushed us aside. 'Look you to Iain Ban,' he insisted. 'He is shot in the shoulder and has lost a deal of blood.'

'I'll be right enough,' muttered Iain Ban through clenched teeth, 'but sorry I am that I am not in at the finish.'

'You have done more than enough,' said Roderick Mac-Pherson. 'If . . .'

The rapid stutter of the Sten gun cut into his words, and he made as if to turn and head back to the gorge.

Norman Ross seized him by the shoulder.

'You are done, Roderick,' he exclaimed. 'That leg o' yours is laid open to the bone.'

Seumas Stewart came forward with his silent, cat-like tread and snatched the rifle from Norman's hands.

'Look to the boy, Tormod,' he called, 'or you will have Duncan Mor to answer to,' and so saying he made off for the gorge.

'Tinker or no, he is a cool fellow that one,' said Norman Ross.

Roderick MacPherson stretched out in the bracken alongside Iain Ban, and Hector and Norman and I squatted down on our heels facing them.

'Are they still holding out in the bothy?' asked Hector.

Roderick nodded. 'They have the Sten gun mounted in the window,' he said, 'and the walls of the bothy make a grand fort.'

'Right enough,' added Norman Ross. 'I believe those walls are every inch o' three foot thick, and solid stone forby.'

'It is some job,' sighed Hector. 'I doubt we will need to wait for the polis.'

'Not if Duncan Mor can help it,' retorted Roderick. 'The big fellow is after crawling round to the back o' the bothy. He has soaked rags in petrol, and if he can come up on them unawares, he is for firing the roof o' the bothy and smoking them out.'

As Roderick spoke, we heard the steady fusillade of shots and the answering chatter of the Sten gun.

'The boys are doing their best to cover him,' went on Roderick, 'but if the Major's men get a sight of him it is the end o' the big fellow.'

None of us spoke, and I suppose we were all thinking the same thing. What if Duncan Mor was seen and shot down? It was Norman who first saw the glow in the sky, and then we all saw the slowly ascending column of thick black smoke.

'He has done it!' cried Hector. 'That is the tarred felt going up.'

'Aye, they are finished once they are forced out of the bothy,' said Roderick grimly.

As if in confirmation of his words, all we could hear was some desultory rifle fire. The Sten gun was silent.

'Well, well,' exclaimed Hector, 'it has been some night, right enough. Mind you, I can hardly believe that the Major is at the back o' this lot. Such a nice, friendly fellow, and him so keen on the bird-watching.'

'I'm thinking the police will need an awful lot o' proof,' added Norman Ross.

'But the proof is in the Lodge,' I cried excitedly. 'It's in the safe, in the Major's study.'

I thought of the metal deed box I had seen him take out of the wall safe, and his words to Dr Reuter, and I turned to go. I would see to it that the proof was at hand, when the police came.

'Where are you away to, Alasdair?' Hector MacLeod called sharply.

'To the Lodge,' I answered over my shoulder, 'to get the proof.'

'Wait you,' cried Hector. 'Duncan Mor said . . .'

'Duncan Mor will understand,' I called back. 'He will need to have proof for the police.'

Hector shouted something after me, but I didn't hear what he said.

I ran all the way to the Lodge, straight up the gravelled drive from the main road. The front door stood wide open, as they had doubtless left it in their haste to get to the shore, and the dim hall light was burning. I crossed the hall quickly and hurried up the passage to the Major's study. The door was slightly ajar and the light streamed out into the passage. I smiled to myself, visualizing the hurried departure the Major had made, leaving doors open and not even stopping to switch off the lights. Still smiling to myself, I opened the door and walked into the study.

'Good evening, Master Cameron,' said Major Cassell. He too was smiling, but it was not a pleasant smile. 'Come in and close the door,' he went on. 'I hope you won't try anything foolish like trying to run for it, or I'm afraid I should have to shoot you.'

He leaned back in his desk chair, and it was then that I saw the black revolver in his right hand. I closed the door slowly, backing against it to make it shut, my eyes never leaving the gun in his hand.

'Come over here and sit down,' he commanded, indicating a straight-backed chair in front of the desk.

I moved across to it like a sleep walker, my legs moving stiffly and my hands held a little way in front of me, as if to ward off any movement of the gun.

'It is lucky for me that you never stop to think, Master Alasdair,' the Major went on, in the same low, conversational tone. 'But this time there is no fool to leave a key in the lock. This time, my friend, you have me to deal with.'

'I thought you were at the shore,' I muttered. The words slipped out involuntarily. I suppose I must have been thinking aloud.

He felt for a cigarette with his left hand, and when he lifted the lid the cigarette box played the Christmas Carol, 'Silent Night'. The tune jangled through my head, and he must have read the expression on my face, because he said mockingly: 'All is calm; all is bright. Is it, Master Alasdair?'

Suddenly he snapped the lid shut, and lit the cigarette, all with his left hand. The revolver never wavered.

'So you thought I was at the shore,' he said slowly. 'No, my friend, I expected trouble tonight, and I stayed here. My doctors tell me that I have a weak heart. Too much excitement could kill me.' He laughed shortly. 'And I am afraid mine is a rather exciting life.'

Sitting there, a few feet away from him, I could hardly believe that I had once chatted and laughed with this man. The ready smile had vanished and his mouth was compressed in a hard, ruthless line. He no longer spoke in short, clipped sentences, and whilst his English had no trace of an accent, it was not the English of slurred consonants and long vowels so typical of an officer and gentleman.

He saw my eyes waver from his face to the door, and he said: 'I shouldn't try anything rash if I were you. You are not dealing with a soft English army officer. You are dealing with Colonel Zaborin, the Head of the Soviet espionage system in Western Europe.'

My obvious astonishment seemed to amuse him, and he continued: 'Do you not think I played my part well? Major Cassell, the stupid, good-natured army officer, who was silly enough to sit up all night bird-watching. It was a good joke, was it not? The fools were so busy laughing they never thought Major Cassell might be watching for something other than birds.

'I have worked well for Soviet Russia, Master Cameron. Reuter will be the third atomic scientist I have smuggled out of this country. The third! And there have been others – not scientists – but almost as valuable to us. But of course there is your famous Intelligence Service. What did they do about it?' He laughed harshly. 'Nothing. They were baffled.

'It is the simple schemes that succeed, my friend. Simple and well planned. My scientists walked into Euston Station carrying a brief-case. They were wearing a neat business suit, like dozens of other professional men, and they disappeared into a cloakroom. When they came out they were dressed as sportsmen, wearing heavy tweeds, homespun stockings, and studded shoes. A seat had been booked for them and their baggage was waiting on the rack. The baggage of a sportsman. Rods and guns and the like. A better disguise than a false beard, eh? And they journeyed to Skye. Ransome was the first of the scientists. Then Hunt, and now Reuter. Simple, eh? Just another visitor to Major Cassell for the shooting and fishing. A hospitable man, the Major.

'Then at midnight on a Saturday – always on a Saturday, Master Cameron, when all good Skyemen are indoors preparing for the ordeal of their Sabbath – my men were taken aboard a submarine bound for Murmansk. A precious cargo, eh, and all done so simply.'

I saw his fingers tighten around the butt of his revolver, and I stiffened back in the chair.

'But for you, my friend,' he said softly, 'I could have completed my mission here undetected. If Beaton had disposed of you as he was instructed, Reuter would not have needed an armed guard tonight. I heard the shots. They will have had to kill some poor fools of crofters, and not even I can explain that away.'

'When I last saw Dr Reuter,' I burst out triumphantly, 'he was lying flat on his back with two men standing guard over him.'

A vein in his forehead started to twitch, but he never raised his voice.

'So your friends have got Reuter, eh?' he said thoughtfully.

'Yes, and all the rest of your gang,' I said boldly.

'In that case I must thank you for providing me with a way out, Master Cameron,' he said smoothly. 'Your friends would like to shoot me, yes, but they will not shoot you. You and I will take a walk to the shore, and I don't think any obstacles will be placed in our way.'

'But . . .' I started, when there was a clattering of feet in the passage outside and the door was swung back violently on its hinges. Duncan Mor stood framed in the opening.

Looking at him with a glad smile of recognition, I was happy that I was on his side. His great figure filled the doorway, and what reassurance I found in his imposing bulk. He must have run all the way from the shore, but his breath came evenly enough despite the quick rise and fall of his chest. He was soaked to the waist, and his trousers clung wetly to his legs. His shirt was stained red with blood, and I saw that he had a long, jagged cut across his cheek. In his right hand he carried a rifle.

I suppose it took me only a fraction of a second to take in these details, and at the same time the Russian snapped: 'Drop that gun, or the boy dies.'

I looked into the muzzle of his revolver and saw that his finger had tightened around the trigger, and I gazed at that crooked index finger like one hypnotized. There was a dull thud as Duncan Mor let his rifle slip to the floor, and only then did I manage to tear my eyes away from the unwavering barrel of the revolver in the Russian's hand.

'Kick that rifle away,' he ordered, 'and then get back against the wall.'

Duncan Mor kicked the rifle across the room and backed slowly to the wall. He met my eyes and showed his white teeth in a reassuring smile.

'Well, Alasdair Beag, we managed it right enough,' he said calmly. 'They are finished, the lot of them, but I only wish I could have got my hands on the Red Fellow before the bridge went up.'

'Not finished,' corrected the Colonel grimly. 'Not all of them. You have forgotten me.'

'Not at all,' retorted Duncan Mor contemptuously. 'You are finished along wi' the rest of your crowd. You'll never blast your way out wi' that wee pea-shooter in your fist.'

'I think I will,' said the Russian evenly. 'I took good care to prepare for all eventualities. I have been in touch with the

Commander of the submarine that was to pick up Reuter, and she will lie out in the Sound until two a.m.' He glanced swiftly at his watch. 'It is now ten past one. We have plenty of time, my friends.'

'Time for what?' asked Duncan Mor grimly.

'Time for us to get to the shore and for you to row me out to the submarine,' said the Russian calmly.

Duncan Mor threw back his head and laughed his great, booming laugh, and I stiffened in my chair, appalled by the incongruity of the scene. The Russian was crouched forward tensely, the revolver clenched tightly in his fist, and I was sitting bolt upright in the straight-backed chair, dazed with fright, whilst Duncan Mor was shaking with laughter, his head thrown back and his hands on his hips, in a relaxed, almost careless attitude.

I could not understand the reason for it until I saw a dull flush spreading over the Russian's face, and the nervous twitching of his mouth. Without a weapon in his hand Duncan Mor had succeeded in shaking Colonel Zaborin's confidence.

'Perhaps you will laugh some more if I squeeze the trigger and put a bullet through the boy,' he rasped. 'Enough of this foolery, MacDonald. I have no time to waste. You will lead the way to the bay. Master Cameron will be a few yards behind you and I shall be directly behind him – with this revolver in his back. One false move on your part and the boy dies.'

'Good enough,' said Duncan Mor soberly. 'But the boy stays on the shore. Myself will row you out to the submarine.'

The Russian laughed. It was an unpleasant laugh and it revealed his thoughts more eloquently than words.

'The boy goes with us,' he stated.

'And what guarantee have I got that he won't be shot the minute you board the submarine?' demanded Duncan Mor.

'You have no guarantee, and you are in no position to ask for one,' said the Russian flatly. 'My actions will be in accordance with my duty to the Soviet State.'

'And if I refuse?'

'If you refuse – and I will give you five minutes to decide if you want to condemn the boy to death – I will pull the trigger. Master Cameron is about seven feet away from me, and this pea-shooter as you call it, is a very effective weapon.'

'I know your kind, Cassell,' barked Duncan Mor. 'There would be no coming back for either of us, if we stepped into that coble.'

'The choice is yours,' said the Russian shortly. 'You have four minutes.'

'You could shoot the boy, right enough,' went on Duncan Mor, in a quieter tone, 'and maybe you could shoot me, too. But you haven't a chance of getting away.'

'I know how to die,' said the Russian curtly. 'But at least I would have the satisfaction of disposing of a bungling idiot who has ruined my plans,' and he directed a look at me of such concentrated venom that I felt the goose-pimples rising on my flesh.

I thought I had been afraid before, but at that moment, for the first time, I knew the meaning of real fear. Colonel Zaborin would shoot me down like a dog, and enjoy doing it. There was no mercy in those cold, unblinking eyes.

'But what if twenty odd men, all armed, came bursting into the Lodge?' persisted Duncan Mor. 'You couldn't kill the lot o' them; you would be dead meat before you could squeeze that trigger a couple o' times.'

'Why do you think Communism is on the march all over the world?' said the Russian fiercely. 'It is because it is greater than the life of any one of us. We Russians would never let an idiot of a boy stand in our way, but you would. If any attempt is made to take me, the boy goes first. But you would be afraid to sacrifice him. That is why you British and the Americans are doomed. You place too high a value on worthless skins.' He shot a quick glance at his watch. 'Two minutes.'

'Before we go I would like to know one thing,' said Duncan Mor easily. As he spoke he took several swift paces across the room until the Russian halted him with a menacing jerk of the revolver. 'Tell me, was it yourself had that money put in my house for the police to find, or was it that red rogue of a Murdo Beaton?'

'Beaton placed the money there on my orders,' said the Russian coldly.

'Do you know,' said Duncan Mor, inching forward, 'it was the first time in all my life I was ever accused o' lifting as much as a penny piece?'

'I am not interested in your personal history,' returned the Russian.

As he glanced again at his watch, I saw Duncan Mor take another quick step forward.

'One minute.' The Russian's voice was flat, completely emotionless.

'I swore I would break in two the man who did that to me,' went on Duncan Mor, and I noticed the beads of perspiration on his upper lip. 'I am a man of my word, Cassell, whatever.'

I thought I heard voices in the distance, but neither of them seemed to have heard anything. The muzzle of the Russian's revolver still pointed unwaveringly at my chest, but his eyes were riveted on Duncan Mor's face. As for Duncan Mor, he was standing poised on the balls of his feet, leaning slightly forward from the hips. He glanced at me and smiled, and raised his right hand to his head and let it fall again to his side. I thought he was brushing back a lock of hair, but it was also the gesture he always made whenever we parted.

Colonel Zaborin drew a deep breath.

'You have got exactly thirty seconds,' he said, in the same even, controlled voice.

I was paralysed with fear. It gripped my stomach so that I was almost physically sick, and my tongue felt like a dry rag in my mouth.

'Thirty seconds is it?' said Duncan Mor, smiling still. 'Well, well, many a better man than me had less.'

I don't quite know how it happened, but Duncan Mor launched himself forward in one swift leap, and even as he started to spring, his long right arm reached out and grasped the back of my chair, upending it. I was catapulted out of the chair across the room. As I fell, I felt the hot blast of the revolver and was almost deafened by the report.

I struck my head on the floor, half stunning myself, but I tried to struggle back to my feet. As I raised my head, I saw that Duncan Mor's broad back was between me and the Russian. Then the revolver spoke again and the room was full of the acrid smell of cordite. The shot must have caught Duncan Mor in the chest, for he half spun round and seemed to crumple at the knees. His hands were at his sides and I saw them clench and unclench, then he took a step forward and half sprang, half toppled over the desk. His hands sought Zaborin's throat and the Russian crashed to the floor beneath his weight.

I struggled to get to my feet, but my legs seemed to have turned to rubber. An ornate silver inkstand on the desk had been overturned in the struggle and the ink was dripping steadily on to the carpet, forming a little black pool. I watched it inanely, feeling the room swimming about me.

Once again I thought I heard voices, and somehow or other I raised myself to my feet. The voices seemed to draw nearer and I was sure that I heard footsteps clattering up the stone steps of the Lodge.

I took an unsteady step forward, wondering why the two figures behind the desk were so still. The floor seemed to come up to meet me, and something like a shooting star exploded before my eyes. I sank into a black pit and knew no more.

Chapter 24

WHEN I opened my eyes again I was lying on a sofa in a strange room. The light hurt my eyes and I shut them again quickly. My forehead seemed to be on fire and my head was throbbing madly. I felt weak and sick and dizzy.

I opened my eyes again, shielding them with my hand against the glare of the light, and looked around the room. Hector MacLeod was standing with his back to the fire. He crossed quickly to the sofa and bent over me.

I noticed with a shock of surprise that he seemed suddenly to have become a very old man. His face was grey with fatigue, anxious and careworn. For the first time I noticed the sagging pouches of skin under his eyes and the deep wrinkles that lined the corners of his mouth.

'How are you feeling, Alasdair Beag?' he asked, attempting a wan smile.

'Fine,' I said, 'except for my head. It's aching a bit.' I shivered. 'And it's awfully cold in here.'

Hector drew the blankets up to my chin. They had been draped over my legs and I had not even noticed they were there.

'The doctor from Staffin is here,' said Hector. 'He will be in to see you in a wee while.'

I tried to blink away the white spots that kept dancing in front of my eyes.

'Where am I?' I asked.

He looked at me thoughtfully. 'At the Lodge,' he said slowly.

The memory of all that had happened in the Major's study came flooding back, and I cried: 'Is Duncan Mor all right? And the Major? He didn't get away, did he?'

Hector MacLeod scrubbed at his bristly chin with his fist. It made a sound like sandpaper on wood.

'Duncan Mor saw to the Major,' he said at length. 'No, no, he didn't get away. When we got to him his neck was broken. He was dead, a bhalaich.'

'And is the doctor seeing to Duncan Mor?' I wanted to know.

Hector swallowed, and said in a strangled sort of voice: 'Aye, that's it. The doctor is seeing to Duncan Mor.' He patted my head awkwardly. 'Just you rest now, Alasdair Beag. It is rest you are needing.'

I watched him as he walked back to the fire, noticing once again how old and tired he looked. He took out his pipe and stared at it absently, then thrust it back into his pocket again. I shut my eyes thankfully and I believe I would have gone straight to sleep if the doctor had not come into the room.

The doctor was a tiny man with a face like a wrinkled gnome. He sat on the sofa and took my pulse and chatted about my father whom he said he had known well. He had a cheerful, easy manner, and he did not seem a bit like a doctor, not even when he started to ask the sort of questions doctors always ask.

Hector MacLeod accompanied him to the door and they stood there for a few moments, talking together in low tones, and the doctor handed something to Hector. Then they shook hands and the door closed behind the little man.

Hector came back to the sofa. 'We will get you home now, Alasdair,' he said. 'The doctor says you are suffering from shock and nervous exhaustion, but you will be right enough after a good long sleep.'

He helped me to my feet and wrapped the blankets around my shoulders. Once I was on my feet the sickness rose in my throat, and I was grateful for the strength of his supporting arm as we made our way to the door.

Calum Stewart was waiting outside the door, almost as if he had been on guard there, and he smiled at me and took my arm on the other side. As we crossed the hall I glanced down the passage and saw that the study door was closed.

'I'd like to see Duncan Mor before I go,' I said.

'Not now,' they said in unison, and hurried me out of the Lodge.

There were several cars parked outside the Lodge, but I was too tired to ask what they were doing there. The three of us climbed into the back of a black police car, and I noticed that the constable in the driving seat was the man who had tried to arrest Duncan Mor. He nodded to me as I got in, and I felt more than ever that I was sleep-walking; ever since I had entered the Lodge there had been an unreal, dream-like quality about the events of the night.

We drove to Achmore in silence. I was too weary to speak and I suppose the men were tired too.

When we got to the cottage I was surprised to see that Donald Alec MacDonald was sitting on the bench. Mairi and the cailleach were still up. Mairi's small face was pale and drawn and there were black shadows under her eyes. Hector asked her to heat a glass of milk and she went off obediently after an anxious glance in my direction. The cailleach was sitting hunched forward in the rough wooden chair, holding out her hands to the peat fire flames. Donald Alec MacDonald spoke to her in Gaelic, but if she heard him she made no reply. She seemed to be withdrawn within herself, lost in brooding thought.

When I had undressed and got into bed, Hector MacLeod came in with a glass of warm milk. He handed me two white tablets.

'The doctor says these will make you sleep,' he said, 'and there is to be no getting up in the morning until we have seen how you are.'

I swallowed the tablets and gulped down the warm milk. A dozen questions rose to my lips, but my body was desperate for sleep. I felt my eyelids drooping, but I forced them open again.

'Does Mairi know about . . . about her father?' I asked.

Hector MacLeod was tiptoeing carefully out of the room, and at the sound of my voice he swung round. He looked at me for a long time before he spoke, and I felt my eyelids start to droop again.

'Aye, she knows,' he said gravely, 'but she is wise beyond her years, that one.'

He swallowed, and I thought he was about to go on, but he turned on his heel and left the room abruptly.

I rolled over on my side, and I believe I was asleep before he reached the kitchen.

It was exactly two o'clock in the afternoon when I woke up. I lay on my back rubbing one foot against the other, drowsily content, letting wakefulness steal over me slowly like the wash of an incoming tide. It was the low murmur of voices in the kitchen that finally roused me. I leapt out of bed and threw on my clothes and dashed across the lobby to the kitchen.

I stopped short in the doorway. All the men of Achmore were crowded into that little room. Hector MacLeod, Calum Stewart, Lachlan MacLeod, Donald Alec MacDonald, Roderick MacPherson; they were all there. Even Iain Ban MacDonald, with his arm in a sling.

They all looked at me, but Hector MacLeod was the only one who spoke, and I noticed that his face still had a grey, drawn look.

'What are you doing out of your bed?' he demanded.

'But I feel fine,' I protested. 'I'm . . . I'm just hungry, that's all.'

Mairi was sitting in a corner and she rose without a word and made me a big bowl of brose. I sat in to the table and took the brose, and ate several girdle scones and drank two cups of strong sweet tea.

All the time I was eating, the men were strangely silent. They did not even speak to one another, and I thought at first that it was on account of Mairi having lost her father that they were so subdued.

When I had finished my breakfast, I looked round the ring of silent faces and the first faint, gnawing doubt crept into my mind.

'How is Duncan Mor ?' I asked.

Nobody spoke.

Hector MacLeod bit his lip. Calum Stewart looked down at his boots. Lachlan MacLeod, that dark, silent man, I didn't expect to speak, but even his eyes refused to meet mine, as if afraid of what I would see there. Donald Alec MacDonald stared fixedly at the ceiling. Roderick MacPherson chewed at his nails. Iain Ban MacDonald fingered the bandage of his sling.

The six men of Achmore were silent.

'How is Duncan Mor ?' I repeated shakily, the bitter gall of fear gripping my stomach and rising up in my throat.

Nobody spoke.

I looked from one to the other of these men I knew so well. Some of them, like Calum Stewart and Donald Alec MacDonald, were big men. All of them were strong men. Like Duncan Mor they worked with their hands, and like Duncan Mor they feared no man. They would stand their ground and look prince or pauper in the eye, but not one of them would look at me. I know now that every one of them would willingly have faced the Devil himself rather than answer that question.

It was left to Mairi to speak. She was standing at the other side of the table clearing away the dishes. She put down a cup and saucer with unsteady hands, and I saw her hands grip the edge of the table.

'Duncan Mor is dead, Alasdair,' she said, in a voice that was little more than a whisper.

'No,' I cried. And again: 'No.' And yet a third time, 'No.' I blinked back the hot tears that flooded to my eyes. 'He can't be. He' – and my voice broke – 'he just can't be.'

Hector MacLeod drew a long breath. 'Aye, Duncan Mor is

gone,' he said solemnly, 'and death comes to us all through time, but as long as any o' the one of us is left, then the big fellow will live, too. Do you think I can ever be looking across to Mealt without seeing him there? Do you think I will ever make a ceilidh again without hearing that great roar o' a laugh of his? No, no, Alasdair Beag, it is the ones who have nothing to leave but their money-bags who are dead and gone. Death can never finish the likes o' Duncan Mor, not in these parts.'

'But if only he had waited,' I said miserably. 'If only he had waited. Surely he must have known that you would all follow him to the Lodge?'

'Duncan Mor arranged it himself,' said Roderick Mac-Pherson. 'We were to wait by the main road while he went on alone. If he was not back in ten minutes we were to storm the Lodge.'

I sat quite still in my chair, not seeing any of the faces around me, only the Major's study and the gun pointing at my heart. Duncan Mor's voice came back to me. WHAT IF TWENTY ODD MEN CAME BURSTING INTO THE LODGE? I saw the tightening of the Major's lips and heard again his icy reply. IF ANY ATTEMPT IS MADE TO TAKE ME THE BOY GOES FIRST.

Somebody was speaking, and I jerked my head round. It was Iain Ban.

'You may be sure Duncan Mor knew what he was doing,' he said simply, 'and I am thinking he is well pleased with his work.'

'Aye,' assented Lachlan MacLeod, that man of few words. 'The big fellow was never the man to leave a job unfinished.'

Hector MacLeod rose to his feet. 'The funeral is the day after tomorrow,' he said. 'We will need to get the word round.'

Little did I know, at that moment, what 'the word' would bring.

I don't know how I would have got through the rest of that day had it not been for the constant coming and going of people. Mairi and the cailleach and I were never alone in the cottage for more than five minutes, and I had no time to think.

Willie The Post came in to say that they had had a telegram at the post office to say that my mother would be arriving that night. When she came he was going to take the cailleach back home with him, for his mother was her first cousin, and he thought she would be happier staying with them.

When I asked about Mairi, all he would say was: 'Ach, your mother will be wanting to look after the lassie,' and I suspected there was more in the telegram than he had revealed.

That afternoon the police came to see me. There was an inspector with a lot of silver braid on his cap, and a sergeant. The sergeant took notes while the inspector questioned me. It went on for a long time, dealing with everything that had happened from the day I arrived in Skye.

When they had finished questioning me, the inspector cleared his throat importantly, and said: 'Sir Reginald Gower, the Head of Military Intelligence, is coming to Portree tonight. He has expressed a wish to see you, so I shall send a car for you at ten tomorrow morning.' He fingered his collar, and added: 'I don't want you to discuss this with any of your crofter friends. Sir Reginald's visit is to be kept strictly private. The instructions from London are that there is to be no publicity.'

After that he seemed to thaw a little, and become less like a policeman. He shook hands with me and wished me luck, and smiling broadly told me not to forget the Police Force when I was old enough to leave school and be thinking of a career.

It was a little after seven o'clock when my mother arrived with Willie The Post carrying her luggage. Willie only stayed for a few minutes, then he left with the cailleach, leaving my mother, Mairi and I, together in the kitchen.

'How on earth did you get here so quickly?' I asked.

'Well, you seem to have become awfully important since you came to Skye,' answered my mother, smiling at me. 'I had a visit from Sir Reginald Gower, and he told me everything that had happened. I flew to Inverness with him and came on from there by car. Sir Reginald told me that he was looking forward to seeing you tomorrow. I'm . . . I'm awfully proud of you, Alasdair.'

I had expected my mother to be worried and anxious, and I had been preparing myself to answer her flood of questions, but none came. She turned to Mairi and before long the two of them were chatting together as if they had known one another always. It all seemed so topsy-turvy, my mother behaving as if a sudden flight to Inverness and a dash by car to Skye were an everyday occurrence, but then everything had been topsy-turvy during the past few days.

When I went to bed that night Mairi and my mother were still talking together. It had been arranged that Mairi would stay with us in London, and we were to leave immediately after Duncan Mor's funeral.

The Police Inspector was true to his word. Punctually at ten o'clock the next morning a police car arrived for me. I felt a little frightened as I sat alone in the back and was driven into Portree. The car stopped outside a hotel overlooking the bay, and the constable who was driving went in and spoke to the manager.

The manager escorted me upstairs and knocked softly on a door at the end of a long corridor. When a voice called 'Come in,' he stood aside to let me enter.

As I stepped forward, I heard the door click quietly shut behind me, and I walked slowly across the room. A man was sitting in a deep armchair with his back to me. There was a coffee table in front of the chair and he pushed it aside and sprang to his feet. In two quick strides he had reached me and shaken me warmly by the hand. The first thing that occurred to me was that he looked more like a crofter than a peer of the realm. Perhaps it was his open, sun-tanned face, or it may have been due to the fact that most of the crofters I knew had the natural, easy dignity that one somehow associates with titles. At any rate, I liked him on sight.

He was not a big man; in fact, he was rather small and sparely built, but the power of his personality was such that it seemed to magnify his physical stature. He had deep-set grey eyes and a broad, humorous mouth, and an eager, bird-like way of holding his head a little on one side. He was wearing an old tweed suit with leather inserts patched on the elbows, and leather cuffs, and a soft shirt and plain woollen tie. There was nothing about him to indicate the fact that he was a sort of super policeman, except for his unmistakable air of authority and those keen grey eyes. I had an uneasy feeling that he could see through to my backbone.

'Well, young Cameron, sit down,' he said. His voice was surprisingly deep for so small a man and free from any exaggerated accent.

When I sat down I noticed that the coffee table was littered with dozens of fish hooks and flies.

Sir Reginald saw my eyes on them and said, smiling a little: 'You and your friends seem to have done all my work for me, so I might as well do a spot of fishing while I'm in Skye.'

I mumbled something, and he said: 'D'you like fishing?'

I told him that Duncan Mor had taught me how to fish.

'Duncan MacDonald, eh?' was all he said.

I nodded, feeling a lump rising in my throat at the mention of his name.

'I would have liked to have had the honour of meeting your friend MacDonald,' he said slowly. He paused and lit a cigarette, leaning back in the chair and blowing smoke rings, his eyes on the ceiling. 'You know he was shot at very close range,' he went on, his eyes still on the ceiling. 'The doctors tell me that any normal man would have been dead within seconds, but Duncan MacDonald stayed on his feet long enough to put paid to Cassell. That was a man for you, young Cameron. He must have had the heart of a lion.'

'Duncan Mor wasn't afraid of anything,' I said, keeping my eyes down, afraid of making a fool of myself.

'Tell me about him,' said Sir Reginald simply. 'How you came to meet him. How you got involved in this affair. Everything.'

I started off in a halting fashion, and then, as my confidence grew, I became absorbed in the telling of the tale and almost forgot that the man I was speaking to was the chief of MI5. I told him my story from the very beginning, exactly as I have set it down here, and he listened without a word, but his alert grey eyes never left my face.

When I had finished, he said reflectively: 'It makes a good story. Major Cassell – or Colonel Zaborin of the Russian Military Intelligence, to give him his real name – was a very clever man. He succeeded in fooling us for a long time, but it never occurred to him that he could be out-witted by a boy and a bunch of crofters. It's the old story of the professional despising the amateur. We were always a nation of amateurs, young Cameron, and I hope to God we always will be. I shouldn't be saying this, but it has always been the amateurs who have pulled us through.

'Of course, we weren't asleep. After Ransome disappeared without trace, we had Hunt and Reuter watched day and night. Our agent succeeded in sticking to Hunt and tracked him as far as Lochailort. Unfortunately, it was a case of the watcher being watched, and you know what happened to him. He didn't live to tell his story.'

'There's just one thing I've never understood, sir,' I said hesitantly. 'Why didn't your agent let me know that Hunt was at Achmore Lodge, instead of writing Hunt at the Hill of the Red Fox?'

'The answer to that one is simple,' replied Sir Reginald. 'Our agent wasn't even aware of the existence of Achmore Lodge. You must remember we were working in the dark. Our information was of the sketchiest. We knew that Ransome and a member of the Foreign Office were working in Russia for the Soviet Government, and that Russian agents had succeeded in smuggling them out of the country. The one real scrap of information that we succeeded in picking up was that the leader of the Soviet espionage group went under the code name of Red Fox.

'Well then, to go back to our agent who was trailing Hunt. He knew that the train was bound for Mallaig. It was logical to assume that Hunt was making for a rendezvous, prior to leaving the country, and what better place for that rendezvous than the Island of Skye? If it were Skye, then Hunt must be making his getaway by sea. For Skye, mark you, although it is only fifty miles long, has a coastline that stretches for thousands of miles. A long, lonely coastline.

'I think our agent must have borrowed a map from somebody on the train. A good proportion of the passengers would be going to Skye, and a fair number of them would be climbers and hikers – people who always carry maps with them. His next step, unless I am greatly mistaken, would be to study the map – particularly the coastline – to look for a likely place for getting a man away unobserved. It is my opinion that he saw the hill marked on the map as the Hill of the Red Fox. A hill that was only a few miles from a bay in an isolated part of the island. I think he took a chance on its name. It might have been a coincidence. On the other hand – and as events proved – it might not.

'Put yourself in our agent's shoes, young Cameron, when he discovered that he, too, had a man on his tail. He had to shake him off, or his life wasn't worth tuppence, and at the same time he had to try to get a message through, in case the worst happened. For all he knew, Hunt was guarded by several men. He could trust nobody. So he passed a message to you – a schoolboy. Who would suspect a schoolboy of carrying a message on behalf of MI5? Nobody. Unfortunately' – and here his eyes twinkled – 'or perhaps I should say "fortunately", instead of handing the message over, you acted in a rather unorthodox fashion.'

I had had a question on my lips all the time he was speaking, and when he paused to light a cigarette, I presented it.

'But how did Dr Reuter get to Skye without being traced, sir? You said he was being watched day and night.'

Sir Reginald grimaced. 'We were fooled by a very simple

ruse,' he said wryly. 'Reuter hired a car from Marwell to London. He paid it off near Euston Station and went into a café. Our agent followed him to the café and took a corner table that commanded a view of the entire room. Reuter had coffee and biscuits, then he went to the lavatory. As you know, Reuter was an easy man to keep an eye on; he had a very distinctive limp and he was carrying a shiny new brief-case. Well, a limping man came out of the toilet carrying the same brief-case, paid his bill and took a cab to Victoria Station. From Victoria he went by train to Dover with our man hanging grimly on to his tail.

'Of course, you have probably guessed by now that the man on the Dover train wasn't Dr Reuter at all. He was a double, made up to look like Reuter, wearing identical clothes and simulating Reuter's limp. The switchover took place in the café's toilet. Doubtless, once the coast was clear, Reuter made for Euston Station and followed the same process as Ransome and Hunt. Believe me, Colonel Zaborin was a most thorough organizer. I've been through all the documents we found in Achmore Lodge, and the whole operation was planned with military precision.'

'Did you get all the proof you wanted, sir?' I asked.

Sir Reginald nodded. 'In addition to the documents we found, Reuter has made a full statement, admitting everything. It seems that the Russians were holding his wife as a hostage, although if he is to be believed, she was a fanatical Communist and had been urging him to join her. Of course, we didn't know that his wife was living; he had told us she had died in a Nazi concentration camp.

'One of the three men who were holding out in the bothy has since died of his wounds, but the other two have made complete confessions. They were British-born Communists, and will pay the full penalty.

'The only local man involved was Murdo Beaton. He was paid handsomely for taking them out by coble to the submarine. The Sound of Raasay is a dangerous stretch of water and a local man was needed to handle the boat. Not only that, if they had been seen, the presence of a local man would have disarmed suspicion. Needless to say, when Zaborin's mission was completed, Beaton would have been disposed of.'

'Has he . . . has he been found yet?' It was difficult to put such a question into words when it concerned somebody you had known and lived with.

'No, he has not, nor is he likely to be,' said Sir Reginald firmly. 'There is no doubt that he was killed in the explosion on the bridge. No man could have survived that. His body was swept out to sea, and I am told that the off-shore currents are such that it is unlikely to be recovered.'

I could not repress a shiver, thinking how close I had come to sharing the same fate.

Sir Reginald went on to give me some more information; information that I am not at liberty to repeat here. When he had sworn me to secrecy, he rose to his feet and stood looking down at me.

'You have lost a good friend, young Cameron,' he said slowly, 'and unless I am much mistaken you will be lucky if you ever meet his equal again. I cannot speak on behalf of Her Majesty's Government, but I can tell you that when I return to London I shall be making my report directly to the Home Secretary. I shall make the strongest possible recommendation that the George Cross be awarded posthumously to Duncan MacDonald.'

'I just can't believe that Duncan Mor is dead,' I cried.

I suppose wise men think alike whether they be humble crofters or powerful men high up in the counsels of the nation, because Sir Reginald Gower's reply was much the same as one that Hector MacLeod had made to me.

'The brave don't die, Alasdair,' he said gravely. 'Their deeds out-live us all.'

Neither of us spoke again, although he walked with me out of the hotel to the waiting car. I was grateful for his silence. I knew that, although he had never met Duncan Mor, he knew him as well as any man.

Chapter 25

A CHILL wind blew from the north-west sending the white clouds scudding across the sky and lifting the waters of the Sound in an angry swell. From where I was standing on top of Cnoc an t-Sithein, I could see the waves breaking over Rudha nam Braithrean in drenching clouds of spray.

Not a spade would break the ground in Achmore this morning; not a peat would be stacked, or a blade of grass cut. And it would be the same in all the townships for miles around. It would be the same in Garos across the moor, and Rigg, that lonely township watched over by the Old Man of Storr, and Ellishadder of the little loch.

But I could see people on the road. Some of them in twos; some of them in little groups of three and four. All of them making their way to the house by the river in Mealt. They came from the north and they came from the south. Over an hour ago I had seen some of them coming from the west, tiny black dots on the green of the hill as they made their way through Bealach na Leacaich from the Long Glen.

I scrambled down from Cnoc an t-Sithein and ran back to the cottage. All the men of Achmore were waiting for me, looking strangely unlike themselves in their blue suits and stiff white collars.

Hector MacLeod took a large gold watch from his waistcoat pocket and studied it.

'It is time we were making a move,' he said gravely, and with that we set off.

I shall never forget the sight that met my eyes when we passed through the gate in the dike at Mealt and looked down to the river. There must have been over two hundred men gathered around Duncan Mor's house.

Hector MacLeod led the way through the waiting men, shaking hands here and there when he spotted a familiar face, and we followed him into the kitchen. I sat on the bench, with the men of Achmore on either side of me, looking across at the photograph of the crew of the *Empire Rose* which hung above the mantelpiece.

Somebody must have tidied the room. There were no old coats draped over the back of the bench and the table under the window had been cleared of snaring wire and tools. The minister, a small, white-haired man, was leaning on the table looking out of the window.

More and more men filed into the kitchen, standing closely shoulder to shoulder, and I could see through the open door that the lobby was also packed with men. Nobody spoke. There was only the sound of breathing and the clearing of throats and an occasional cough.

The minister turned round from the window and clasped his hands, and heads were bowed as he said a prayer in Gaelic. My eyes were still closed when the voice of the precentor, a deep bass, launched into a psalm. The psalm was taken up by all the men in the kitchen and those in the lobby and all those outside. I did not understand a word of it, but I have never felt such sadness as was contained in that psalm. The voices rose and fell, rose and fell; the sound sobbing away like the wind in the dark corries of the Storr, and rose again, like the crash of the sea against the black basaltic rocks.

Then the minister read from the Bible, his voice slow and sonorous, rising and falling; always rising and falling, like the murmur of the everlasting sea. He closed the Bible reverently, and once again the deep voice of the precentor took up the words of a psalm.

The voices slowly ebbed away into silence, and Hector MacLeod urged me to my feet and I followed the rest of the men out of the house. The polished oak coffin was brought outside and laid across two chairs and the men of Achmore took up position on either side of it. All the other men walked up the croft in a column two abreast. After they had gone about twenty yards, the first six men halted and let the column proceed between them. They stood a few yards apart, facing one another, and I saw the same thing happen again and again, until the column was out of sight on the track leading to the main road.

Hector MacLeod took the cord from the head of the coffin and placed it in my hand.

'The son should lead the father,' he said quietly, 'and Duncan Mor was a second father to you, Alasdair Beag. It is right that you should lead him on his last journey.'

And with that the men of Achmore, three on each side, lifted the coffin from the chairs. With myself leading the way, the cord clutched tightly in my hand, we made our way slowly and solemnly up the croft.

When we came abreast of the first six men they relieved the bearers, and the men of Achmore took up their place in front of me, walking two abreast. Another twenty yards and the next six men took over, and so it went on, every man in his turn having the honour of bearing Duncan Mor.

Down below me, where the ground sloped away from the road, I could see the river surging forward in its eager rush to the sea, and beyond the river the curving line of hills of the Storr Range. Cattle were grazing by the side of the track, and an old woman in black stood outside the door of her cottage on the other side of the river, watching that solemn procession.

And every so often another six men stepped forward to relieve the bearers. Old men and young men, some of them not much older than myself. Men I had never seen before. They came from Aird and Breackry and Culnacnock; from Digg and Ellishadder and Flodigarry. They came from Garos and Hungladder and Idrigil; from Kendram and Linicro and Maligar. They came from North Duntulm and Ord and Portree; from Rigg and Stenscholl and Totescore. They came from Uig and Valtos and distant Waternish. They came to carry Duncan Mor and no King ever made his last journey like that.

When we came in sight of the little graveyard above Rudha nam Braithrean, the men formed up in a long, long column on either side of the path. I never saw the faces on either side of me, for my eyes were blinded with tears.

I stood by the side of the grave, no longer conscious of the people around me, the tears streaming down my face. Hector MacLeod took my arm and I did not know what to say when I saw that his cheeks were wet. We stood with heads bowed until it was all over, then we made our way back to Achmore, neither of us speaking.

I left him at his house, and he said: 'You will never see his like again, Alasdair Beag; no, not if you roam the length and breadth of the wide world.'

I crept into the cottage and changed my clothes. I could hear my mother and Mairi talking in the kitchen, but I did not want them to see me so I tiptoed across the lobby to the door. Once outside I did not stop running until I had reached Cnoc an t-Sithein.

I lay back on the green turf, shading my eyes against the sun and watching the white clouds go chasing across the sky, for all the world like galleons in full sail. How often I had come to this green mound when I wanted to be alone with my thoughts.

The Hill of the Fairies! If only it were true! If only I could whisper my wish to a little man decked all in green, and have it granted. What would we not do together on a day like this, Duncan Mor and I. North to the Quiraing, south to the Storr, west to Loch Liuravay. We would go striding through the heather, and if you have never footed it through the Highland heather you have never lived. Not for us the long miles on weary roads, but the joyous tramp over the moors, where the miles are forgotten and there is only the scent of bog myrtle and wild thyme and the spring of the heather forever urging your feet onwards.

But there was no little man in green. He belonged to the peat fire flame and the long winter nights when tales are told.

I got to my feet and made my way across the moor to Mealt. Without any conscious thought on my part, my feet followed the track to the hill. I looked straight ahead into the dark face of Sgurr a' Mhadaidh Ruaidh, topped by a delicate white circlet of cloud.

I crossed the river before I came to Loch Cuithir and made my way up the south side of the basin of the loch. All around me towered an immense wall of rock, broken here and there by shelves of green, speckled with the white dots of grazing sheep.

I climbed up the hillside by the banks of a tumbling burn until I came to the Achmore fank. I sat down with my back against the wall of the fank, my arms clasped around my knees, looking across the moor to Achmore with the Island of Rona beyond and the hills of Applecross in the distance.

I thought of the day I had spent at the shearing. There had been laughter that day; the hills had resounded to it, and snatches of song, and the constant bleating of sheep and the steady snip-snip of shears. But now all was silent. The fank was empty and the men were gone; one of them never to return. I looked upwards and my eyes were drawn to the sheer north face of Sgurr a' Mhadaidh Ruaidh.

It happened like that. One moment I was looking across the moor to Achmore, thinking of making my way back, and the next I had decided to climb the Hill of the Red Fox. Perhaps all the really important decisions are made like that, in as little time as it takes you to turn your head.

I scrambled to my feet and pressed on up the hill. When the ground became too steep for a direct assault, I went on in a series of zigzag paths, as I had often seen Duncan Mor do. It took the strain off my legs and I made quicker progress for all that.

When I was more than half-way up I paused for breath, and turned to look back. I could see as far as the fertile plain of Staffin with its clusters of white houses and green crofts and Flodigarry Island lying off the coast. Looking across the moor

I made out the winding course of Staffin River and followed it with my eyes to the bay. Away to the north I could see the whole serrated ridge of the Quiraing, and from where I was perched Loch Mealt, that tiny loch separated from the Sound by a narrow neck of land, looked like an inlet from the sea.

On and on I went up the steep sides of the hill. It was like climbing up the inside of a gigantic bowl, for the hills swept round in a tremendous, overhanging wall encircling Loch Cuithir. The only way to get to the top of the ridge was through the gap formed by Bealach na Leacaich.

As I got higher the hillside became barer and I had to scramble over patches of scree. Once, hesitating too long to secure a foothold, I slipped and started a miniature landslide. I suppose I only slid down for about fifteen or twenty feet, but I was badly frightened. I watched a boulder I had dislodged go hurtling hundreds of feet down the hillside until it crashed against a massive rock and shattered in fragments.

I went on again, stepping quickly and lightly across the screes, the way Duncan Mor had taught me. One light toehold, then a few quick steps before the gravel and stone could start to slide beneath my feet. Up and up I went until it seemed that I could go no higher for I was under a protruding lip of bare rock fully twenty feet high.

I glanced down and my head reeled. It seemed impossible that I could have climbed so high. I felt like a fly on a window-pane; if I were to take one foot off the ground surely I must go crashing down. Forcing myself to keep my eyes up, I saw the dip in the ridge of the hill formed by the Bealach. It lay to the south of me, and the only way I could reach it was by scrambling along under the overhanging wall of rock.

It was easier crossing the screes now that the angle of the hill was so acute, for I could balance myself with my right hand. I was afraid to look down, but I carried on doggedly, sliding on to my knees now and then, but always moving forward.

At last I came out through the Bealach, leg weary and sweating for all the cold wind that whistled around my ears. I was on top of the ridge of hills. On the west side the ground fell away in a gentle slope to Glenhinisdale. I sat on top of an old dry-stone wall and not even stout Cortés could have gazed around with more wonderment than I.

I was facing south and on my right lay the long valley of Glenhinisdale, cut by the silver ribbon of the River Hinisdal. I could see Loch Snizort and Loch Snizort Beag, Loch Greshornish, the slender chain of the Ascrib Islands, and even distant Waternish Point. In the far distance I made out the flat tops of MacLeod's Tables and Loch Bracadale.

I looked round to my left, across the Sound of Raasay, and saw the blue hills of the Outer Isles topped by a long roller of white cloud. The full range of the Quiraing curved away to the north.

For all my tiredness I tramped swiftly across the green springy turf on the ridge. The wind cut through my thin clothes like a knife, chilling and invigorating me at the same time. There were sheep grazing on the ridge and they lifted their heads and gazed at me, then wheeled round and galloped off as I drew near. Two black hooded crows circled slowly overhead then winged their way south.

The ridge narrowed as I neared the summit of Sgurr a' Mhadaidh Ruaidh, and on the north side there was a gigantic cleft in the rock. I crawled forward on my hands and knees and lay flat on my stomach looking down the gap in the rock. It was as if it had been split with a giant axe, and I gazed down a sheer precipice to Loch Cuithir over a thousand feet below. I crawled back to the south side of the ridge, where there was a gentle slope to the moors, before I went on again.

I ran the last few yards to the summit of the Hill of the Red Fox and threw myself face down on the close cropped turf. The whole of Trotternish was spread out below me. I could see the River Mealt winding through the flats on the start of its long journey to the sea, and all the townships for miles around.

I don't know how long I lay there. The sky was clear when I reached the summit and the mist was settling on the Storr when I turned to go. All I know is that I no longer felt lonely and miserable. I had climbed the Hill of the Red Fox, just as Duncan Mor had said I should, and I felt a wild, unreasoning surge of joy.

It happened when I was making my way down the south side of the ridge. People say that the light plays strange tricks with your eyes in the hills, that the shadows falling on the bare rock can take on the shape of a man. Perhaps what they say is true. I only know that I suddenly lifted my eyes and saw him.

He was standing on a ledge a little way above me, the wind rippling his grey hair. I saw the flash of his teeth as he smiled and the sweep of his arm as he waved to me. I shouted his name and started forward, and then the sun came through the clouds and the shadows lifted and I was gazing at the bare rock above the ledge.

I knew then that wherever I went in Skye the shadow of Duncan Mor would always be by my side.

GLOSSARY OF THE GAELIC
WORDS AND PHRASES

CHAPTER 1
Duncan Mor: Big Duncan
Alasdair Beag: Little Alasdair
Alasdair Dubh: Black Alasdair

CHAPTER 5
a bhalaich: O boy

CHAPTER 7
cailleach: old woman
Cnoc an t-Sithein: Hill of the Fairies
Sgurr a' Mhadaidh Ruaidh: Hill of the Red Fox

CHAPTER 8
strupag: A snack, usually consisting of a cup of tea, bread and
jam, scones, and biscuits

CHAPTER 9
Ceud mile failte agus slainte mhath: A hundred thousand
welcomes and good health
Iain Ban: Fair John
bodach: old man
Failte do'n duthaich: welcome to the country
Murdo Ruadh: Red Murdo
ceilidh: A gathering in a house for entertainment
an duine bochd: the poor man
port-a-beul: mouth music
Ruairidh: Roderick
Ist: Quiet
Oidhche mhath, Eachann: Good night, Hector

CHAPTER 11

a dhuine dhuine: O man man
A Thighearna bheannaichte: O blessed Lord
Rudha nam Braithrean: Brothers' Point

CHAPTER 13

Oidhche mhath mata: Good night then

CHAPTER 15

feadan: chanter
Domhnull-nam-Faochag: Donald of the Whelks

CHAPTER 17

A Chruthaidhear: O Creator

CHAPTER 18

truaghan: Poor creature

CHAPTER 22

Ruairidh the Leodhasach: Roderick the Lewisman

CHAPTER 23

Seall, Alasdair: Look, Alasdair
Co tha'n sud?: Who is there?
Thigibh an so: Come here
Tormod: Norman

Master of Morgana

ALLAN CAMPBELL McLEAN

'I stopped, panting, straining my ears for all they were worth. Above the loud thumping of my heart, I was certain I could hear the sound of hurrying feet scuffing the loose gravel on the road. I took to my heels. I was half-way down the road before I caught sight of him . . . Right away I knew he was my man.'

At that moment, sixteen year old Niall knew that his brother's near fatal fall was not a mere accident. Someone had fully intended Ruairidh to die when he fell deep into the gorge. But why should anyone want to rob quiet and solitary Ruairidh of his life? Move by move Niall is bound tighter in a web of intrigue and suspicion.

Set against the lonely, rugged background of the Isle of Skye, this is an immensely gripping adventure story for older readers.

The Hill of the Red Fox and *The Year of the Stranger* by Allan Campbell McLean are also in LIONS.